Angel Hunters
Struggle for the Cylinder

Gary Fisher

DEDICATION

To my wife, Gloria

For being brave in the dark and strong in the light you allowed us to transcend the traditional friend and lover into the closeness we now experience.

We were destined to be together in this creative spiritual union and this new cycle of life is only in its infancy.

Without you, this story would be a memory of forgotten words in a manila folder defining an un-pursued dream.

Thank you for believing in me.

We both thank God for His love, which passes knowledge.

Shader, I love you.

Prologue

Thousands of years ago while the great angelic war raged

In heaven, as Satan pitted himself against his creator, a secondary struggle erupted. With the silver cylinder containing one of the angel's favorite gifts from God as the prize. The elite from each opposing side battled, without the constraint of time, to control the cylinder. Near the end of that final confrontation, over something God had meant to be pleasurable and entertaining, He imposed his judgment. A third of the angels were banished from heaven, and along with the cylinder they plummeted to earth.

The cylinder crashed, and was buried intact, penetrating deep into the planet's crust near what is now known as Whispering Pines California. Whispering Pines is the current location of an archeological dig by Professor Jacob Winston Kendall.

Professor Kendall was in his mid-fifties. For the last twenty years he was the head of the anthropology department at San Francisco State University. His dignified weathered face reflected many years of outdoor exploration, and teaching college students had etched a few facial lines of their own. He had what the students called the scruffy chic look. Whatever his look, the female students lined up to take his classes.

God gave him an abundance of talents and desires, even though Professor Kendall didn't have much time for God. He wasn't even sure God existed. His late wife Beth and his daughter Sara's strong belief was the only reason Kendall ever considered God as being real. And that's all it ever amounted to, a consideration. He made decisions as a scientist---see it, calculate it, believe it.

It took him a long time to deal with Beth's life ending car crash eight years earlier. Sara was the one that got him through it. His daughter and his work consumed his time. Sara, second in command at the dig turned out great, but his work became more of a challenge.

Professor Kendall remained stuck in the middle of his third book on the lives of the Indian tribes of northern California, and at a crossroad in his life. Money for the dig ran perilously low, and it had been years since his discoveries amounted to more than mere words on a page. He kept trying, dreaming he could discover something his colleagues failed to find. He hoped for something that would bring him new goals, new adventures, and new meaning to his life. When things did change, it wasn't going to be like he wrote it on the chalkboard in his mind, and even more surprising than how the dig site came about. And a substantial inheritance of the family's empire. As it turned out, Mr. Bryant was Kendall's college roommate.

The two were close friends in college, although several years had passed since they took time to revisit their younger days. The professor contacted Spencer about the use of the land and he was more than happy to oblige. Indian artifacts did not register on Spencer's priority scale. But Professor Kendall was high on a short list of people Spencer would go out of his way to help. Under contract, Kendall was allowed to keep any and all artifacts he found.

The professor's home in Clear Lake was only forty miles away from the dig, but he treated this excavation as he would a trip to Egypt. The group would live and eat at the site. Tents for shelter and campfires for cooking gave the students a genuine exposure to fieldwork. The professor and his crew of experienced students had been working on the site for almost a month.

Two sites were being excavated at the dig about a mile and a half apart. Site one yielded some broken pottery, bone fragments, and beads. The only thing coming out of site two was buckets of dirt. And the second site was the one Kendall felt inexplicably drawn to. He would discover later all things are by design, and even though he didn't know God, God knew Professor Kendal.

Chapter One

It was late in the afternoon on an early August day and unusually hot for northern California. The professor scraped the ground with a flat blade shovel stopping to locate a red headed woodpecker tapping in the tree above him. The life of an archaeologist was not quite as romantic as one might think, he thought, as he wiped his sweat from his brow.

Ethan, one of his students walked by. "Found the holy grail yet?"

"Not yet, Ethan. And northern California would not be the best place to look. Besides, I'm not Indiana Jones."

"Who knows Professor, keep looking."

Kendall had to smile. "Keep looking? That happens to be my mantra."

Work continued until it was past time to retire to the campsite for the evening. Losing what light they had, a halt was issued to the crews to end the dig for the day. The nightly glow of the campfire would replace the glow of the computer screen or the TV for the junior archeologists. Entertainment would be left up to the imagination and two guitars. The pow-wow around the fire seemed extra rowdy that night with students singing made up songs about working on the Kendall expedition.

Professor Kendall was about to excuse himself and settle into his tent when a strange man wearing a long black coat suddenly stepped out of the darkness into the softened light of the campfire. The music stopped abruptly as Ethan stood, with guitar in hand. People were reaching for pickaxes and other makeshift weapons that were part of the expedition's equipment.

There was an eerie silence until the stranger spoke. "Professor Jacob Winston Kendall," the stranger said. The stranger stepped forward never taking his eyes off of the professor. His voice had an odd sound that instantly grabbed the attention of the students and Professor Kendall. As the professor stood, he felt the presence of evil settle with unconditional disregard. Ethan sat, while the others farm implement weaponry lowered to half-mast.

"Yes," said the professor. "What can I do for you, sir?"

"It's what we can do for each other, Professor Kendall."

"Have we met? How do you know my name?"

The stranger pointed. "I know everything about you." As the man's finger extended, the campfire flame self-imploded leaving only the glowing smoky embers to give the already conspicuous gathering an appropriate ghostly atmosphere.

At this point, one of the students stood and exposed the only firearm available to the crew. He picked up the shotgun and pointed it at the stranger. "Mister," the student said, "I don't know who you are or what you want. But I think it best you leave now, before I'm forced to use this."

"Billy," the professor said. "Put down the gun."

Billy never took his eyes off of the strange man, and listened as the professor spoke again.

"Put the gun down now, Billy."

Billy lowered the barrel of the weapon but stood his ground as the conversation between the two men continued. Refusing to let go of the gun and never taking his eyes off of the man that stood at the outer edge of the shadows, Billy remained resolute.

"You have something that belongs to me Professor," said the man.

The professor cleared his throat. "And what might that be?"

"You know full well what it is and I want it." His tone became more threatening. The folks around the campfire had blank stares or quick head turns looking to someone else for an explanation. His voice spread chills for some, and anger for others. Billy once again trained the shotgun on the strange man standing before him.

The professor's eyes remained locked with this demanding uninvited guest, while peripherally; the barrel of the shotgun came back into view. No protest lodged this time, as the professor felt truly confused. "I have no clue what you want".

The stranger forced a puzzled look all the while knowing the professor spoke the truth. The purpose of this campsite visit was to see, up close and personal, the ones he would soon draw into battle. Any blurring of the truth or reality he could conjure would be a bonus. The stranger had made contact, and for now, satisfied to retreat and wait. "Perhaps our conversation is premature," he said. "We will talk again soon, Professor Kendall." And just as suddenly as he appeared, he disappeared. He took a step back into the shadows, and he was gone. As soon as his exit registered with the group, the fire flashed back to a healthy flame.

There was a moment of total silence and then everyone seemed to be talking.

Ethan blurted. "Hey, Billy, what were you going to do, shoot him?"

"I don't know, but it seemed like a good idea at the time."

Kate and Rachel spoke in unison, "Who was that guy?"

One of the other students, Cooper, chimed in. "I'll tell you one thing, no way he was a local boy."

"Local boy," the professor said. "I'm not even sure he was from this planet. We need to stay alert. Billy, I want you to assign people to stand guard. Pick four crewmembers using two shifts, and put them on the perimeter of the camp. Everyone else try to get some sleep."

As Billy chose the guards, the professor just watched with admiration of Billy's pluck to protect the group, and thought. *I'm glad the boy stood his ground during what just happened, even though I'm not sure what did happen. I guess that's why the other students listen to him. He seems wise beyond his years and it doesn't matter if he's right or wrong, if he believes he's right, you're going to have to fight to change his mind.*

Kendall attributed this to his less than perfect upbringing. Not knowing his real parents, and being raised by the system made him grow up faster than other kids. But it gave him an inner strength. His natural leadership abilities were enhanced by his military experience. The professor hired Billy several times for his expeditions even though Billy's major was in computer science. He liked the professor, and he didn't mind digging in the dirt.

Sunrise of the next day at the site greeted everyone as they were rising from sleep with the events of the night before still fresh on their minds. Professor Kendall sipped his first cup of coffee, and contemplated the course of action for the day. He stood alone just outside the camp watching the sun make its way above the hills. The magnificence of the golden sky seemed to make all the concerns about this project disappear. The weather would soon be turning cooler, he thought, but questions about the night before still haunted him.

Sara's Morning Prayer came to a close at the campsite and Professor Kendall could see from where he stood the group preparing themselves for the day. As he turned his thoughts to the events of last night, the day was the furthest thing from his mind as the vision of the unwelcome guest in the long black coat with the absurd questions crowded his mental process. *What's the connection between this dig and the strange things of which the man in the shadows spoke? What do I have that belongs to him? Why didn't I ask him his name? Why didn't I ask him a lot of things?* Kendall, being an expert at compartmentalizing his thoughts filled his concerns in his recycle bin and spoke out loud to himself. "If I'm to know, I will know. If not, then it meant nothing."

When he turned to walk to the camp he saw Ethan approaching. Ethan was an enthusiastic athletic student with a full head of dark flowing hair, and a smile he was sure had gotten the attention of Sara.

Ethan waved. "Hey, Professor Kendall, what's on the agenda for today, sir?"

"More hard work. We have to continue the dig at the first site but I feel we must focus more on the second site. Just a feeling, but we have some unfinished business there. Anyway, it looks like a long day ahead of us, Ethan."

"Let's do it. I'll gather the crews for the morning briefing."

The morning briefing came after the Morning Prayer Sara led the crews in each day. If for some reason Sara was not present at the expedition, there was no prayer; at least not formally, because Kendall did not pray. Not formally. Everyone was milling around as the professor walked up, seeing his young crew drinking coffee or orange juice and talking among themselves. Until Professor Kendall spoke. "Good morning campers."

It wasn't like they came to military attention, but they did stop talking and responded, "Good Morning Professor."

"This will be a quick meeting so pay attention. Let me start off by talking about the incident last night. Anything I could say about that encounter would only be conjecture. I can tell you I am more than a bit intrigued. While we don't have time to sit and discuss this now, I am open to any and all input. You can approach me during the day if any theory comes to mind you think will shed some light on things. Now to the work at hand, the first site has yielded some pottery and jewelry and we have collected a considerable amount of data. There will be much work to do in the lab once we get back. So let's keep at it, and thank you for your hard work."

The professor began to assign jobs. "Ethan, Cooper, pick two other students and come with me and Billy to the second site. The rest of you know what to do here, if not, check with Sara."

Professor Kendall watched as the young men picked their two cohorts. He knew whom the boys would pick.

Cooper looked around like he was trying to decide. "Let's see, who's our next contestant? Rachel Grant, come on down."

Rachel smiled, rolled her eyes, and gladly joined the group. Ethan, not to be outdone, was next to choose. Ethan pointed. "Kate Parker, you have won an all-expenses paid trip to dig site number two, plus a slightly used shovel."

Kate came forward, carrying on the joke, as if she was elated.

Kendall shook his head. "I see you made some outstanding choices there, men. Go ahead; get ready and head out. I'll be right behind you."

The professor took a few steps, stopped, and scanned the area for his daughter. He noticed Sara busy giving out assignments, but he called her anyway. "Sara."

"Yes, dad."

"Talk to me a minute before you get started."

Sara held up her index finger to relay just a minute, and turned back to talk to the students. When she finished she walked to her father who was pacing in a semi-circle. "Have a lot on your mind this morning Professor?"

"Yes, thanks for asking Number One, a little more than usual. So, who do you think that guy was that walked into camp last night?"

"I have no idea. He said you had something that belonged to him. It was freaky. I don't know what to think." Sara paused. "So, what do you need this morning?"

"I need you to make sure the eastern quadrant gets taken care of today."

Sara smiled. "Dad, I know that."

"I know you do, hon. I'm just concerned about a lot of things. We only have so much time and so much money."

"All I can say, in God's timing Dad. And according to the word, He's always on time."

The professor took a deep breath and looked straight into her eyes. "I hope you're right, otherwise our next dig could be in our own back yard."

She held his gaze. "Just go dig and let God take care of the rest."

The professor gave her a hug. "Good luck."

They turned to go to their respective jobs, when Sara looked back. "Hey, Dad, luck is not a factor."

Sara did not believe in luck. She knew things happened for a reason. And sometimes you can't reason why things happen. But you have to keep moving forward in what you believe is God's will---because God knows the reason, and has all the answers.

Billy readied the water cooler and then gestured as if he were herding cats. "We're burning daylight." The group quickly began gathering supplies and loading the old jeep Cherokee. Backpacks and food flew into the rear compartment in preparation to leave.

Billy singled out Cooper. "Could we get going this morning please sir? We're already behind schedule."

"All right, let's move it," Cooper said, mocking Billy.

Rachel and Kate laughed at his act and piled into the back seat.

Ethan positioned himself between the two girls. "We're ready back here. What's the hold up?"

Cooper started the jeep, and they embarked on their mile and a half journey into the forest.

Billy was in the front seat with a hand held GPS, a detailed survey map, and the graph of the site. It was the same map and the same graph he had been looking at for a month. They were not going to get lost. But he was concerned by the amount of units that were producing artifacts. They needed a breakthrough today, so Billy was eager to get to work.

Billy had a pleading sound to his voice as he spoke. "Cooper. Try to miss some of the lower hanging limbs you acquainted us with yesterday. And stay away from those tight spots and underbrush this time okay?"

"Sure thing, chief." Then Cooper targeted and clipped the side of a small bush.

Billy was so involved in studying his map he missed the driving stunt. He wanted to be able to have everything straight in his mind before Professor Kendall got to the site. Billy felt it was his job to answer the professor's questions and give him detailed facts, so Kendall could make the right decisions.

Cooper turned half around in the seat, "Hey, what scripture did Sara read at the prayer session this morning? It was cool."

Kate waved her hand in the air like a third grader trying to impress her teacher as she said, "It was Psalm 139:16."

Billy interrupted. "Hey Cooper. Can you drive and listen without climbing into the back seat? And take a left up there between those two rocks."

"Yeah, sorry Chief."

"Don't call me chief any more Cooper, okay? "

While the boys were sparring, Rachel reached into her backpack and retrieved her copy of the Living Bible. "Never leave home without it," she said, as she showed it to Ethan and Kate.

Ethan laughed. "Sort of like that credit card thing, huh?"

"Yeah, except without the interest charges." Rachel smiled as she thumbed through her page worn Bible. "Here it is."

"Read it out loud," Cooper yelled, over the drone of the jeep engine and the bouncing of each and every rut he tried to overcome, sometimes with very little success.

Rachel started reading the Psalm. "You saw me before I was born and scheduled each day of my life before I began to breathe. Every day was recorded in your book."

"Wow," Ethan said. "That's pretty heavy. It's kind of like God knowing that every hair on your head thing."

Rachel considered the response. "Well, sort of. But it's more like that before you ask scripture. Kate, you know the one I mean."

Kate knew the scripture by heart, "its Matthew 6:8. For your father knoweth what things you have need of before ye ask him."

"That's it," Rachel said. "It has to do with a divine order to things."

"What about the free will wild card?" said Cooper.

"Good point, Mr. Wild Card," Kate said.

"How does the will to choose mess up divine order?" asked Cooper. "We obviously don't always make the right choice."

Kate lowered her Bible. "I think you can totally mess up the will of God for your life."

"Been there, done that," said Cooper under his breath.

"What?" Billy asked.

"I thought you were asleep, chief," Cooper said.

"I'm going to pretend I didn't hear that", and Billy went back to studying his maps.

Kate continued. "The apostle Paul said, sometimes *he* did the wrong thing even though he knew what was right. God knows we all can miss it. God can also fix it."

"God knows each and every one of our lives and its destiny," said Rachel.

"Yeah, and it's my destiny to always be a thorn in Ethan's side," Kate said, poking Ethan's ribs with her elbow.

Ethan gave her a look, smiled, and rubbed his side.

Rachel, still thinking about the scripture said, "Let's see what destiny holds for us today."

Billy rolled up his maps. "Cooper, pull the Jeep up to the tents on the east side of the dig and back in so we're in position to leave later."

"Okay, will do." Almost referring to Billy as chief again but stopping just in time, as he laughed to himself. "We are almost there. Put your seats in the upright position, your tray tables up and locked, and please fasten your seat belts. I hope you have enjoyed your flight and you will consider flying Cooper Airlines in the near future."

"Fat chance," shouted Kate from the back seat.

"The in-flight movie wasn't bad," Ethan said.

"Yeah," said Rachael, "but the food was the worst."

"I thought the navigator did a heck of a job," Billy said. They all laughed, and piled out of the vehicle.

Sara Kendall was in charge of site one and was to remain there most of the day. She felt they had found the majority of the artifacts in the area, and wanted to go to the second site. But she stayed and kept looking. Professor Kendall's departure for site two was delayed due to some equipment issues, but his A-Team had been dispatched. He never called the five students the A-Team to their face, but he thought of them that way. He could always depend on their decision-making, especially as a unit. Billy seemed to be the true leader.

Everyone began unloading equipment. Billy could see site two from where he stood and the workers already on their location. He looked up from the survey map, now unrolled on the hood of the jeep, and saw the foreman Juan Perez heading his way. He noticed there was something extra in Juan's step as he approached.

"Ola, Juan."

"Ola, Mr. Billy."

Billy gazed back to the site map. "So, Juan, you've been working for Professor Kendall for a long time, huh?"

"Oh, Mr. Billy, I have been with Mr. Kendall for nearly twenty-two years. Mr. Kendall is a good man."

"Tell me Juan, do you have your best men on the units Kendall wanted done this morning?"

"Si, I do. They've been working for an hour now, and they find something I don't think is from an Indian tribe. Look, Mr. Billy." Juan pointed to the spot where his crew stood.

Billy turned to look, and the sun reflected off an object, which hit Billy in the eyes like a luminescent spear. "It looks like a mirror, Juan."

"No mirror, Mr. Billy. It is metal."

Billy and Juan walked toward the crew.

"We stop digging when we find this."

A five-inch square portion of the object lay exposed in the ground. It was a brilliant silver color with raised ribs running across the surface.

"This couldn't have been buried for long with the metal remaining this bright. Are you sure it's metal, Juan?"

"Sounded like metal when we hit it, and we make no dent either."

Billy put his maps on the ground and climbed into the dig site to get a closer look. The object was buried in about three feet of hard clay. Billy touched it with his hand and it did feel like metal. "Hum, that's strange, I can't tell what it is. The chrome looking finish is really strange." He turned to Juan. "Juan, we will take care of this, no need to use your men on this unit." I'm gonna put Cooper and Ethan on this. Okay?"

"Si, Mr. Billy. My men have already refused to dig any further, and don't want nothing to do with this."

Billy felt some sort of superstitious overtone in Juan's voice as he reached for his walkie-talkie.

"Professor, come in."

"Yes, Billy, what is it?"

"Are you on your way, sir?"

"It will be at least an hour before I can leave here. What do you need?"

"Juan found something metal over here the GPR didn't pick up. We may need some special equipment before we proceed"

"That's unusual. The ground penetrating radar didn't pick up metal? What is it?"

"I don't know, but you need to get over here."

"I'll be there as soon as I can."

Sara also heard the transmission and responded. "Dad, you need some help?"

"I'm not sure. But when you're free, grab the photo equipment and meet me at site two."

"Will do, see you soon."

Cooper and Ethan finished unloading the supplies and headed toward Billy to see what was going on. Rachel and Kate were not far behind.

"Hey, Billy, what's up?" said Cooper.

Billy pointed. "It's what's down. Check it out."

They all looked at the strange piece of metal breaking the surface of the soil.

Ethan reached down to feel the item. "It's sure not a piece of pottery."

Cooper couldn't resist. "My guess. A front bumper off a 57 Chevy."

Kate walked up. "Did we find a 57 Chevy?"

Rachel was with her. "That was a good year. I think Professor Kendall has one of those."

Billy wasn't amused. "The professor owns a 1948 GMC pickup, Rachel. Now let's get some brushes and trowels, move some of this dirt, and let's see what it is."

They carefully started removing the earth from around the object. After about thirty minutes of brushing and scraping, a little here and a little there, a shape began to emerge. It looked like an elongated football, about three feet long. With only a portion visible, the exact shape was unknown.

"What is that?" Cooper said.

"I have no idea," said Billy.

"Something alien would be cool," Rachel said.

"Could be a time capsule," said Kate.

"Or a bomb," Ethan said, jokingly at first, until everyone looked at each other and wondered.

"What if it is a bomb?" said Rachel.

"Let's stop where we are," Billy said. "Professor Kendall is bringing extra equipment to try and get some readings. The only thing we do know is we don't know what it is."

Someone knew what lay buried only inches below the surface. He hovered invisible about eighty feet above the group enjoying their confusion. It was Dante, the campsite intruder from the night before. His rank extended into the hierarchy of fallen angels. And it wasn't just a supervisory position. There was a lot of blood on his hands. His essence defined warrior, with the scars to prove it.

Satan chose him for this mission of retrieval because of his willingness to cross the ancient boundaries, and fearlessly break all the rules of angelic involvement with humans. A being so loyal to his master, he was privileged to be present during the violation of the forbidden fruit. But his main concern; was a personal claim on something within the cylinder.

Dante tarried while floated upright with his head bent looking down, and his wings stretched as if there were a panel of Olympic judges waiting to score his performance. The temptation of seeing the silver metal peaking from the earth was too much. A smirk flashed across his face. He straightened his back, raised his head, and dove headlong off his imaginary platform. The smirk turned into a scowl and his eyes widened with cruel intent as he plunged downward toward the prize he longed to possess.

Just yards from his goal, as victory dominated his thoughts, he saw two enormous angels appear on either side of the object. Invisible to the group, they both stared straight at him each with one arm extended and a hand up like an angelic gatekeeper, and the authority that came with it. Dante pulled up, flew directly between the two manifesting a swirling gust of wind that everyone around the site felt, even though they saw nothing. He came to rest inches behind Billy looking over his shoulder. Dante focused on the two figures, slowly tilted his head and viewed them as a predator would view his prey. The angels turned to face him, never losing their pose.

"Angels of Light, be damned," said Dante. "Prepare yourselves for a fight. Your God will not keep me from this."

The angels did not reply, but simply dropped their arms to their sides and stood motionless.

Dante yelled, "Has fear taken your voices?" "Do you not know who I am?"

For a moment the angels remained still until one of them in a deliberate, yet subtle move, raised his right hand and drug it across his left cheek in a slashing motion, and said. "Do you not remember me?"

Dante stepped back in amazement, as he raised his hand to touch the ancient scar that marked the left side of his face. A thousand gruesome images of battles almost forgotten flooded his entire being as his hand clinched into a fist. It became clear he stood face to face with the angel who had cut him centuries before. Dante, in a proud manner, stroked the scar once more. "This I remember. This I will avenge."

Dante again spread his magnificent wings in an almost ballet like fashion, and rose from the ground. He reached out, touched Billy's hair, and flew away.

Billy was shaken. He sensed a dark presence from the gust of wind and feeling the brush of his hair made him struggle to keep his composure. Billy looked around to see who touched him. No one was there. "Did anyone touch me?"

"No," said Kate.

"Not me," Ethan said.

"I felt a strange wind blow through here," added Cooper.

"I'm feeling something deeper than wind," Rachel said. "I think we should pray, now."

The crew gathered, held hands, and forming a semi-circle, Ethan led them in the prayer of protection, Psalm 91.

"He that dwelleth in the secret place of the most high shall abide under the shadow of the Almighty. I will say of the Lord, He is my refuge and my fortress: My God; in him will I trust. Surely he shall deliver thee from the snare of the fowler, and from the noisome pestilence."

As they continued the prayer, what the crew could not see was their semi-circle was actually a full circle. The two angels had joined the group in prayer and could not help smiling at one another as they recited verse 11 and 12.

"For He shall give his angels charge over you, to keep you and all your ways. In their hands, they shall bear you up lest you dash your foot against a stone."

Chapter Two

About a hundred miles south and twenty floors up from the Whispering Pines excavation, Spencer Jennings Bryant sat at an oversized mahogany desk and gazed out the corner office windows at the San Francisco skyline. The sun swept across the surface of the desk, highlighting a collection of objects that reflected the diversity of his life. A photograph of Spencer, Kendall, and Beth anchored the right corner. The picture was taken while Spencer and Beth were dating, but years before Kendall and Beth were married.

In the center of the desk was a handwritten note encased in Plexiglas reading; *if you find this note, Spencer Jennings and Carson Taylor are alive approximately 200 miles west of the large island in the Philippines, Luzon.* Spencer's plane had made a crash landing on the beach. He had written the note, put it in a bottle, and threw it in the ocean. Two days later, the bottle with the note still inside washed back onto the beach, followed by a Coast Guard cutter that rescued them. The note had nothing to do with the rescue, but whenever he read it, it gave him hope.

Spencer looked back to the desk and the work that needed his attention. On the left was a stack of briefs and acquisitions. Decisions had to be made on which fire to put out first, and which deal would make the most money. Instead, he focused on the legal pad in front of him, covered with crude drawings of an invention he had been toying with for months. The phone rang.

"Yes, Donna," he said, as he continued to look at the drawings.

"Carson Taylor is on the line for you."

"Put him through, Donna."

"Good morning Spencer."

"Morning Carson, how are you today?"

"Doing good, but I have some information I think you need to hear. I have it on good authority that your professor friend may have found something we need to think twice about letting him have."

"Kendall?"

"Yes sir."

"We gave him permission to excavate that land, and that's all there is to it."

"But, Spencer, I'm not sure exactly what he found, but I think ..."

"I don't care what you think, Carson, leave Kendall alone. Unless he finds gold or uranium, drop it. Call me back with the projections from the Texas plant." Spencer hung up the phone.

Carson sat with the phone to his ear for a few seconds, with an, Oh well, expression on his face, looked up at the man facing him and put the phone back in its cradle. "I tried."

Dante sat still with no expression, staring at Carson from a large leather chair, not liking what he heard.

Dante spoke in a calm reassuring tone. "Carson, you do understand your success would not have been possible without our help. You must realize your position as vice president, houses, cars, boats, and even that beautiful wife is a result of your alliance with my master. You were hand-picked for this moment in time, and you knew this day would come. Every iota of power, deception, and if necessary even violence must be utilized to complete this mission. This is not a threat, Carson, only a reminder of your agreement. Assist us successfully retrieve the object, or your life and the lives of your family will be history."

"I understand, Dante."

"It disgusts me to think we need to rely on a human to finish this work."

"I'll get it done, what else can I say," pleaded Carson.

Dante caressed his scared cheek. "I have a plan on how to get started."

"Please enlighten me sir."

"We're going to have to do something about this Christian gang of Kendall's. They have no idea what they have found."

"For that matter neither do I."

"If you will allow me to continue," Dante took a cleansing breath. These kids have a significant prayer covering but I think I can get to a certain individual. Several, small, seemingly unrelated events have been set in motion that will culminate in a serious mistake. This will give you a chance to reclaim what's mine."

"Divide and conquer, sir?"

"Exactly, one of our greatest weapons. According to their book, every kingdom divided against itself is brought to desolation; and every city or house divided against itself shall not stand. Next, you're going to have to make sure Spencer does not get in the way. If he does, it's up to you to take care of him. Understand?"

Carson reluctantly trained his eyes on Dante's face, and said, "I do."

Spencer still doodled on his legal pad, realizing he had to change gears and do some real work. Spencer's real work consisted of finding a solution for each opportunity and delegating responsibility to his team. He spent most of his time trying to enjoy his life. Spencer believed, you're born, you die, and that's it. No heaven and hell stuff for him. As a result women were a big part of his life and lots of them. He never stayed with a woman long enough to learn her middle name. Beth was the only woman he had ever loved, but he knew early he was never meant to be with one woman. He did regret not having a child and sometimes felt a void in his life even if for the reason, there would be no little Spencer to take over the family business.

Spencer used his money to try and eliminate these feelings. He would fly his private jet to Chicago for a hot dog from his favorite vendor, or drive his 32 Ford coupe 300 miles north to Grants Pass Oregon, to eat a bowl of chili, at the diner where his father took him as a child. These things did fill his time and temporarily made him happy, but God also had a plan for Spencer, and by letting Kendall use his land he had unknowingly taken the first step.

* * *

Professor Kendall was minutes away from the second site negotiating the rugged terrain in his 1948 GMC pickup. The truck had been specially built to his specifications with a frame up restoration. It had four wheel drive with an eighteen inch ground clearance, power steering, disk brakes, air conditioning and even a built in GPS system. Everything except a DVD player, but the professor considered installing one.

He had been in the relic hunting business long enough to know, not to get excited until he was sure of what had been found. He was calm as he listened to the CD of Cream's "Sunshine of Your Love" and enjoyed his off-road experience.

Sara, on the other hand, was about a mile behind her dad on a four wheel drive all-terrain vehicle going hammer down for the horizon. Her pack was loaded with several cameras, a sketchpad, and even a Geiger counter. She felt a rush of adrenaline and was not sure if it was from the ride or the sense that something special was about to happen. At any rate she could not get there quick enough.

Kendall arrived at the site and saw the group standing, and holding hands around the hole. He had no idea what was taking place. He got out of the truck and Billy was the first to greet him. "Glad you could make it Professor."

"Wouldn't miss it for the world. What's with the holding hands?"

"Prayer. Something weird just happened and I don't know what it was. Come look at this."

Kendall looked down at the shining object and felt a tinge of excitement. This is certainly different, he thought. "There's a portable G.P.R. unit in the back of my truck."

"I got it," Cooper said.

"I'll help," said Ethan.

"What do you think, Professor?" Kate asked.

"I don't know Kate. It has a certain aesthetic quality doesn't it?"

Cooper and Ethan got to the truck just as Sara flew around the corner and skidded to a stop.

"Safe!" yelled Cooper.

"No way she was out by a mile," Ethan said.

"Good slide, Sara." Cooper laughed as she dismounted her ride.

"What's going on guys?"

"Oh, just you're run of the mill flying saucer," Ethan said.

"Not Grover's Mill?" asked Sara joking.

"Orson Wells radio show, right?" Cooper said.

Sara shrugged. "Yeah, that's right Cooper, but H. G. Wells wrote the original book. The Orson Wells show only panicked the entire eastern seaboard. At any rate, it's not funny if you have to explain it."

"We're taking the ground penetrating radar over now," said Ethan.

"I'll grab my cameras and be right there."

Rachel and Billy assembled the radar unit while Cooper and Ethan cleared the shovels and utensils from the area.

Kendall knew the truck mounted radar unit originally scanned the area, but for some reason, didn't pick up a reading. Human error was the likely suspect. This time there would be no mistake. Kendall gave a thumbs up. "We should determine size and how deep it might be."

Billy switched on the machine and moved it slowly from one end to the other and back again. "Am I doing something wrong Professor?"

"Let me try Billy." He took the unit and with the same motion moved it across the object one direction, and then back the other direction. "There are no anomalies at all showing on this screen. Does this thing still work?"

Cooper laid a shovel down next to the professor and said," Try this."

Kendall moved the radar unit across the shovel and there it was, shovel handle, shovel blade, and two bolts securing them together.

Kendall scratched his head. "This machine is working."

"Just not on whatever that is," said Billy.

"I brought a Geiger counter dad," and Sara held up the unit.

"As strange as this is I suppose we should check for radioactivity." Kendall said.

Sara turned on the Geiger counter and approached the object. Not a movement, not a sound, the machine registered nothing.

"How do we precede, Professor?" asked Billy.

"By faith," Sara said.

"Oh, I was talking to the other professor, your dad."

Sara's eyes cut toward Billy. "I know you were. But I know what the answers going to be."

Professor Kendall looked at Sara gave a slight smile, and turned back to look at the object.

"Like she said, carefully continue to dig, and let's see what happens."

The object rested on the side of the hole where Juan's crew had been digging, so Ethan and Cooper started clearing dirt from the topside. Sara was shooting photographs. Kate was taking notes on the event, while Rachel was drawing sketches of the scene. Professor Kendal and Billy were observing.

The students had more in common than college or working with Kendall. They played in a rock & roll blues band. As a group, Rachel, Kate, Cooper, and Ethan had been close friends for about four years. Billy had met them a couple of years later when he auditioned, and got the position as drummer for their band, The Alpha State Troopers. They also enjoyed playing tennis, and were all good players at different levels. Cooper was the tennis aficionado. He competed in amateur tournaments, but he could not devote enough time to the game to think about turning pro.

Cooper and Ethan's friendship started much earlier and they had been close since grade school. In the sixth grade, their first dig site was in Ethan's neighbor's back yard looking for buried treasure. The main thing they accomplished was the digging of a big hole. They declared it a successful dig when the ground gave up the bones of a large cat. The bones momentarily held their interest, and only served to delay the reality of repairing the somewhat desecrated lawn just minutes before the owner returned home. Even now it was still known and referred to as the infamous dead cat dig.

Something sparked in the boy's spirits that day even if they were too young to realize its potential or put it into words. They shared the same desire for adventure and discovery from that point on. A bond formed between the two that would last a lifetime.

The memory of cat bones resurfaced as the boys gingerly removed soil from around the body of silver metal. After about fifteen minutes of digging Cooper stuck a long trowel in the ground over the top of the object to try and detect its size or shape. He gave a slight upward pressure. He continued to push, probably harder than he should have, and the silver object rolled out of its earthly grave like a newborn baby. It fell about a foot just missing Cooper and Ethan, and lay there at the bottom of the hole rocking back and forth.

It seemed like time stood still as everyone froze, with their eyes glued to the rocking cylinder waiting for something to happen. Nothing did, except the slow rolling motion of the cylinder as if it was perfectly balanced in some kind of perpetual motion experiment. Words were not coming easy for the crew, but one voice seemed to sum it up.

"Oops," Cooper said, as the cylinder finally slowed and stopped. "I guess I pushed a little too hard that last time."

Ethan grabbed the trowel from his hand. "You think?"

Professor Kendall exhaled deeply. "You didn't quite go by the excavation handbook, Cooper. Get out of the hole, and let's see if there is any damage."

Cooper stepped up onto level ground and walked away from the group with a look of disgust on his face. Rachel followed. She eased up beside him and put her arm around his shoulders. "Boy Cooper. I haven't seen that look on your face since you lost the finals tennis match to that San Diego dude."

"Terry Green," said Cooper. "He made me look bad and blew my shot at the state championship.

"He blew your shot?"

"Okay, I blew it; I stayed out all night partying, and then ran out of gas half way through the match."

"It will be alright, Cooper. You'll get another chance."

"Yeah and soon. We're playing an exhibition tennis match for a charity event this weekend."

"What kind of event?"

"Some kind of sports deal, spotlighting different sports and sports equipment manufacturers with all the proceeds going to charity. That friend of Professor Kendall's is putting it on. I can't remember his name."

"Oh, the guy who let us excavate this land?" Rachel said.

"Yeah, that's him," said Cooper.

"Spencer something. Spencer Bryant, that's it."

"I think so. At any rate, I'm supposed to see some guy named, Carson Taylor, to get the final details."

"So get some sleep the night before, okay?"

"Yeah, and don't pry on any foreign objects in a hole either," Cooper said.

"Follow me, Cooper, I have something that will make you feel better."

Cooper raised his eyebrows. "And what might that be?"

"Ice cream."

"Ice cream, out here?"

"Come on, let's go. Something cold and sweet will help."

"I guess it couldn't hurt."

* * *

Dante rambled on about some gory battle in heaven before the third of the angels fell. Carson didn't enjoy the graphic nature of the story and his thoughts wandered. Ranging from how this whole thing got started, to what he might have to do to fulfill his obligation to these evil forces. Carson had what was known in World War II as the 'two thousand yard stare.' An expression describing an empty look, after the visual buffet of war filled your senses to overflow and by the time you realized you had seen enough, you'd seen too much.

Dante became aware that his minion's mind drifted and was about to reach out and slap him, when every cell of the physical body Dante inhabited tingled with excitement. He suddenly sat up on the edge of the chair, raised and turned his head, then froze like a mannequin in a department store window. The move brought Carson back to reality and he almost laughed out loud. Dante reminded him of a squirrel running across the lawn, then screeching to a halt with that look on his face like he had just lost his car keys.

"Are you ok, sir?"

Dante's face began to come back to life. First a blink, then two, then his eyes moved around the room, as if he was trying to remember where he was. "The sun is shining on the face of the cylinder."

"I'm sorry?"

"It has been unearthed Carson. I will give you specifics on your assignment later, but for now I must go." And without a nod or a twitch of the nose, Dante vanished.

Carson mumbled to himself, "He comes here, gives me no information at all except oh, by the way, you may have to kill your boss---no goodbye, no see you later, just I must go and then poof."

Carson remembered the information Spencer had requested and pulled up the spreadsheet on his computer. With a few keystrokes, the totals were complete and he sent them to Spencer as his phone rang.

"Hello, this is Carson."

"Carson, what about the projections from Texas?"

"I just sent them to you, Spencer, and I believe you will be pleased."

"Let's see here."

Carson could hear Spencer pecking at the computer over the phone.

"Looks pretty good, Carson. We're up a few points from last year. By the way, what's going on with the Sports Expo Charity Event?"

"I will be leaving this morning to see that everything is proceeding as planned."

"Clear Lake, isn't it?"

"Yes sir, nice part of the country."

"Yes it is. The home I grew up in is a few miles north of there. It's secluded and vacant. Why don't I send Donna over with directions and the keys?"

"That would be great. Thank you sir."

"I may be there a day or so early. Kendall lives up that way, and it would be nice to catch up on things."

"About what was said about Kendall earlier, I wasn't trying to pry in anybody's business, but he may have found something, how shall I say, unique."

"Ok, Carson, but do me a favor, make sure this charity deal goes well and if and when I see Kendall, I'll talk to him."

"Will do; see you in a few days."

Carson knew the title of yes man fell somewhere in his job description, but he didn't mind. He figured it came with the territory and from where he sat, the territory looked pretty good. He made more money than he ever believed he could and besides, he had some yes men under him too. He enjoyed the money but was addicted to the power. Power was something Carson strived for early in his life, and the reason Dante recruited him just out of high school.

Carson's high school experience was normal except for one thing. He was vertically challenged. He had an average looking face, not ugly, not handsome, but kind of plain. He made good grades, had some close friends, but he was always shorter than everyone else. His height bothered him sometimes and making himself taller was not an option, but he could make up for it with confidence. Confidence in himself that he could do anything he put his mind to, and he was just as good as or better than anyone. At some point he became over confident. This is where Dante entered the picture and manipulated Carson into a blood oath.

Carson could remember Dante using phrases like, you may never see me again, this will not have any negative effect on your life, and the big one; it is totally your decision. He simply didn't have all the facts back then, kind of like now. For the present there was only one thing he could do and that was the job in front of him. He picked up his briefcase, and with all the confidence he could muster he walked out of the office for his date in Clear Lake.

Chapter Three

Back in Whispering Pines, Professor Kendall and Billy were in the hole on their hands and knees inspecting the silver cylinder, and trying to draw some kind of conclusion as to its origin. Dirt and some small rocks, which clung to the metal surface, impaired a detailed visual analysis. But now that the cylinder had been unearthed, they were able to distinguish a definite shape.

Billy considered the cylinders contour. "It has the same proportions as a blimp, just on a smaller scale. It could also be described as a stretched football."

Professor Kendall snapped into teaching mode. "So, geometrically speaking, what is the shape of a football?"

Billy was quick to answer. "There is some debate on that, Professor. One school of thought would call it a prolate spheroid, and another, an ellipsoid."

Ethan had to rebut. "A long shiny thing works for me."

Kendall laughed. "I see your education has been put to good use, Ethan. Let me have your tape measure. Kate, write this down please."

"I'm ready, Professor."

"The length from tip to tip is forty-two inches. The width at the center is eighteen inches, which tapers down to a point on both ends. I can get the circumference once it's moved, but for now, let's brush this dirt away and get a better look."

Billy started brushing the dirt from the center out.

"The surface looks like it was tooled in a machine shop," Sara said. "The ridges running across the length of the object are very precise. Get a measurement on those, Dad."

"Okay, write this Kate. The grooves are one quarter of an inch wide and one quarter of an inch deep. The width of the raised portion is also one quarter of an inch. Definitely not random, this was well thought out."

Billy was making progress with the loose dirt on the cylinder, when he said, "Hey, there's some kind of writing here."

Everyone's attention was on Billy as he spoke. "Let's see, what does this say, yeah, Bob's Machine Shop, El Paso, Texas."

Professor Kendall's heart dropped as he stared at Billy waiting for the punch line.

"Gotcha, Professor."

The professor just shot him a look, and shook his head.

"Good one," said Ethan.

"I have my moments," Billy said.

"More like nanoseconds," said Sara, as she walked back a few steps to get a wide shot of the new find.

"Do you think there is anything inside, Professor?" Kate said.

"I don't know, I don't see any visible signs of an opening. It could be solid, and if so, we could have a very unusual boat anchor. Ethan, give Billy a hand here, I need to get some tools out of the truck."

Ethan stood and applauded.

"That's not the kind of hand I meant," said the professor.

"Here I come," said Ethan, as he jumped into the hole next to Billy.

Billy had removed most of the loose dirt, and was searching for a tool to clean the impacted dirt from the grooves. The first tool he saw was the trowel, the tool of the day. The one Cooper has used to inadvertently dislodge the cylinder. Billy picked up the trowel and lightly slid the tip into one of the grooves. Sara screamed, "Stop! You're going to scratch it Billy. There could be something in one of those grooves, like a switch or a latch, or something."

"Chill out, Sara. I'm being careful."

Sara put her hands on her hips. "If you're going to use the trowel, you might as well poke it with a stick."

Professor Kendall was returning from the truck with some small scraping tools when he heard Sara's remark and stopped in his tracks. "Poke it with a stick? What is that, Sara, something I missed in the latest archeological journal?"

"It's from the old science fiction movie, 'The Blob'."

"Here she goes again," Billy said, "always with the movie analogies."

"That's right Billy---classic fifties science fiction, Steve McQueen's first movie, and a giant Jello creature eating teenagers. Well, anyway, it all started with a guy poking this meteor with a stick, which struck me as a totally male move. If you don't know what it is, just poke it with a stick."

With Rachel's help, Cooper had cleared his head, and they rejoined the group, both eating Popsicles.

"Where's my Popsicle?" said Kate.

Rachel waved the Popsicle. "The blue cooler in the jeep. One of Juan's guys brought them back from town yesterday."

"You okay, Cooper?" Kendall said.

"I'm alright Professor. Is there any damage to the shiny, silver, whatever it is?"

Billy answered. "No damage. You could probably drop this thing off a five-story building and not scratch it. But be sure and don't poke it with a stick."

Cooper and Rachel just looked at each other and did not ask.

"Here Billy, try these." Professor Kendall pitched Billy a zippered bag with the precision tools inside.

Billy unzipped the bag, and held up a tool which looked like something a dentist would use to clean your teeth, and in fact, it was.

Billy held up a tool. "This okay, Sara?"

"Yeah, that will do, since I don't see a good stick anywhere close."

Billy grinned. "I do. Hey, Cooper, give me that Popsicle stick."

"I'm not done yet."

"Well, hurry up."

Cooper gulped down the last of his frozen treat, almost got brain freeze, and threw the stick to Billy. Billy cleaned the stick by rubbing it in the dirt, pulled out his pocket knife, and with two cuts, he tapered one end of the stick to just about one quarter of an inch.

Billy waved the stick at Sara. "Guess what I'm going to do?"

"Okay, everybody, all together now," said Sara.

"POKE IT WITH A STICK!" everyone said and laughed, as Billy went about cleaning the grooves of the cylinder with his homemade tool.

Kendall's team went about their jobs like they found silver cylinders every week. But the feelings, which they kept in check, ran the entire spectrum of human emotions. This was something new, and nothing like they had ever seen before.

Dante had seen the silver cylinder. But it had been thousands of years since he touched it, smelled it, and his desire to claim it escalated as he grew near the site. Dante flew in and touched down in the forest just out of sight of the crew. He closed his eyes, concentrated, and morphed himself into human form. Which meant, he made his wings invisible and brought his eight-foot height down to six. He combed his hair, straightened his collar, and went casually strolling into the clearing.

Kate saw him first. "Look, Professor." She pointed toward the tree line.

They all looked and saw the mysterious stranger they encountered the night before, still wearing the full length black coat, and getting closer with each decisive step.

Dante was not only pure evil, but also had the look: jet-black hair, and dark intense eyes that seemed like they were looking right through you. A woman would describe him as ruggedly handsome. Rugged because of centuries of being a warrior, and of course the scar, a prominent feature that added a sense of dread to his otherwise unblemished complexion. Then there was that smile, or more like an eternal smirk. Which seemed to never leave suggesting he always knew something you didn't?

Dante defiantly approached the site and sized up the situation. He could smell the fear from some of them, but from a few, he sensed a determination to do whatever necessary to protect the others and the cylinder. Dante could see the two angels still guarding each side of the hole, but he knew they were invisible to the group. He also knew the angels would not make a move unless he threatened the believers. He could not have been more wrong. Dante was fifteen feet into the clearing when both angels rose off the ground and started flying in a circle over the group---one going clockwise, and the other counter clockwise. He didn't miss a step as he heard the whooshing sound of the angels flying overhead. He was prepared for this encounter, and continued toward them. At this point, it was more like a game for Dante. Scare them a little, gauge their faith, and, oh yeah, lie his wings off to get what he wanted; the cylinder and its contents.

"No one move," said the professor. "Try and stay calm."

They all obeyed the professor's command. The only move Billy made was to visually locate the shotgun, and gauge his response if he needed to retrieve it. Sara also looked toward the weapon, then to Billy and gave him a nod.

Dante stopped facing the professor.

Kendall spoke first. "I'm sorry, sir, but have we met? I mean, besides your intrusion in our camp last night?"

"Forgive me, Professor. My name is Dante. We have a mutual acquaintance who informed me of your excavation in this area and is in part responsible for your permission to be here."

"Are you talking about Spencer?"

"Well, actually, an employee of Spencer's, who is aware of an unfortunate event perpetrated against me years ago."

"What do you want?" shouted Billy.

"Take it easy, Billy," the professor said. "Let him talk."

The angels, still flying above, remarked as they passed each other. One said, "That's a mistake."

"Free will," said the other.

Dante crossed his arms. "Billy, is it? I like a man who gets to the point, so I will do the same. Have you found an object you cannot explain, perhaps in the hole directly behind you, Professor?"

Sara spoke up. "I don't like this, Dad. I think this, Dante, is up no good, and quite frankly, I think he's evil."

Dante turned his gaze to Sara. "Now Sara, is that nice to talk about someone in the third person when he is standing right in front of you? And that evil remark, nothing could be further from the truth."

"Yes, obviously we have found something we cannot currently identify," the professor said.

"If you will only allow me to look," said Dante, "I may be able to help you in that respect."

The group could no longer hold their tongues.

"Don't do it, Professor, "said Ethan.

"Tell him to take a hike," Cooper said.

"Let me hurt him," said Billy.

"Think about it, Dad," Sara said.

"Who is this guy?" said Kate and Rachel in unison.

"If it will shut you up, and get you out of here go ahead," said Professor Kendall.

The angels guarding the scene remarked again.

One said, "Another mistake."

"More free will," said the other.

Dante's mouth almost watered, as he took the six steps toward the hole to view the object of his century's old mission. He bent over the hole and surveyed the cylinder like he was studying a Michelangelo sculpture.

Billy was still kneeling in the hole next to the cylinder, and Dante was just too close for comfort. Billy instinctively picked up the infamous trowel and held it in front of him with a defensive posture. Dante moved only his eyes to meet Billy's, and there was that smirk on Dante's face, which made Billy grasp the trowel even tighter.

Dante looked back to the cylinder. "Yes, that's it."

Billy knifed the trowel in the ground at Dante's feet shouting. "What's it?"

Kendall held up his hand to Billy. "Easy son." Then turned to Dante. "But please explain that remark sir."

Dante stepped away from the cylinder fearing if he didn't, he would grab it and fly away, only to have an angelic fight on his hands. He knew that lying was much easier. "Yes, an explanation is in order. You see I am an artist, based out of New York. I wouldn't expect you have seen any of my work, as much of it is sold to private collectors. This object which lies here before you is one of my creations."

"What," said Sara?

"No way," Billy said.

Dante put his hands together as if praying. "Please, I know this sounds strange. But I was just getting started out here in California about thirty years ago. I was commissioned to come up with a piece that was very simple, yet beautiful. During the creation of the piece, I was intimate with the buyer's daughter, which turned out to be a huge mistake. The relationship did not work out, and in a jealous rage, she stole the piece, and I never saw it or her again. I heard rumors from her friends she buried it somewhere in the Whispering Pines area. I hadn't thought of it for years, until I became aware there was an archeological dig on going in this area. You must understand, my curiosity could not be controlled, and I had to discern if the rumors were true."

"What a crock," said Cooper.

"That's not going to fly," Ethan said.

"I'm not buying it, Dad," said Sara.

"Who is this guy?" Kate and Rachel said in unison.

"It could explain why the object is here, and why it doesn't look very old," said Professor Kendall. "You must also understand, I cannot simply take your word on this. We have a legal right, and will take this to a lab to be studied. If your story is true, I suspect science will give us the answer."

"I would be more than happy to pay you for the piece," Dante said. "How does fifty thousand dollars sound?"

"Sounds like you want it pretty bad," said Sara.

"Well, my work has been good to me and you can't put a price on sentimental value, can you?"

"Sentimental value, my Aunt Tillie," Cooper said.

Kendall held up his hands. "Hold on everyone, let's take a step back here. I'm more interested in who led you to us. What did you say his name was?"

"Well, I didn't say, Professor, and I don't see what that has to do with anything. If you must know, his name is Carson Taylor."

Rachel whispered to Cooper. "Isn't that your contact for the charity match?"

"Yeah," said Cooper. "This thing just keeps getting stranger and stranger."

* * *

Carson had made it home and was in the upstairs bedroom of his beach house packing his suitcase. He was preparing to embark on a journey to help raise money for charity, plus deceive and destroy anyone his master deemed necessary. He felt like a secret agent with an unknown mission as he took a long look at the ocean view from the bedroom window. He didn't know how long he'd been looking at the waves rolling in and out from the shore when he heard a voice.

"You need some help, Carson?" His wife called out from downstairs.

"No, I've got it under control, honey, I'm almost done."

The packing he had under control. It was his nerve he worried about. It had been a lot of years since desert storm, and even though he had battle experience, he had never killed anyone. Maybe things will work out, he thought, and his life could go on as planned.

Carson focused back on the suitcase and took inventory. Shirts, pants, underwear, socks, everything was there.

His wife called out again, "be sure you take a jacket. It can get cool at night up there, even in the summer."

"Okay, thanks," Carson replied.

He pulled a jacket from the closet, neatly folded it and put it in the suitcase.

"And jacket," he said to himself.

He then pulled a duffle bag from a secret storage spot under the floor of the closet, and took another inventory. He unzipped the bag, and began; nine millimeter automatic, five extra clips, smoke grenades, C4, detonators, and in a wooden case, a disassembled 22 caliber sniper rifle.

"Yep," he said out loud, "everything I'll need for a week in the country." He loaded the bags in his Hummer and came back in the house to tell his wife goodbye.

"I love you, babe," Carson said.

"I love you too. Have a good time this week."

Carson didn't say another word he just kissed her. He kissed her with all the passion in his being, like it was the first time they had ever kissed. He knew it could be the last. He walked out the door, waved goodbye and got into the truck. He was about to turn the ignition, when he saw a folded piece of paper on the floor he hadn't noticed before. He picked up the paper, opened it and couldn't believe his eyes.

"How does that guy do it?"

The note said: *This afternoon, three o'clock in Clear Lake. The Lake Bakery and Cafe. Be there.* It was signed Dante.

Carson folded the note, put it in his pocket and left his palatial beach house for Clear Lake.

* * *

Dante was truly on a fishing expedition with this Christian gang, as he had dubbed them. But he was growing weary of the banter and the smart remarks from the young ones pushed him past the point of rational thinking.

The angels circling the group seemed to be getting closer, only a foot or so above his head, and the sound of them passing also grew louder. Whoosh! Whoosh! Whoosh! Dante's urge to let them all know exactly whom they were dealing with, and to just plain show off the power he possessed could no longer be controlled.

"I see we are not reaching any agreement today," Dante said, "but there is one thing I would like to show you."

He waited for the precise moment when one of the angels was directly overhead. Then without warning his angel body materialized. He shot straight up into the air, knocking one angel to the ground, flew over the group side-swiping the other angel, who also crashed and rolled across the dirt. Moving like an out of control cruise missile, he zoomed back over the amazed group and stopped about ten yards out. He hovered erect in mid-air with his hands on his hips like a circus performer who had just performed his greatest stunt. Everyone was speechless, not to mention terrified, and needed time to process what had just happened. Everyone, that is, except Cooper.

"No, you did not just fly straight up into the air like Superman late for a date with Lois Lane."

"That I did, Coop, that I did. But this Superman, although I do like his outfit, is only a children's comic book fantasy. I am real."

Dante held his position suspended ten feet off the ground, displaying a slight up and down motion, he used only for effect. Dante knew he could not out fight both angels, but was confident he could out fly them. He was known from Heaven to Hell for his flying abilities. He once, back in the day, beat the archangel Michael in a race. There were accusations of cheating on Dante's part, which he denies to this day.

Billy, ready to make his move for the shotgun only four feet away, knew he had to act fast. He had a problem. He was in the hole, and once he got to the gun, Kendall would be directly between Dante and himself. His eyes met Sara's, who already had a "do it" expression on her face, and that was all he needed. He dove out the hole, grabbed the gun, and threw it.

As the shotgun sailed through the air, Sara flashed on her favorite classic western, "Rio Bravo". There was a scene where two gunmen outside the town's hotel held John Wayne at bay. His rifle leaned on the hotel porch, unreachable and useless. Inside the hotel were Ricky Nelson and Angie Dickerson. Seeing the sheriff's predicament, Ricky had Angie throw a flowerpot through the window to distract the gunmen. Ricky ran out, tossed the rifle to the sheriff, and the bad guys were done. Sara knew it was John Wayne time, as the shotgun came within reach.

Billy's throw was perfect. She caught and pumped a shell in the chamber with one hand, leveled the gun, and "Bang". The shot hit Dante directly in the chest, which pushed him back several feet. His body went limp, but was still floating above the ground. Sara pumped the shotgun again, took aim and Dante started to laugh.

"Whoa, good shooting, Tex. But the thing is these earthly weapons cannot harm me."

The two bushwhacked angels recovered and headed straight for Dante as if being shot out of a cannon. Dante went ballistic, climbing toward the heavens with the angel's right on his tail. He maneuvered beyond the limits of the most sophisticated aircraft in existence. At an incredible rate of speed, he zigzagged, made ninety degree turns, and flew straight down toward the earth, then turned to fly just inches above the ground, all with the angels still behind him. Dante was slowly and purposefully moving them away from the group.

"Does this strike anyone as being totally unreal?" said Kate.

"He looks like he's fighting with something invisible," Ethan said.

"Angels," said Rachel.

"Let's don't get carried away," Kendall said.

"What, do you see a mini-jetpack on his back, Dad? This guy is not human."

Exactly the point Dante was trying to convey, and he was about to make his most devious and lasting impression of the day.

The dogfight between Dante and the angels was about a hundred yards out from the group. Dante was flying at least a hundred miles an hour, with the two angels hanging in about five feet behind him. Dante made his move. He hit the brakes, jogged left, then right, bashing both angels and again sent them tumbling. He made a beeline back to the dazed group. Rachel and Kate knelt and were praying. Billy, Cooper, and Ethan wanted to do something, they just didn't know what. The only logical reason Professor Kendall's scientific mind could come up with to explain the incredible display was mass hallucination. Sara was just plain mad.

Dante was hurtling above the treetops, and it wasn't two seconds before he flew up behind Sara, wrapped his left arm around her neck, and grabbed her forehead with his right hand. He wasn't standing; he was floating, extended parallel to the ground, with a death grip on Sara, as he spoke. "You know, little lady, I could snap you like a twig. And pulling that trigger has made me dislike you even more."

Sara stood, trying not to move, and unable to speak. She could barely breathe. The others felt helpless and horrified by this unbelievable sight. As the last few words came out of Dante's mouth, the two angels rushed to Sara's side, inches from Dante's face.

One said, "That would be a mistake."

"No free will for you," said the other. "Your limbs will be hanging from the trees if you attempt to hurt her."

Sara knew what to do, and she mustered all the strength she could, took a deep breath, and screamed. "No devil from hell can hurt me, because Jesus is my Lord."

Dante leaned in and whispered in her ear. "Devil from hell, huh. That could not be further from the truth. I was created in heaven. I do not wish to hurt you; however I do think a lesson is in order."

Dante threw Sara to the ground, and rocketed upward spinning like a top. Bellowing a hideous laugh as he flew higher and higher. He grew smaller and smaller until he disappeared into the clear sky.

Rachel and Kate ran to Sara and turned her over to check her condition. She was conscious but seemed to be in shock.

The angels stayed with the group and started praying and praising God, as they flew over and around them, leaving a white transparent trail to protect them. Kendall's team had little time to recover when Billy said, "What's that, Professor?"

"Where, Billy?"

"Up there, out of the west."

They all looked up to see a rolling black cloud growing exponentially as it grew closer. The wind started to blow and became so fierce it was difficult to stand. The cloud was directly above them and the beautiful day of moments ago had now turned ominous and dark. Then it happened. CRACK! BANG! A bolt of lightning exploded out of the clouds, lit up the area like the Fourth of July, as it hit Professor Kendall directly in the head. The professor's body jerked with electricity then went limp. He dropped to the ground and slid into the hole at Billy's feet.

Kendall's collapse signaled the end of the sudden turbulence. The wind stopped blowing and in an instant the darkness was replaced by blue skies and sunshine. The sun reflected off the silver cylinder onto Kendall's lifeless body.

Billy fell at the professor's side, and checked his pulse. "He's not breathing!"

Chapter Four

Spencer Bryant, unaware of the fate of his old friend and the demonic alliance of his second in command, had weeded out the critical briefs and finalized their respective course of action. He remembered important information concerning the charity event he had forgotten to give Carson. The Nike reps needed some special attention and he wanted to make sure Carson had his shoe size. He called Carson's cell phone. The phone rang, with no answer, and finally went to voice mail. "You have reached Carson Taylor of Spin-Corp, please leave a message". Spencer was not big on leaving voice mail messages, so he hung up and tried to call again with the same result. Spencer surmised Carson must be in a bad area for phone reception and would call him again later.

Carson was about 60 miles north of the Golden Gate Bridge, just off the 101; on the north side of Santa Rosa, and his phone reception was perfect. He had received both calls from Spencer and on the second call, when he saw Spencer's name on the display, he pitched the cell phone in the passenger seat of the Hummer and continued to drive. The worm had started to turn for Carson. He had never ignored a call from Spencer, who had been a good boss to him over the past fifteen years, but in the last few miles he traveled over roads he had driven countless times, he came to realize Spencer was no longer his boss, and Dante was. Boss, he thought, more like sub-ruler of the earthly realm or maybe wicked general was a more appropriate term, because his confidence was high at some point in his unsure future, there was going to be a battle.

Something snapped in Carson's spirit when Spencer's name lit up his phone. Like some kind of evil anointing had been poured from a five-gallon bucket saturating every pore of his body. He could feel it in his hands as he grasped the wheel of the Hummer. He could smell it, tickling his nose as it permeated the cab of the truck.

A strange thing struck him about the evil feeling, not just that he liked it, but is was familiar. He had felt these same exact feelings years ago and was aware that the decision he made at that time had brought him to where he was today.

He then had a simple yet powerful realization. As he looked at all the traffic around him, some exiting, some merging, some traveling in his direction and some heading the other way---he became keenly aware they were all there at that instant because a decision had been made. The type of car they drove, whether or not they were married, did they like their jobs, could all be traced back to a chain of decisions that shaped their lives. Some he supposed as was his case, had made that one, big, heart stopper of a decision, which changed the course of a life for better or worse. This was an odd freeing experience for Carson. Free from his job, free from his wife, and free from his whole life, all of which only minutes before he could not have imagined giving up. But the stark reality was, there was no going back now. Carson had definitely gotten out of the boat.

The next thought he had, on this escalating evolution of evil, was to do something to prove himself worthy, something bad. Professor Kendall and his group were first to come to mind, but they were the main event. He needed a preliminary bout to get his juices flowing, so he drove and waited. Waited for destiny to bring him an unsuspecting victim, then he would make his decision. He verbalized his concept. "Decisions and destiny, free will and fate. How opposite yet intertwined these forces are, and how does one affect the other." Carson was caught up in his own thoughts when he noticed the low fuel light glowing from his dashboard; he had forgotten to fill up. Destiny had brought Carson to this point without fuel, now a decision was made to exit the freeway to find a gas station. This would ultimately give him the opportunity for his immediate goal---to prove himself worthy of the evil anointing.

* * *

Professor Kendall and the silver cylinder lay side by side in the man-made dirt cavity, both of which had yet to reach their full potential in God's plan. The professor had been successful in his own right, but he possessed no vision of God's plan. His prospects were not good because in his current state, he had no vision at all. The cylinder was still waiting for the predetermined time to come into the world, and be solely dependent on external forces to help it reach its full potential.

The group knew Sara's take on potential. "The thing about potential, it's like a seed," she would say. "If it sits on a shelf in an unopened package, it's still just a dormant spark in a paper prison. But if it's planted in good soil by environment, watered by the will, and has the sunlight of the promise in God's word, it will grow and bear fruit." The cylinder's potential had been put in the hands of the believers. Kendall's fate was in the hands of God.

Billy was trying to find some kind of life in the professor, and when the statement that Kendall wasn't breathing hit the group, Kate ran to the hole. "Move over Billy, let me see."

Kate verified Billy was correct and started CPR. She had been trained on the technique as a lifeguard in high school, but had never used it and hoped she was doing it correctly. Sara hearing the news about her father felt a shot of adrenalin pump into her system and she jumped up walked a few steps, only to fall and kneel at the edge of the hole. "Somebody call 911."

"Your phone, Sara."

Sara handed Cooper her phone as she starred down at Kate trying to revive the man she loved and respected more than anyone in the world.

"I'm having trouble getting a signal," Cooper said, "I'll go up on that hill and see if it's any better."

"I'll try the Ranger Station," said Ethan. "I programmed the number when we first got here. It's ringing. Still ringing."

"How you doing Kate?" Sara said.

"The best I can but still no response."

"The Rangers aren't answering. It's just ringing."

Sara felt helpless and disoriented. "What are we going to do?"

Billy looked up to see Cooper on the hill with the phone to his ear and yelled, "Any luck?"

Sara remembered the earlier conversation with her dad and said under her breath, "Luck is not a factor."

Billy saw Cooper raise both hands in the air to relay the cell phone signal was no better on the hill and Cooper started back down.

"We can't let him die," said Sara.

Billy looked at Ethan redialing the Ranger Station and Ethan just shook his head.

Professor Kendall had not moved for more than ten minutes. It seemed like an eternity, and for someone who had no oxygen flowing to his brain, it was.

The two angels standing on each side of Sara had done their jobs. They had protected the believers. Professor Kendall was unsure about God, and therefore the weak link. The two angels had limited power over the professor and could not bring him back to life, but they could do one small thing to help.

"This is not happening!" Rachel said.

Sara agreed, "No, it's not. Move Kate."

Kate moved and Sara took her place, not to perform CPR, but to lay hands on her dad and pray. As Sara got into position, putting her hand on his chest, closing her eyes, and lifting her head up toward the heavens, she appeared to move Kendall's arm and his hand was now touching the side of the cylinder. In reality one of the angels had bent down and slid his arm to contact the cylinder.

Sara let the prayer fly. "Father, in Jesus name, do not let this man die. We have been given authority according to the sacrifice of Jesus and..."

Sara stopped speaking. She heard a melodic sound coming from somewhere close. Everyone heard it. She looked over and realized it was coming from the silver cylinder, which was not silver anymore. It had started to radiate a deep blue color and the sound was growing louder as the cylinder became brighter. The cylinder had transformed into what looked like a liquid form, preserving the same shape, but it now engulfed the professor's hand. No one moved or spoke. As Cooper returned, even he had nothing to say as he observed the aqueous blue, fluorescent object. It was emitting some kind of melodic tones with the light being hypnotic and the melody replacing their fear with a peace they could not understand.

Their trancelike state was broken as the professor took a long, deep reviving breath and opened his eyes. He was back. So was the cylinder, silver, shiny, and seemingly impenetrable.

Professor Kendall opened his eyes and saw Sara bending over him. She cried and laughed at the same time. Sara pounced on him and gave him a bear hug, "Dad, you're alive."

"Not for long if you don't let me breathe."

Sara rose up wiping her tears and slapped him on the arm. "You scared me."

"I'm sure I didn't do it intentionally, by the way, what just happened?"

To say the group was astonished would be an understatement. Stuff was happening way too fast to digest the morning's events in the natural, but in the Spirit, they all knew they had witnessed pure evil and a healing miracle in a small span of time. They gathered around the professor, elated to see him sitting up and asking for water.

Billy handed him his canteen, "Glad to have you back, Professor."

"Back from where, Billy. Did I pass out?"

Billy looked at the others and didn't quite know what to say. "Well, sort of."

"Man, this water tastes good, but I have a metallic taste in my mouth."

"Probably from electricity," said Cooper.

"Or the cylinder," Ethan added.

Kendall gazed at each of their faces. "Electricity"?

"Okay, Dad, take it easy. You were struck by lightning."

"How could that be, there's not a cloud in the sky," as he held his hand up, doing his best Vanna White imitation.

"It's true, Professor."

"Yeah, it zapped you."

"Lit you up like a Christmas tree," the group assured him.

"No way," said Kendall, as he patted and checked his body, starting at his neck and working down to his legs. "What the..."

Kendall's eyes focused on the charred hole, the size of a golf ball, on the end of his right boot and had obviously come from the inside out. His sock was burnt and missing in the same area, and you could see his wiggling toes, which looked untouched.

"There's a hole in my boot."

"You were well grounded," Cooper said. "Electrically speaking, of course."

"So, where was I hit?"

"In the head, Dad."

"Although I see the hole where the lightning reached the common ground, I don't think you could survive a lightning strike that intense."

Sara reached in her backpack and handed him a small mirror. "You didn't."

Kendall took the mirror unaware of its purpose, and contemplated Sara's conclusion. "I didn't what?"

Sara just pointed at the mirror, then at his face, back and forth several times, until he got the message to look at himself. He resembled an exploded cartoon character with his burnt hair sticking straight out all over his head, and he thought he saw a little smoke rise from the singed strands.

"You probably won't like this, and God knows you are not going to believe me, so I'm just going to say it. You were dead, no pulse, not breathing for ten minutes until the cylinder sucked up your arm and brought you back to life. It was just like 'The Blob', only good, not bad. Your hand was inside the cylinder."

"The last thing I remember was the sunrise, and yes, coffee. The coffee was good this morning." Kendall looked over at the gleaming metal object, and reached out and touched it. "What's this?"

"Okay, that's it, Dad; you're going to the hospital."

"But I feel great. In fact, I haven't felt this good in years. The knee pain that's bothered me has disappeared. The only thing I have a problem with is my memory."

"Dad we need to get you checked by a doctor."

Kendall was emphatic, "No. Maybe I don't know what this thing is laying next to me, but I do know, at least I feel it's our responsibility. Somebody help me up."

Sara knew when he had that tone in his voice; she wasn't going to change his mind. "Have it your way. But if you drop dead on the way home, I may just kick you out of the truck and let the wolves have you for dinner."

Kendall smiled and knew Sara had come by her stubbornness honestly.

Billy decided it was time to move on. "If you two are finished, let's get a plan on how to proceed."

Kendall and Sara stared at each other, then Kendall spoke, "Go ahead, Sara, make the call."

"Cooper, Ethan, there's an anvil case in the tent big enough to accommodate the cylinder. Everyone here, pack your gear. Juan and his crew will close up the site, and we'll go back to our lab and get to work."

Billy questioned her. "The lab at the university?"

Kendall's tone became even more stern. "No. Not the university. We need to go somewhere more private. Take it to the lab at my house."

"I agree Dad. There is sufficient equipment to get started."

The group knew the plan was final, as Juan called out to Sara from the tree line. Juan and his men had witnessed Dante's mysterious spectacle and were not coming any closer than necessary. Sara went to discuss the details of closing down the site with Juan. The rest of the group started gathering tools and packing.

Professor Kendall found himself alone, and looking down at the cylinder. He pondered how he could feel so alive and alert and yet his analytical mind was totally void of any scientific data. Something to process mentally as to how, or why, he was standing in a hole next to this silver, metal cylinder.

Chapter Five

The cylinder was also on the mind of Carson Taylor when he pulled into the gas station for fuel. He knew Dante and the cylinder were connected, and he was somehow part of a scheme to reclaim it. Beyond that, he was on a need to know basis. Carson did know he had to show up at the charity event, and sooner or later, he was going to have to talk to Spencer.

It would be sooner. His phone rang, still laying in the seat next to him. He did not have to look to know it was Spencer. This time he would answer.

"Hello, Spencer. And what can I do for you?"

"First of all, you can answer your phone when I call, and do you have my shoe size for the Nike group?"

Carson overlooked the answer your phone remark. "Yes, I do. Ten and a half, right?"

"Yes, ten and a half. Be sure to take care of the Nike reps and all the reps for that matter."

"Will do."

"You have the layout on how the booths are to be placed. If you think any adjustments need to be made, take care of it."

"Booth adjustments, check."

"The trucks should start rolling in day after tomorrow, on Thursday. You will have a day to prepare the grounds, and a day to set up. We'll kick it off Friday around 10:00 A.M. and I think we have scheduled more than enough events to last three days."

"I'm sure we will be okay sir. Make sure you call the radio station and coordinate times for the live broadcasts."

"Yeah, thanks, I'll do that. Have you heard the spots on the radio?"

"I sure have. *Come to Clear Lake this weekend for three days of sports fun and sun. Meet some sports legends and some up and coming players in their field.* Sounded good."

"I should be there sometime Friday. Take care, Carson."

"You too, sir," and they both hung up. That wasn't so bad Carson thought. I guess this evil thing will be easier to hide than I anticipated. It should be since lying is a large part of the evil M.O.

Carson slipped his company credit card into the slot, put in his pin number and started pumping gas. He could not really remember, but his uncle would talk of a time when you pulled into a gas station and three or four attendants would come out, pump your gas, check your oil, clean your windshields, and even check the air in your tires. That would be nice, he thought, as he started to the rear of the Hummer. He opened the cargo door and pulled the nine-millimeter handgun from the duffle bag. Maybe the gas station attendants would clean your gun for you or offer target practice from your car. He opened the side door and placed the gun in the console. He did think about target practice on the pumps, but there were too many cameras these days. He knew his movements were being recorded right now, but he had done no wrong although he wanted to hurt something, even if it was a gas pump.

Carson kept his cool as he put the nozzle back and walked inside for a soda. He got about four steps when he heard screeching automobile tires from behind. The sound startled him and good thing it did because when he stopped and looked back, the car was inches from him. He braced for impact but the car slid, blew right by, and continued its' erratic course out of the station and down the road.

A voice from the adjacent island called out, "Wow, are you okay, mister?"

Carson's feet felt glued to the concrete, so he turned his head and said, "Yes, I'm okay."

The voice came from a girl filling up her red Mustang convertible. By Carson's best estimate she was in her early twenties. She was a gorgeous blonde, dressed in a short plaid skirt, white blouse with black high heels. It struck him as a racy catholic school outfit, and without thinking, he said, "Do you go to Catholic School around here?" He couldn't believe what he said. He was not really forward with women especially in that manner.

The young lady just laughed and said, "No, I'm a waitress downtown. It's the uniform of the day."

In Carson's mind, she looked like the victim of the day. Could she be the opportunity to do something evil just for the doing of it? He felt he had as much to prove to himself as he did the principalities and powers.

"That guy barely missed you," she said.

"Yeah, no kidding. Be careful out there," and Carson's mind rushed back the speeding maniac that could have crushed him. His feet were not so stuck to the ground as they were before, so he continued with his plan. Go get a drink.

He visualized the car going by him over and over in his mind with the front tire almost running over his foot. He did not notice who was driving, or if there were any passengers. But he did see the car up close and personal. It was a gray color. Not a shiny gray, but that flat battleship gray like a primer. That was it. It was primed and definitely an older, classic Chevy. He guessed around 1963. It sat low to the ground, and the rims could have cost more than the car itself. They were huge, about twenty-two inches and chrome with a hand polished finish he saw his reflection in as they glistened past his feet.

"A dollar forty-nine," he heard.

He looked up and came back to the present. He had gotten his drink and now the clerk was expecting him to pay.

"Yeah, here you go." Carson opened his billfold and threw two dollars down on the counter.

The clerk picked up the money. "I guess those two dudes rattled you, huh?"

"I guess they did. You say there were two males?"

"Yes sir. They were laughing and acting a fool. It seems someone was looking after you."

Carson agreed by shaking his head, and walked out. Someone was looking after him. In fact, there were two. Dante had dispatched two fallen angels to trail Carson and help only when necessary. This was a test for Carson and his reborn evil anointing. Dante wanted to make sure he could count on him later.

On his way back to the Hummer, he noticed the sexy catholic waitress had left. I guess she wasn't my victim, he thought. No problem. There would be plenty of chances to do this thing he felt he had to do, although no details came to mind. He was clearly driven, and this implanted urge would not go away until his bad deed was done.

The immediate decision was which way to drive. Carson decided to take the scenic route but there really was no other way in this part of the state. It was all scenic. He decided to take a secondary back road. A back road to the back road. He started the truck and was back on his route to Clear Lake.

Back at the site Professor Kendall was still standing in the hole next to the cylinder, and he was still alone. Everyone looked busy. He walked to his truck, and sat down on the passenger side watching the flurry of activity before him. He could see Cooper and Ethan carrying the case that would house the cylinder for transport back to Clear Lake. Sara was confirming to Juan, or mainly his men, once the cylinder was removed, they would have nothing to fear. Rachel and Kate were taking more photos and doing general clean up. Billy was in the far corner of the site, and he seemed to be looking for more Indian artifacts. There was no doubting Billy's dedication.

Professor Kendall was simply trying to think. Trying to remember anything of the morning events. What popped into his head was an event about eight years' worth of mornings past. He could picture his wife, Beth, on that rainy day driving to San Francisco late for an important meeting. He could imagine her thoughts preoccupied with things, other than her driving, as the large rock dislodged from it's perch and rolled down the mountain striking the blue Tahoe.

The professor figured she never knew what hit her. When the rock struck her SUV the vehicle started to swerve violently, going over the edge, and began to roll over and over down the side of Chapel Canyon. By the time the truck came to rest at the bottom of the canyon, Beth was gone. Kendall could only hope she had not suffered and her death quick. He also wondered if there really is a God, how could he let this happen to such a good woman who believed in Him.

He wished he could see her again. He wished hard closing his eyes. He laid his head back on the seat and his mind went blank; he fell asleep and began to dream. The professor found himself in the past. He starred out the window from the front seat of his 1966 Fairlane GT at a white, blank movie screen. He recognized the familiar place of his youth---the Buckner Drive-In movie theatre. He looked around at the people coming back from the concession stand with refreshments. Some had brought their own food. One couple sat on the hood of their car leaned up against the windshield having a picnic. He could see the concession stand from where he parked, and the outdoor seating area. There were about twenty or so wooden chairs, and a few were occupied with people waiting for the movie to start. Speakers hung close by on the side of the building so the movie could be heard.

Standing under one of the speakers a figure was looking and waving at him. The figure's waving action changed into a slow and steady, come here movement with the arm. Kendall knew that whoever it was motioned to him. Because now when he looked around he was the only other soul in the place. He got out of his Fairlane GT, which he was glad to see again because he loved his first car, looked up, and the waving person was not there.

He could hear a familiar, squeaking sound coming from the area right in front of the Drive-In screen. In the distance he could see a play- ground area with swings, a slide, merry-go-round, jungle gym, and teeter-totter. The sound was coming from the chain on the swings that were in much need of an oiling. The figure was now swinging up and down on the swing set and still signaling him to come. In the next moment he was swinging alongside the stranger. Their swings were out of sync, and Kendall could only see the back of a woman's head as she swung by out in front of him. She was way too familiar to be a stranger, and he was sure as she spoke. "Whatcha you doing here Jacob?"

They were now swinging side by side and there was no mistake. It was Beth.

"Beth, you look beautiful, and where is here?"

"At the Drive-In silly. Isn't it fun? I can't remember the last time we did this together.

"Yes you can. It's where we first met. I remember thinking, what's that good looking high school girl doing on the swing set?"

"She was trying to get the attention of that handsome high school boy,"

"You were not?"

"I was and it worked."

Kendall and Beth were laughing like a couple of kids, and swinging higher and higher. They were both at the limits of the swings capacity for height when Beth said something strange.

"I want you to know I'm okay, Jacob. Things happen for a reason, but you are not supposed to be here now. So be thankful for second chances and remember."

"Remember what?"

The next thing Kendall new, just like when he was a child, at the highest point of the swings arc he jumped. He was not sure why he jumped but it felt great free falling toward the earth. It felt great for a few seconds until he realized he was past the spot where he should have hit the ground. He looked back for Beth but everything around him was black. Black was not really an accurate description. It was a blackness that had weight or substance and it was pulling at his clothes, and skin.

While waiting to land, as the falling continued, the pulling at his body felt more like human hands, now grabbing and pinching. The assault on his body became more intense and he could see arms and hands coming out of the darkness, but they did not look human. The hands were larger than normal with yellowish colored skin and the long skinny fingers were tipped with two-inch razor sharp nails. His limbs were being pulled in opposite directions, and the knifelike fingernails were ripping his flesh. His wonderful dream about Beth had turned into a nightmare, when he heard a voice out of the darkness.

"Dad. Dad wake up."

Kendall's body jumped and he opened his eyes to find Sara at the window. He rubbed his eyes and looked at his daughter. "I guess I fell asleep."

"We're ready to move the cylinder and I knew you would want to be there."

"Yeah, the cylinder, of course I do."

"Of course you do. You forgot all about it didn't you?"

"Ask me about yesterday, I remember yesterday."

Sara reached into her bag, and handed him a brush, "You can't expect me to go anywhere with you looking like that."

The professor did his best to groom his lightning hairdo but he never was meticulous about his appearance. So as his grandmother used to say, he gave it a lick and a promise. The professor exited the truck, with the bad dream still vibrating his head and walked with Sara to the cylinder.

"Is it safe to move, Sara?"

"I would have to say yes. It's not radioactive, and it doesn't look like anything military."

"Do you have any idea where it's from or what it might be?"

"Other than we dug it up this morning, then it saved your life, oh yeah, it could be a work of art."

"Art? You mean like the Venus De Milo or Mona Lisa art?"

"Don't strain yourself Dad. I'll try to fill in the blanks later, not like you're going to be receptive."

Professor Kendall did not rebut Sara's comment as he knelt down in front of the cylinder. Ethan and Cooper were at each end of the cylinder and Billy was holding the lid to the case open ready to receive the ancient silver object. Kendall reached out and stroked the cylinder in an almost compassionate manor, "Does anyone know how much it weights?"

Cooper responded, "We're going to find out. Are you ready Ethan?"

"Ready."

"On three. One, two, three."

The boys lifted, and with very little effort the cylinder was cradled inside the foam rubber of the anvil case.

"That wasn't bad," said Ethan. "I guess it's not full of gold."

"How much did it weight?" Sara said.

"What do you think Cooper, fifty maybe seventy five pounds?"

"That sounds about right."

Sara was glad the cylinder was safe in the case. She was also relieved it did not explode, shoot lightning bolts, or release a plague of locusts when they moved it, but she was itching to leave. "Is everyone about ready to go?"

"So, where are we going?" said Billy.

"We should stop by site one, and pick up our personal stuff..."

"No, I mean where are we going to take the cylinder?"

"I thought we settled that," Sara said.

"To my house," injected Kendall. "Cooper, Ethan, would you put it in the back of my truck, please?"

"Yes sir," and they carefully picked up the case and walked to the truck.

Billy walked in the opposite direction of Cooper and Ethan, and looked back," Can I talk to you Sara?"

"Sure Billy, what's up?"

"I would be talking to the professor about this but after what he's been through..."

"Okay, and?"

"I'm not so sure we should take the cylinder to the house."

"Why not?"

"I think we're obligated to take it back to the school. It's because of school money we are out here, right?"

"Partly, but most of the donations for this dig were private. They were given directly to dad and without his friend Spencer we would not be on this land. This is private land."

"Well, at least we should contact the proper authorities."

"Did you not see what happened here today? Who are we going to call, Ghostbusters? I know we can call Gabriel or the archangel Michael. Do you have their phone numbers?"

"You don't have to be disrespectful, but maybe the military should take a look at it."

"The military, that's great. Have you never seen a science fiction movie? The military can never stop the alien invader, or they take what you've found and you never see it again."

"Why are you so intent on not telling anyone about this, it could be nothing?"

"You're right, it could be nothing. But after what happened this morning you know it's something."

"What about the other members of the team back at site one?"

"I think the least people that know about this the better."

"I think your wrong Sara. Everyone should know about it. The world should know about it."

"Billy, did it not cross your mind that we, us, this small group, on this day, in this spot, were supposed to find the cylinder? Are the words fate or destiny in your vocabulary? We need to get it to our lab, analyze it, and go from there."

"I think we are going to agree to disagree, but you're in charge. I won't say anything, but I don't have to like it."

"Well, you can like it or not, but we need you Billy."

"I guess it's nice to be needed. I'll go get the Jeep if that's OK with you. Billy walked off.

Sara went to her father who saw the conversation, but could not hear.

"Billy didn't look like a happy camper. What was all that about?"

"I don't know why he has his shorts in a knot over what to do with the cylinder."

"What does he want to do?"

"Turn it over to the school or the military."

"Which we may do."

"Dad!"

"After we study it of course. We need Billy you know."

"I know, and I told him."

"He is one of the most talented computer programmers I've seen."

"More like programmer slash hacker."

"That could be useful too."

"All right, let's get out of here, I need some food."

A few minutes later, Sara was behind the wheel of the GMC pickup pointed in the direction to leave. The truck was packed, the engine was running and Professor Kendall sat next to her wondering what she was waiting on. Sara was leaning forward in the seat looking out the side window. She could see Billy driving the old Jeep Cherokee slowly down the hill and stop for the others. Rachel and Cooper got in the front seat, and Kate and Ethan got in the back. They were all laughing and shoving one another into the vehicle. She saw Billy crack a smile and knew he would be okay.

"Kids," she said. "What are you going to do?"

"You are going to be patient, and teach them everything you know, any way they will listen."

"That sounds like sagely advice, Professor, but here's some more. We all better get ready to go back to class. Because the thing in the back of this truck is going to make us all think it's the first day of school."

Chapter Six

As he drove, Carson Taylor had visions of school also. Only it wasn't so much school as it was the woman in the schoolgirl uniform, who spoke to him at the gas station. His mind was racing with the things he could have done with her before she became his test victim. His fantasy turned into regret and then anger, because he let the opportunity get away. If it wasn't for those crazy guys in that gray Chevy, things might have been different. Now he was mad at the out of control driver that almost smashed him. He did not see which way the girl in the red Mustang or the gray Chevy went, but he knew he had seen them twice; the first and last.

Time was not a concern for Carson. It was just after noon on Tuesday, and the event did not start till Friday. He was planning to dump most of the set up on the locals and the charity, so the next appointment he had to make was The Lake Bakery Cafe, three o'clock. He planned to be there early because patience was not in Dante's make up. The thought of Dante made him shudder. Here he was thinking of how tough he's going to be, and one picture of Dante made his skin cold. So what do you call that he wondered, when the mental image of a supernatural being with a mean streak from the pits of hell brings you back to sanity?

Fear. Because somewhere on some time worn parchment Carson Taylor's signature was locked forever. Locked in a universal struggle for souls, and Carson had picked sides. He did not choose wisely. He had not read the book. He decided on a few good years at the top, in exchange for eternity. He could have had a long prosperous life with a heavenly eternity, but he did not know that. The truth be known, back when he made his decision he didn't believe in either side, good or evil. Until early that morning when Dante showed up in his office he wasn't sure he was on a side, but it was real now. The most real thing he had ever felt. He knew there was no way out. He was in bed with evil so be evil and enjoy it. Have fun being bad and go out with guns blazing.

As he rationalized his predicament it was all sounding like a bad gangster movie, but he was getting more comfortable with his probable future. He started to relax. His grip on the steering wheel loosened up as he rolled his head from side to side and stretched the muscles in his neck. He noticed the tension in his upper body had eased up and a smile came across his face, until he topped the hill. He could not believe his eyes. There, on a scenic turn out, about fifty yards off the road sat the gray Chevy. The peace he was starting to experience was now gone.

He went into commando mode as he applied the brakes and turned off the road. He stopped the Hummer a few feet behind the gray Chevy. Carson opened the console and starred at the nine mm automatic he had so conveniently placed. He didn't think about it very long before he reached in and grabbed the gun. He checked the clip, took the safety off and chambered a round. There was no activity around the gray Chevy and he wasn't sure if anyone was inside as he got out of the Hummer. The gun was still in his hand but he concealed it behind his back and walked to the car.

Carson did not know what was about to go down but he was prepared. He was walking slow and bent down to look inside the Chevy's window. There they were, two of them. The driver had long thin dark hair and his seat was leaned back like a La-Z-Boy recliner. The passenger sat upright and wore a long black headband that hung down behind the front seat. Carson stopped about three feet from the window in view of the two men, "How's it going there gentlemen."

The driver was the only one that spoke, "Pretty good Pops. What has you on this lonely stretch of road?"

I'm on my way to Clear Lake. I decided to stop and check out the scenery."

"That could have been a mistake," the driver said and smiled. The passenger started to snicker out of control and put his hand to his mouth in a feeble attempt to stop. The driver slapped his arm, "Shut up man."

Caron knew the type, young and invincible with no respect for anyone. "So, do I look familiar to either of you?"

"Yeah Pops you do. You remind me of that Jackrabbit we saw a few miles back. Only you're not as tall. So what do you think dude," as he turned to the passenger and tapped him on the arm. The passenger, who was still snickering, said nothing. He just pulled on his ear. The driver turned back to face Carson. "Oh yeah, your ears may be a little bigger than the rabbits'.

Carson was bubbling inside and he knew it would be no loss to society as he reveled and pointed the gun at the young men.

"Hang on man, we were only playing around."

"Playing around, huh. You almost ran over me back at that gas station."

"Was that you? Well we missed you didn't we." They both let go a distasteful laugh that filled the air with rebellion.

That was it for Carson; he lost control and pulled the trigger. Pow! Pow! He fired one shot in the head of each wise guy and they both sagged down in their seats. Pow! Pow! He put one more round in each chest for good measure. Just as the echo of the last gunshot faded through the hills he heard the sound of a police siren. He could not see a vehicle but the whaling sound was close, to close for him to run, and headed his way. He stuck the gun in his pants, leaned over with his hands on the grey door of the Chevy, and pretended to talk to the two dead men inside. About thirty seconds was all it took and the California Highway Patrol came over the hill. Go down guns blazing, he imagined. The Trooper drove by and continued down the highway.

Unbelievable he thought, but that cop had to have seen me. The Hummer and the old gray Chevy were too distinct, so he had to get rid of the evidence. The dead men's car was parked on a downhill grade facing a fifty-foot drop into a ravine. This was too easy. Put the car in neutral, a little push, and bye-bye bad guys. He leaned into the car pulled the gearshift down into neutral, got a tight grip on the window frame and pushed. The car did not budge. "Emergency brake," he said out loud and again reached into the car. He slid his arm down along the door panel but this time a hand lunged out and grabbed him tight around the wrist. Carson looked over to find the driver starring back at him. "I wouldn't do that if I were you. We need to talk."

* * *

After a five-minute stop at site one grabbing a few things and giving very little reason why they were leaving, Sara was leading the way northwest toward Clear Lake. Her normal driving habits were about the same as one of the Andretti boys on the final lap of the Indy 500. But having her father in the truck had slowed her down a bit. She kept the GMC humming about five miles above the speed limit. In the mirror she could see Billy and the others in the Jeep trying to keep up. She noticed they were all talking and gesturing but there was no question Dante's supernatural show was the subject of the conversation.

She wanted to talk about what happened that morning but her dad's memory was fried, and aside from that, she didn't know where to begin. Now was not the time. She looked over at him; awake but not speaking and there was an uneasy silence between them. Small talk was the way to go.

"Nice weather," she said?

"Yeah, can't argue with that."

"Billy, Ethan, and Cooper have been a lot of help this year."

"Yes they have."

"Kate and Rachel have really gotten the hang of things. I think we're a good team."

"The two girls have pulled their weight and more."

"I think Rachel has a thing for Cooper, have you noticed?"

"I've noticed you give special attention to Ethan."

"Dad, he's at least ten years younger than I am."

"More like fifteen."

"Thanks a lot. He does have something that attracts me but it would never work. He's still a kid."

"You do need to think about settling down Sara. You're not getting any younger."

"O.K. enough with the age references I'm only thirty three. When I meet the right guy I'll know it, just like when you met mom."

"The last conversation I had with your mom was an argument that morning right before she left."

"Oh Dad, don't."

"Toast."

"What?"

"Toast. We argued about the toast. I wonder if things would have been different if I had just kissed her before she walked out the door."

"You can't think her accident had anything to do with you. I miss her too; more than you know but none of it was your fault."

"I know that now."

"You do, good."

"She told me about an hour ago."

"That's it, we're going to the emergency room."

"Don't panic Sara, it was in a dream. It seemed so real but I think she was there because she didn't want me to worry."

"So, you feel better?"

"I think she's in a better place."

"What's this, Professor Jacob Winston Kendall saying he believes in heaven?"

Sara was trying to lighten things up with the heaven question, but when she looked at her dad she saw a man who was seriously contemplating his answer.

"I'm pretty sure it wasn't heaven where I saw your mom. We met on some kind of neutral ground."

"Neutral ground, what does that mean?"

"The location looked like a Drive-In movie theatre but my theory is, it was somewhere in between."

"You're kind of talking in riddles Dad. In between where?"

"As far as I can tell between heaven and hell or between life and death. You are not exactly catching me at my best and I'm sorting this out as I go, but I don't believe it was a dream. I think the dream was actually my memory starting to return. The memory of what happened while I was dead."

"You saw mom when you were gone? That's good. I know she's in heaven. Who do you think first taught me about Jesus?

"I know who is responsible for your belief, but before, I could never really accept the whole Christ thing. Seeing Beth was a pleasure but what happened after that has opened my eyes."

Sara was tired of the question and answer game but she decided to play one more round, " So what happened?"

"After I was with her a minute or so she said something kind of cryptic and I started to fall. There is no doubt in my mind now Sara. I was falling straight through the gates of hell. So the simple answer to your earlier question, yes. Professor Jacob Winston Kendall does believe in heaven because he's already been to hell.

* * *

At the same time Sara was learning of her father's revelation, Carson Taylor was in the midst of discovery himself. The man he had shot twice not only had a death grip on his wrist, but he wanted to talk. Carson instinctively pulled the pistol from his pants as the revived gunshot victim shook his head. He lifted Carson's arm and threw it out the window. "That gun didn't do the job before and it won't help you now. Put the canon away Carson?"

Carson stepped backwards as the driver and passenger of the grey Chevy both exited. He could barely speak as the two men came toward him. "Do I know you guys?"

"You mean besides our little run in at the gas station? Let us introduce ourselves, you can call me Rob," said the driver, "and you can call him Bob, " as he pointed to his grungy friend. Bob just smiled and waved.

"Rob and Bob huh?"

"Well, what's in a name anyway C.T. but here's a truth for you. You're in big trouble boy. Dante is not going to like this."

"Dante?"

"Yeah, you know, tall scary guy, black coat, big scar on his left cheek."

"How do you know Dante?"

"Hang on to your socks there Carson because me and Bob, we're both angels."

"You're two of Dante's soldiers, aren't you?"

"Give the man a cigar, we have a winner. As I hope you can tell by now, we were not the intended victims. That urge you had to do something bad to somebody, well that somebody was that pretty thing driving the Mustang."

"But if you had not tried to run over me I might have concentrated more on her and less on you."

"It's kind of funny how things work out, isn't it Mr. C. You see if I had not done some trick driving back at the gas station she would have never noticed you and you would have never spoken to her. The fact is my action gave you a chance to take your action, which was kill the girl."

Bob finally spoke, "You messed up dude."

"What was this, a test?"

"I don't know, why don't you ask him." Rob nodded at the Hummer.

Carson looked and saw Dante sitting in the passenger seat of the truck smoking a cigar.

"Good luck man, you're gonna need it," Rob said. Rob and Bob got back into the Chevy.

Carson reached way down inside for strength to walk the few steps for his face to face with Dante. He stopped at the drivers' side window and looked in. Dante was immersed in the pleasure of his cigar but he paused long enough to speak. "Get in."

Carson was no stranger to a butt chewing by his boss but before he never had to consider his boss might reach over and snatch his heart out of his chest. He opened the door sat down in the seat and closed the door behind him. He looked straight ahead, silent and did not move. Out of the corner of his eye he noticed what looked like a black tennis ball in Dante's left hand. Dante was still getting off on his cigar that was about to choke Carson. Rob had started up the Chevy and with Bob at his side they were headed up to the main road.

"Did they call themselves Rob and Bob?" Dante said.

"Yes, they did sir."

"Clowns. I do not know why I keep them around."

Dante gave a lingering look at the smoldering tobacco he held between his fingers before he continued. "I do enjoy a good cigar now and then. How about you Carson?"

Carson was trying not to cough. "No sir, not really."

Strange thoughts were coming to Carson. Was Dante going to punish him by choking him with cigar smoke? Carson just sat there glancing at Dante having a relationship with his cigar, and spinning the black ball in his hand. Carson saw the brake lights on the Chevy light up as they stopped before pulling out on the main road.

Dante took one long puff on the cigar, closed his eyes and savored the twirling smoke drifting above his head. "I suppose you wonder what's going to happen to you."

"It had crossed my mind and if I might say..."

"Hang on a minute Carson."

Dante pitched the cigar out the window, got out of the truck and spotted the Chevy just getting on the highway. He tossed the black ball up in the air, caught it with his right hand, then reared back and threw it with all his might. The ball made a whistling sound as it rocketed at the grey Chevy. The impact was about half way down on the door. Carson could hear it crash through the metal, then two groans, then out the other door. The Chevy slowed to a stop in the middle of the road. Then a strange thing happened with strange being relative at this point. The black ball flew back to Dante who caught it, but it made a squishy sound as it hit his hand. Carson knew what made the ball sound that way, angel guts. Rob and Bob were surely dead this time. Dante got back in the Hummer, pulled out his handkerchief and wiped down the ball. "Good help is hard to find. You with me Carson?"

"Yes sir."

"Drive."

Carson buckled his seatbelt and when he looked up he saw something stranger than the returning ball trick. The Chevy was glowing a bright gold color and starting to melt. It took about thirty seconds and the entire car had disappeared, melting into the road. Carson watched as Dante finished cleaning the ball and stuck it in his coat pocket.

"Let's go Carson. Go up here and take a right. There is something I need you to see before I go."

Carson pulled out of the scenic parking area and took a right. He was just happy to be alive.

* * *

Sara had been driving about ten minutes in total silence. The small talk Sara had started with had turned into a serious conversation. She was concentrating more on what was said than her driving. She glanced in the rear view mirror and saw the Cherokee about three feet behind her. Cooper had both hands in the air signaling what's up. The others were smiling and motioning her to go faster, all except Billy. He had a look on his face like he had gotten in the wrong line at the grocery store, the slow line. She looked at the speedometer and it read about fifteen miles an hour under the speed limit. Sara punched the GMC's accelerator and in a few second she was a hundred yards in front of the kids.

Kendall was surprised by the sudden burst of speed, pressed against the seat, head touching the rear window and a tight grip on the trucks interior. "Warn me next time will you?"

"Sorry."

Sara checked the mirror this time with no surprises. Billy was following at a safe distance and she was back into her driving. At this time she did not want to talk any more about the cylinder, her dad's death and resurrection, or Dante. But she could not help be amazed at the human spirit. It could take extreme circumstances and download them as a common occurrence. God had hardwired man to believe the unbelievable and to change the unchangeable. Sara could only believe, with God all things are possible.

They were about twenty minutes from Professor Kendall's home, located on the northeast side of the lake, and the conversation in the Cherokee was much lighter. Kendall's death had come up but the emphasis was more on his coming back. Billy and the gang had plenty of time to talk about the supernatural stuff they were part of, and started to speculate about what was next.

"Are we there yet?" said Cooper.

"What, are you anxious to get a look at the cylinder under laboratory conditions?" Billy said.

"No, he was being funny," said Rachel.

"No, I want a cheeseburger."

Ethan's eyes lit up. "That's a great idea. I'll call Sara and get their order."

Ethan called Sara and told her they were stopping for food. They would get it to go and meet them at the house. Kate wrote down everyone's food order then her mind went back to the cylinder, "Billy, what are we going to do with the cylinder when we get it back to the lab?"

"Standard operating procedure, I guess."

As the words came out of Billy's mouth he knew how odd they must have sounded. He looked over at Rachel and Cooper sitting next to him and they busted out laughing, including Billy.

"Yeah, I guess standard was not the right word. Basic stuff would be more accurate. The cylinder will have to be cleaned. It still has some dirt and rock embedded in the groves. It should be precisely measured and weighed."

"Fifty to seventy five pounds," Ethan said.

Billy eyed Ethan in the mirror, " Thank you brother Ethan but I think we should use a scale. After that just a good close look under bright light could be a next step. Check for any markings or maybe we could find what's his name's signature somewhere."

"Dante? Yeah right. He's an artist like I'm a superhero," said Cooper.

"He was a demon," Ethan said.

Kate disagreed. "No Ethan, I don't think so. Demons cannot actually be visible on the earthly plain. But according to scripture there are many accounts of people seeing angels. It is very possible Dante is an angel."

They all let Kate's statement sink in and things got quiet in the truck. Kate was right about Dante, but they all wondered just how prepared they were and how this adventure would unfold.

Dante and the two angels of light were prepared and had been for a long time. Just as Dante waited centuries for this day of destruction, the two angels of God had also waited with patience to protect the cylinder and the group. Kendall and his team were still unable to see them but the angels were there. One flew steady behind the rear window of the pickup truck guarding the cylinder and looking through the glass, surveying what was ahead.

The other angel was more animated and he flew with the Cherokee. Flying first on the right of the vehicle then over the top to the left side occasionally peaking in the window at the kids. At times he would fall back behind the SUV and spin around to fly backwards. He looked behind a second or two only to return to the right side and repeat the process again.

They were coming into Clear Lake now and the group would be splitting up. Sara turned left to go to the house and Billy turned right to get food. The angel with Sara turned back to see the other angel who was now on the hood of the Cherokee. He had positioned himself to look like an oversized hood ornament sticking out in front of the truck with his feet touching the hood. "Can I get you anything," he shouted to his partner who was now laughing and holding the top of the GMC letting it pull him down the road.

"Yeah, pick me up a burger."

"You want fries with that?"

They both smiled and waved as they headed in opposite directions. This was a good time for a laugh and they savored it a moment, before returning to guard duty.

Chapter Seven

Carson and Dante were not far from Clear Lake themselves. Carson guessed his role was more important than Rob and Bob for the fact he was still breathing. He had never pondered the creation and death of angels but apparently Dante had control over the death part, or maybe the black ball in Dante's coat pocket held the power. Angels dying, Carson thought. That didn't seem right. Weren't angels immortal? He would come to the conclusion they were not after rethinking the earlier events. But he would have to make sure later when he was feeling more secure about his standing with Dante.

He could remember hearing from somewhere about war in heaven or angelic forces. If angelic forces were like armed forces he could understand that. If the world has the Army, Air Force, etcetera, it would follow the angelic forces were there to fight something. Other angels with opposing views he guessed. He could only imagine Dante was the equivalent of a five star general and the head of the Joint Chiefs of Bad. Carson felt a little proud Dante had chosen him but the resolution of his apparent failure was unknown.

Dante had said nothing for a few miles and was content just riding looking at the scenery---until he reached over and turned on the radio. "Let's have some music."

Carson kept his eyes on the road but felt a bit bolder now, "Angels like music huh?"

Dante pointed out the window and looked at Carson like he was an idiot. Coming up on the right Carson could see an old billboard for the 'Cloud Nine Bar and Grill'. It had a painting of an angel sitting on a cloud playing a harp. With the harp in one hand while strumming with a chicken leg in the other, the signs slogan read; 'Hottest Music and Best Chicken This Side of Heaven'.

"That was really stupid of me. How could I forget two of the angel's favorites, harps and chicken?"

Dante ignored the attempt at humor and had found the remote control for the radio. He was changing stations with great dispatch intent on finding a song he wanted to hear. He clicked onto a classic rock station playing 'Highway To Hell' by AC/DC. Dante started tapping his leg with his hand and even moved his head as he sang along to the chorus. "That's one of my favorites," he said.

Dante was displaying behavior that had Carson speculating, this guy is not so bad after all, and without thinking he asked. "What has you in such a good mood sir?"

"Jerking the slack out of a couple of goldbricking angels always puts a song in my heart."

There it was. That's the Dante Carson was familiar with. He was happy because he had just done away with Rob and Bob. Carson was curious and Dante seemed receptive to conversation so he continued his query. "I thought angels were immortal. Are Rob and Bob dead?"

"Dead as dirt. The immortal thing is kind of tricky with angels. A time existed when no angels died. That changed. All you need to know is Rob and Bob both have a hole in them about this big." Dante pulled the black ball from his pocket and wrapped both hands around the furry exterior.

Carson extended his hand to get a feel of the black angel eradicator. "Does this thing work on humans?"

Dante shoved the ball back in his coat pocket. "You do not want to find out, Carson. Because a direct hit from my black beauty here, well, you remember what happened to the Chevy."

"It melted."

"That would be the simplest description. But with a human body it would be slower and with extreme pain."

"You're right sir; I don't want to find out."

"I do not think it will come to that. If you are a good boy, everything will be fine."

Don't you mean a bad boy? Carson wanted to ask but didn't.

Dante hit the button on the remote and turned off the radio. "Okay Carson, here is the plan. My sources tell me Kendall and the Christian gang will have the cylinder at his home in a matter of minutes. They should start their investigation this evening and I want you there."

"With Kendall? How do I do that sir?"

"No not *with* Kendall. I want you to be stealthy and observe. Sneak around and see what they do. Kendall's lab is in the basement but there are windows so you can see in and shrubs that will give you cover."

"What should I be looking for?"

"When it happens, you will know. Then give me a call at this number." Dante handed him a folded piece of paper.

Carson unfolded the paper and the numbers 666 were written in red ink across the face. "Kind of a short phone number, isn't it sir?"

Dante thought his prank was hysterical. He laughed until tears streamed down his face, "Boy that is the best laugh I have had this century."

"So, what do I do when *it* happens?"

"Just watch Carson. Take mental notes. There are two angels guarding the cylinder so I cannot be present but I will be close. When you have information to report go sit in your vehicle. I will find you."

"I can do that."

"Good. Don't forget about the meeting at the café. I love their apple pie."

Mental note Carson thought, three things angels like, music, chicken, and apple pie. This is making me hungry.

"I will be leaving you to your mission Carson but about a mile down the road is what I wanted to show you."

Carson braced himself and was glad it was only a mile. Maybe his imagination would not have time to make up terrible things that could happen to him.

"It is just around this curve, slow down a little but don't stop unless you have to."

Carson made the bend and saw the Highway Patrol car that had sped buy him earlier. He slowed the Hummer down and as he passed by the Trooper's vehicle, he saw the red Mustang convertible. The left front tire was flat and there were black marks on the highway where the Mustang had skidded off the road. Carson saw the plaid dressed, white shirted, high-heeled girl leaning into her car. "Man, check that out."

"Yeah, she's a looker."

"No not that. I thought I'd never see her again."

"And yet there she is in all her glory. If you had not allowed Rob and Bob to become a distraction, you could have come by just after the tire blew and helped her. If you know what I mean? Rob was right about one thing. He did draw attention to you at the station. The girl spoke to you first. I can only manipulate things to a certain degree and then you need to make the correct decision."

"Did you do that? Run her off the road."

"No it was an old grey Chevy I believe, unfortunate. A couple of low life's driving without proper restraint crashed into her, puncturing her front tire and stopping her. Stopping her for you."

Carson cursed as he hit the steering wheel and watched as the beautiful would be victim slipped out of site in his rear view mirror.

"Let this be a lesson Carson and try not to get so emotional next time. Pull over up here and let me out. I will see you later somewhere around Kendall's place."

Carson saw a dirt road ahead, checked for what was behind him, and pulled over to a stop. When he looked, Dante was already gone. He just disappeared, again. Funny man, Carson thought, as he hit the gas. In a cloud of dust he was off, tired, hungry and about a mile south of Clear Lake, his final destination.

* * *

Sara steered the GMC into the long driveway of Kendall's home. The driveway was bordered on the right by a row of hedges eight feet tall keeping the lot private. On the left there was a gray picket fence that used to be white. The color changed over the years due to rain, wind, and the professor's dislike of painting. Beyond the fence was a large yard with several old oak trees and another section of gray picket fence around the house. The front part of the home was a single story and the rear portion, which faced the lake, was a two-story addition with the lab in the basement below. The oak trees sprawled over the yard and the roof blending in with the natural cedar exterior of the house.

Sara coasted down the drive leading to the separate two-car garage and behind the garage was a tennis court dotted with leaves from the shedding trees. She pushed the automatic door opener but stopped the truck just outside the garage entrance.

"When are you going paint that fence?" she said.

"I think it has character."

"Character huh, that's your answer?"

"That's my story and I'm sticking to it. And speaking of stories, I would appreciate you keeping my death story to yourself."

"No problem dad, but we do need to talk about it later. Do you remember anything else about what happened?"

"Nothing that makes sense. But I had an image of a man in a black coat flying over my head."

"When the rest of the guys get here you are going to be hearing some unbelievable stuff. A flying man in a black coat will be part of the story."

"I'm ready for anything. I don't ever remember feeling as alive as I do now. Let's get the cylinder inside before the kids get here."

Professor Kendall and Sara picked up the case from the truck bed and walked down the stone path to the rear entrance of the house. Inside the door was the mudroom. A room with a concrete floor, hooks for hanging jackets, and a place to sit and change your muddy shoes before entering the main house. The room was painted a bright turquoise including the floor, and an old round Coke sign hung on the wall splashing the room with red. To the left was the door to the kitchen and straight ahead was the door to the basement. Basements were not common in Clear Lake and Kendall's was special because of the extensive lab equipment he had set up. They carried the case down the stairs and placed it on a table in the center of the room. Professor Kendall started to open the case when Sara gently put her hand on the top, "I think we should eat and have a discussion before we get into this."

"Is that all you think?"

"No, I also think we should all stay together at least for tonight. There is plenty of room and I'm sure we could work out sleeping arrangements."

"That's if anyone sleeps. We could pull an all-nighter. I want to know what this is."

"We all do and I'm certain everyone's up for it."

They heard the door open upstairs and Cooper talking, "No, I ordered the burger dry, no mayo or mustard, not plain. Plain is just meat and bread."

"You'll be lucky if you get one with meat," said Ethan.

Billy lifted one of the sacks filled with greasy delicacies and inhaled deeply, "I ordered the triple meat."

"Oh no man," Cooper said. "That totally throws off your bread to meat ratio. Anything over a double meat is a conglomeration."

Billy put the sack on the counter. "So there's a formula for ordering hamburgers?"

"That's right. The Cooper sandwich equation has been scientifically tested through years of trial and error."

"Let's eat," said Kate.

"Where are Professor Kendall and Sara?" Rachel said.

Downstairs, Sara grabbed her dad's hand still holding the latch to the case. "The rest of the team's here."

"Well, why don't we eat and have a discussion before we start."

"I could not have said it better myself." They both headed upstairs.

They walked into the kitchen to find the group digging through bags of burgers like they had found an Incan treasure. Rachel walked over." Are you feeling any better Professor?"

"I'm feeling great Rachel. Is one of those mine?"

"Yeah, Professor, here you go. One all the way with cheese."

After the food was distributed and everyone sat down, there was total silence. That was always a sign the food was really good or you were really hungry. In this case it was both. There were some moans and a couple of 'this is good' remarks but other than that, there was just eating going on. Cooper was first to finish punctuated by a smile, a long sigh, and standing to rub his stomach." I'm going out to the jeep. I have a couple of rackets and I need some practice for my match this weekend. Does anyone want to hit the ball?"

Ethan was still chewing his last bite when he stood up." I could use some exercise."

Billy held up his hand. "Could you get some exercise by bringing me my laptop? I think I'll do a search on silver cylinders."

"Good luck with that, but yeah I'll get it."

Rachel looked at Kate. "Did they just leave without inviting us?"

"I think they did, but that's never stopped us before. Do you have any extra tennis rackets, Sara?"

"There should be three or four in the hall closet but don't use the Spalding in the black case. That's mine."

"Thanks," and both girls ran to the closet so they could be casually standing on the court, with rackets in hand when the boys arrived.

Ethan came back with Billy's notebook and sat it in front of him. "Here you go, chief. Google your heart out."

"Yeah, yeah, why don't you go out and play with the other kids."

"Thank you, I think I'll do that."

Professor Kendall grabbed Ethan by the arm as he went by.

"Don't stay out there to long; we need to get to work."

"Yes sir, Professor."

"But before we get to work Ethan, we're going to talk and see if we can jog dad's memory."

"Sure thing Sara. I'll grab the baseball bat on the way back in."

"We may need it," said Sara as she wiped her mouth with her napkin.

"What?" Kendall said.

"Nothing dad, let's just sit here a minute and enjoy the view."

Billy stood up with his computer," I think the reception is better in the den." Billy just didn't want to be around Sara after their earlier disagreement about where to take the cylinder. He left Kendall and Sara alone starring out the window.

Sara smiled. "When you gonna paint that boat dock?"

"What's it with you and painting today?"

"Must be that episode of Trading Spaces I saw a couple of months ago."

"Yes it has been a while since I've sat in front of the TV."

"Well we have been on safari about forty minutes from here."

"Hey, you know it's easier to keep everyone's mind in the game if we have no distractions. Besides I like sleeping in a tent."

"Sometimes I think you were born in a tent."

Out the window they saw a tennis ball come flying over the fence and land in the backyard.

"Someone hit a wild one," said Kendall.

"It was probably Cooper taking out his frustration on the ball. It's all or nothing with him."

"Speaking of frustration Sara, although physically I feel great, inside I feel sort of empty."

"I'm so glad you said that. You know what that is?"

"Being without four hours of my morning?"

"No, being without God."

"You think?"

"I know. You said earlier you thought you went to hell when you died and possessing great deductive reasoning, you said there was a heaven."

"It's the deductive reasoning part that has me hung up."

"Why? There is more physical evidence for creation than evolution. The mere fact that the universal system is so complex should suggest, even to a scientist, there was intelligent design and I have the book written by the designer."

Sara walked over to the window seat, brought back her mother's Bible, and put it on the table.

"I don't think I'm ready for this Sara."

"What's there to be ready for---God's goodness, God's direction, God's protection?"

"Yeah, but don't I have to be in church, or talk to a preacher or something?"

"Here's the scoop dad. Because of what Jesus did, you can change your life and be born again right here at the kitchen table. The worlds were framed by the words of God's mouth. Your world can be changed the same way. You can accept Christ by believing in your heart and confessing the words with your mouth."

"I wish your mom could see this."

"I think she will. The Bible says there is joy in the presence of the angels of God over one sinner that repenteth."

"What do I do?"

"You just repeat what I say." She then led him in a prayer of salvation with Kendall repeating every word.

"Dear god in heaven, I come to you in the name of Jesus to receive salvation and eternal life. I believe that Jesus is your son. I believe He died on the cross for my sins and that you raised him from the dead. I receive Jesus now into my heart and make him Lord over my life. Jesus, come into my heart. I welcome you as my Lord and Savior. Father I believe your word says that I am now saved and born again. I am now a child of God. Amen.

"That's it?"

"That's it dad. If you believed what you said, you have accepted Jesus as your Lord and Savior.

"I believe it."

"Praise God. Welcome to the family."

There was indeed rejoicing in heaven over Kendall's conversion but also rejoicing in the basement. The two angels guarding the cylinder were literally bouncing off the walls flying around the room in celebration. Kendall didn't feel a lot different. He just sat there with a half-smile on his face as a tear hung in the corner of his eye, but a quick wipe with his hand took away all evidence of emotion. But something was different. If anything it was contradictions. He felt smaller and at the same time bigger for what he had done. The scope and magnitude that there was a creator of the universe, contrasting with the fact that God not only created him but also cared about the small things in his daily life. There would be time to reflect on things but for now the kids came busting in the back door as Billy came from the den with his computer.

"There are several accounts of silver cylinders on the internet."

Kendall wiped his eye again and straightened his head to look at Billy. "And?"

"Well, two things came up with the most frequency. One is a cremation charm so you can wear your dead loved one around your neck as jewelry."

"How romantic," Kate said.

"I'm thinking the cylinder is a little large for a necklace," said Kendall. "What's number two?"

"UFO's. We may have found a UFO."

Chapter Eight

Carson had learned more than he wanted on the trip from San Francisco, but his drive was about over. He saw the Clear Lake City Limits sign and the first order of business was food. For some reason he was hungry for fried chicken and his destination would fill the need. A family owned establishment for almost sixty years. He pulled up and parked in front of the building built sometime in the late fifties.

He sat in the truck letting the road feeling subside taking in the simple architecture of the building. He could see three sets of wooden steps, all leading to a wooden porch running the entire length of the structure. Three separate entrance doors stood beyond each set of steps and light blue paint covered the outside. The sign had the same blue background with black letters reading The Lake Food Store and Bakery Café. Three old lights, the kind with a gooseneck curving down to a round metal shade hung from the top of the sign.

Carson got out, stretched and walked to the door on the far left. The door creaked as he opened it and the smell of fresh baked cookies filled his head as he entered. He was in the grocery section of the store and the food was stocked on the original wooden shelves. The floor was also wood, marred and scratched but with a new glossy finish, creating an atmosphere that let visitors know they were not in Wal-Mart. He always enjoyed shopping at small town groceries especially for bread. He always found a loaf made by a company he never heard of. Butternut and Krusty were two past finds, but he would wait on the bread search.

Carson turned right leaving the grocery area and came to the bakery. It was full of homemade goodies and the source of the wonderful smells wafting through the store. He stopped a second and gazed at the sugar filled glass cases, later he thought. He enjoyed the clip-clop sound his shoes made on the wood floor as he headed for the open doorway leading to the café. When he entered, the smell changed from baked goods to home cooking. The middle-aged woman sitting behind the cash register handed him a menu, "Seat yourself hon, the special today is fried chicken."

"Thank you," Carson said as he took the menu and checked out the seating.

The café was L-shaped with the front part occupied by the regulars. He could tell because there were several conversations going on between several different booths. He decided to go around the corner to the back. A quite relaxing meal was just what he needed. Carson walked through the talking guests; nodding and smiling at a couple then turned the corner to find a few empty booths in the rear. He sat down looking over the menu but already knowing what he wanted. The waitress came over with silverware and a glass of water, "And what can we get for you today?"

"I'll have the special please."

"Fried chicken dinner," she said as she wrote the ticket, "good choice, and to drink?"

"Coffee, black."

"I'll be right back."

The waitress was gone only a minute until she returned with a steaming hot cup of coffee and sat it in front of Carson. He blew on the surface of the full cup before he took a sip and as he did, he noticed a woman sitting alone across the aisle looking at him. It wasn't a stare, but she didn't look away long before her eyes were back in Carson's direction.

She had long red hair cascading around the light complexion of her face and even from where he sat her dark green eyes stood out. Her red fingernails accented the feminine but muscular hands as she brushed her hair from the side of her face. She wore a tight jogging suit and by the shape of her body Carson guessed she must be an athlete. She picked up her coffee cup holding it with both hands and this time starred at Carson over the top of the cup as she took a drink. Carson tried not to stare back, but when he looked away he noticed out of the corner of his eye she had gotten up and was coming his way. With coffee cup in hand she stopped at Carson's booth. "May I sit down?"

"Ahh, sure, I guess so."

She slid into the seat and with her head down looked deep into the cup of java. She picked up the cup holding it between them. "Have you ever noticed these restaurant style cups? I really enjoy drinking out of them. They're so substantial and solid. Not like a lot of things in life, huh?"

"I've never thought of it that way but I get your point."

Carson hoped she was not an escaped mental patient because he wouldn't stand a chance in hand-to-hand combat.

She held out her hand, "My name is Alexandra, everyone calls me Alex."

"I'm Carson," and he reached out to greet her. "What brings you to Clear Lake?"

She grasped his hand, shook it twice and her eyes became piercing as she pulled him closer. "You did."

"I did what?"

She released his hand, leaned back in the seat and took a breath. "Rob and Bob were friends of mine and I hope you had nothing to do with their recent demise.

Carson was dumbfounded. All he wanted was a chicken dinner. "I'm sure Dante had something to do with you being here?"

"He sent me. I'm your new guardian angel."

Carson felt instantly at ease with Alex. Maybe it was because she was a woman. Maybe it was because she was gorgeous. Whatever the reason Carson waited for his dinner and sensed she didn't want to be there any more than he did. "So, have you known Dante long?"

Alex smiled big and looked at him. Carson was talking to her like they were on a first date in high school. Carson smiled back. "I mean, I've had a lot to absorb today but I still don't know very much."

"You seem pretty harmless, what do you want to know?"

"If you're an angel, where are your wings?"

"We make them invisible while out among the masses. My real body is almost eight feet tall. I've adjusted my height down so I fit in."

"Can you adjust my height up," Carson said, stretching his neck.

"Not without breaking something."

"That's okay. But seriously, how long have you known Dante?"

"Thousands of years---too long to count."

"What was it like back then?"

"At that time angels were the only folks in town. Chosen ones of God. Had the run of heaven. Then Lucifer had to get into a pissing contest with the Almighty and that started the angel wars. You know it wasn't an immediate thing. The falling of one third of the angels I mean. That war went on for years in heaven and it continues here on earth today."

"So, where's man in all this?"

"Your kind didn't exist. Angels were around long before man was created; and God conjuring up a new being, that took us all by surprise. Especially a being with traits the rebellious ones wanted. Some angels still ponder the ways of man."

"How about you, Alex. Do you still ponder?"

"I used to. I'm more in an acceptance phase now. The mission we're on has given me freedoms I never had. If Dante has his way, *all* the barriers of supernatural law will come crashing down."

"The mission. Tell me about the mission."

"The cylinder is the mission. That's another long story but we're here because something of Dante's is inside. Something he does not want to fall into the wrong hands."

"But he has supernatural powers why doesn't he just go get it?"

"That was his original plan out of shear ego. After seeing and being close to the cylinder he realized he didn't know how to open it. The Big Man put some kind of anti-evil mojo over it to stop us. That's why he needs you."

Carson opened his mouth to speak when the waitress came around the corner. She carried his dinner and a basket of rolls. "There you go. Can I get you anything else?"

Alex pointed to the crispy fried chicken sitting in front of Carson. "I've changed my mind. I'll have one of those and more coffee please."

"I'll take care of it," and the waitress left.

Carson picked up a chicken leg and was swinging it like a baton while he talked. "He needs me to open it? I can't open it. I don't even know what it looks like."

"I don't know the whole plan. Dante is keeping that pretty close to the vest. But your involvement is crucial. As an angel, I can do things you can't, but as a human, you can do things I can't. Make sense?"

"I guess so but how are we going to get the cylinder open?"

"Dante is counting on this Kendall guy to figure out the opening part. No telling how long that will take."

"So that's why I'm going to Kendall's tonight. To see if they get the cylinder opened."

"I can tell you for years events have been orchestrated to bring us to this point. It's that free will thing that will help us or hurt us over the coming days. But for now, let's take things one at a time. Why don't I shut up, and you enjoy your meal."

Carson was thinking, if your waiting on me you're backing up. He devoured the chicken leg and got lost in Alex's deep green eyes.

* * *

Kendall's basement was alive with the sound of inspiring busy work and passionate milling around. The cylinder had been uncased and put in a large plastic tray to catch anything removed from the exterior. Before moving downstairs the group had prayed and given thanks for Kendall's conversion to Christ. Prayers were also sent for guidance and protection for the group over the upcoming cylinder exploration. Specific prayers were raised for Kendall's leadership and strength to oversee the unknown work to come. It had been a big day for Professor Kendall and it wasn't over.

The sunrise was his last vivid memory with the rest of the morning still a blur. He remembered the sun peaking over the hills and a feeling he followed his calling, but the results were not abundant or fast enough to suit him. Since then things had picked up. He was told how they had found the cylinder, their unimaginable encounter with Dante, the sudden storm with the fatal lightning bolt, and finally the amazing resurrecting properties of the cylinder. Kendall's one memory of the morning was one he wanted to forget. The falling feeling and knowing he was on his way to hell.

By late afternoon the professor was a born again believer. When he died his eternity would be spent in heaven, not in the pit. Eternity was also a new word to scrutinize, and like most people, his mind could not grasp the vastness of the concept. Part of a scripture Sara quoted before came to mind. *One day is with the Lord as a thousand years, and a thousand years as one day.* Did God give man an equation to help understand heavenly time? If so, one year on earth could be translated to three hundred and sixty five thousand years once in eternity. The numbers excited him.

The professor knew he had to put aside the roller coaster of emotions and get down to the business at hand. What to do with the cylinder? The object had him in unfamiliar territory and how to approach the research was going to be a team effort. Kendall and Sara were leaning against the stair railing just outside the lab enjoying the kids attempt to do something, least they do nothing. Sara put it into two words when Kendall asked, "How do we begin?"

"Wing it," she said.

"Another historic scientific term, I love it."

"Well, it's not pottery, bone fragments, campfire remains, or anything porous. It's metal. We can't date it or take a sample and put it under the microscope. Oh, I forgot to tell you, it did not show up on the G.P.R.

"That's great. Billy could be right about a U.F.O. This is sort of sounding like one of your old science fiction movies."

"My hope is there is something inside."

"I think it's something we have to consider. Let's get it clean and see what we see."

Billy had already started the rough cleaning of the cylinder he had begun at the dig. He was still using his Popsicle stick tool. He had a small microphone clipped to his shirt and the wire was running to a digital recorder in his pocket. He gave a narrative as he worked, sounding like a coroner autopsying a body.

"The dirt is coming out fairly easy from the groves thanks to advancements in archeological equipment."

"Ice cream stick," Cooper yelled from across the room.

"Thank you assistant, I will continue now if you are through. The metal shows no sign of scratching or denting, quite amazing really. The surface finish does resemble a chrome car bumper but we are positive now it is not a fifty seven Chevy."

Cooper and Ethan who were standing around waiting for an assignment looked at Billy and smiled.

"Okay, so I was wrong," said Cooper.

Billy's eyes stayed focused on the cylinder and continued his scraping. "Did you hear that ladies and gentlemen, he was wrong, terribly terribly wrong."

Ethan looked at the professor standing just outside the door, "What do you want us to do?"

"For now guys I don't think we need everyone down here. Doesn't one of you need some practice for a tennis match this weekend?"

"Wow, Professor, we can go?"

"Go for it. We will call you when we need you."

Cooper and Ethan shot upstairs as Kate and Rachel shot the professor 'the look'. The look every adult male has seen that encompassed a hundred different emotions all of which ended with the phrase, 'No you did not just say that out loud'. Having lived with two women the professor knew 'the look' all too well. He had been on the receiving end of the penetrating glare many times in the past. However, being skilled at identifying 'the look' did not make him immune. He scrambled to regain his footing. "We can work in shifts. After the cylinder is clean, you both can trade places with the boys. Sound good?"

The girls' faces changed from 'the look' to a look of whatever as they went back to work. Kate was sketching detailed drawings of the cylinder while Rachel was taking more photographs and bugging Billy. "Smile for me good looking."

Billy looked up from his work smiled and held up the wooden tool he was proud of making. Rachel took the picture and the flash had Billy seeing only white for a few seconds. He exaggerated the temporary vision lose and poked around for what was in front of him. In the midst of his gag he accidentally got the stick stuck in one of the cylinder groves and broke his new toy. A sad expression settled on his face and there was a collective "Awh" from everyone.

"Okay, I'm done. No tools, no work."

The professor was quick to come to his aid. "Will someone go eat a Popsicle so we can get this man back to work?"

* * *

Carson had finished his meal and now he was the one doing the starring. He could not take his eyes off of Alex's perfectly formed face. She noticed his gaze as she swallowed her last bite of chicken. "They fry up a pretty good chicken here."

"Yeah they do. I made a joke earlier about angels and fried chicken but you actually ate some."

"One of the earthly perks of the job, eating I mean. Chicken is good but steak, that's my favorite. I like sex too. How does that fit in with your angel profile?"

Carson started fumbling for his keys. "I think we're about done here. I was going to buy some bread and cookies on the way out. Are you ready to go?"

Alex laughed. It was a kind laugh in the light of her just dropping a bomb and the implications of the statement.

"You know Carson; I would never force you to do anything you didn't want to."

"And that's supposed to make me feel better, chocolate chip, how does chocolate chip sound?"

Alex let him off the hook and responded to the cookie question. "Chocolate chip is fine, maybe some oatmeal."

"Let's go see what they have."

Carson could not get out of the booth quick enough. He got hung up on the center pole of the table and almost tripped across the floor as Alex grabbed his arm. "It's good I'm here to look after you."

"Thank you ma'am."

"So I'm a ma'am now. Just forget about what I said, let's get some cookies."

Carson and Alex spent a few minutes picking out cookies. Carson's hunt for unique bread went without success, so he picked up a loaf of Krusty. He also bought peanut butter, grape jelly, and a gallon of milk to make sure he could have a late night snack. He didn't know if the pizza delivery guy made it to his new destination.

The would be villain and the warrior angel left the old store on their way to one of the many homes Spencer owned scattered around the country. Carson put the address to the house in the Hummer's G.P.S. system. He followed every left and right the soothing voice told him to make until it said, "You have arrived, turn right into the driveway."

Carson looked to the right and even with the tracking system he almost missed the turn. "He said it was secluded but this is almost subterranean."

Brush had grown up around the entrance and the white rock road barely visible. As he pulled into the drive the bushes scraped the side of the truck. Past the flourishing foliage about fifty feet ahead was a closed, black iron gate. He stopped next to a keypad and opened his briefcase to look at the directions. He didn't remember seeing a gate code but there it was on the bottom corner of the page.

He knew Donna included the code and he wondered how Spencer could ever survive without her. Carson entered the code and the chain on the gate made a clickity clack sound as it opened. He pulled through to a small box with a red button. He pushed the button and could hear the gate close behind him.

They could only see road in front of them that curved to the left out of sight. The trees were thick forming a canopy blocking out the sunlight and made it seem they were in a tunnel. Alex looked around. "You sure there's a house out here."

"Supposed to be. I've never been here."

They made a left, a right, and another left then Carson stopped the truck. "Well, it looks like there is a house out here."

"Yeah, and a big one."

The home looked to be about 10,000 square feet with a four-car garage beneath what were probably servant's quarters back in the day. The front yard was relatively small with huge trees all around the house shading the massive roof. The house was old but well maintained judging by the rows of sculptured hedges standing like bookends to the long front porch. Carson was planning on staying in a motel but Spencer had really come through. "I think we'll have plenty of room."

Alex leaned over and put her arm around him. "I wonder how many bedrooms?"

"Oh, wow, I'm positive there's enough to have two or three apiece. Hey look at that, the sun is going down. I need to unpack and get ready to go to Kendall's."

"You sure you wouldn't prefer a hot bath first?"

"No thank you. Look at the time. I may not even sleep tonight. Dante will want to know about the cylinder."

Alex had him squirming and she didn't let up, "I wasn't planning on sleeping either."

Carson clapped his hands and rubbed them together, "Okay, we're here. Where are those keys? What did I do with...?

"Looking for these?" Alex had the front door keys dangling from her finger waving them in front of Carson's face.

Carson grabbed the keys and opened the truck door. "Thank you ma'am.

He unloaded his suitcase and was halfway to the door before Alex could yell at him out the window. "All right mister we'll see how long you can keep up this ma'am thing."

Alex was looking at Carson like a new toy. A life sized G.I. Joe to pass the time until the real fun began. The real fun would be taking out Kendall and the Christian gang.

Chapter Nine

Billy had the silver cylinder shinning like a new penny. His first, eyes only, visual inspection had revealed no slots, buttons, or latches. Nothing to suggest the cylinder opened at all. Rachel sifted through the dirt scraped from the grooves for anything unusual, as Kate used the microscope to identify the dislodged small rocks, labeling them as she went. What they found were dirt and rocks indigenous to that part of the country. Nothing special.

Professor Kendall was writing notes on what he could recall, occasionally asking Sara questions to help jog his memory. He did remember his earlier promise noticing Kate looking at her watch with a glance in his direction.

"Why don't you two take a break? Send the boys down if you would please."

Kate walked to the stairs, "That would be a pleasure."

Rachel left behind her.

The girls exited the house into the cool night air to find Cooper and Ethan sitting on the bench inside the tennis court. They walked over with their hands out, "Our turn. Did you have a good match?"

"Cooper skunked me as usual, Ethan said, handing the racket to Kate.

"It was closer than he's letting on, but yeah, I beat him."

"The professor requires your presence in the basement gentlemen."

"Let's go Coop, time to go to work."

Cooper stayed in is seat looked around at the night sky then back at the girls. "What do you have night vision goggles? It's going to be a little hard to see the ball, don't you think?"

Kate pranced over to a metal box in the corner of the court. She opened it, flipped the switch and six lights illuminated the court.

Cooper stood up. "Man, those things work. I thought they were broken."

Kate came prancing back. "I can't take all the credit. My dad was an electrician."

Just as the words left her mouth the court lights flickered and went out. So did the lights in the basement. Cooper saw the lights inside the house were still on then he noticed blackness from the small basement windows behind the shrubs. "Maybe you should give your electrician dad a call?"

Kate did not think it was funny because she knew it would be pitch black in the basement. She also knew the professor would not be happy.

The professor could not see his hand in front of his face. "Billy, Sara, stay where you are so we don't trip over each other. There's a flashlight around here somewhere."

Kendall rummaged through a few drawers until he found the flashlight. He flipped the switch hoping the batteries were still good. The light hit Sara in the eyes, "Let there be light," she said.

"Sorry. Someone must have turned on the court lights without turning off the backyard lights first. I've been meaning to change that breaker."

"I know dad, you can change the breaker the same time you paint the fence."

Kendall handed the flashlight to Sara. "Again with the painting, just shine the light up the stairs."

Sara watched as he opened the door to the mudroom where the lights were on.

"I'll be back in a minute," Sara heard as the basement door closed leaving her and Billy in the dark once again. Sara pointed the light at Billy still standing next to the cylinder. This was the first time they had been alone since their disagreement back at the dig.

"So Billy, have you come to terms with us bringing the cylinder home?"

"We all have to do what we think is right Sara. I think you did that. Time will tell."

Sara trained the light on the cylinder, "Okay, let's move on then. You didn't see any kind of opening?"

Billy rubbed the tense muscles in his neck as he moved back away from the table, "I didn't see so much as a...

What's that?"

"Where?"

"On the ceiling. The reflection. Is that a word? Hold the light a little closer to the cylinder."

Sara looked up as she moved the light. "It could be a word. Is that a *K*?"

"Yeah it is. It says *KEY*. Move the light around some more."

Sara moved the flashlight when the basement lights came back on removing the reflection from the ceiling.

Professor Kendall and the others were on their way back in as he explained the backyard, basement, and tennis court lights could not all be on at the same time. As he finished, he saw the basement lights go off again. The beam of the flashlight could be seen through the window. "What's gone wrong now?"

They all entered the mudroom and Kendall opened the door to the darkened basement. "What's the problem down there?"

Sara turned on the basement lights. "We found something. Come check it out."

Everyone went down the steps congregating around Sara and Billy. Kendall saw nothing obvious. "What did you find?"

"Ethan, turn out the lights," Sara said, holding the light on the cylinder.

Ethan hit the switch and they gazed at the cylinder where the light was pointing. The professor moved closer to get a better look. "I don't see anything special."

Billy glanced at Sara. "Look up Professor."

The group looked up to view the word *KEY* as plain as day reflecting from the cylinder on to the ceiling.

"Key," said Cooper.

Billy nodded. "That's correct chief."

"Is that all it says?" said Kate.

"Is that all," Sara said. "If it says key that means it will open."

Kendall was scratching his head. "But what is the key? Move the light around Sara. See what happens."

Sara moved the light back and forth as the word *KEY* disappeared and reappeared on the ceiling.

"Maybe light is the key," said Rachel. "The thing did glow before."

The professor thought for a moment. "Or maybe light is the key to the key. Turn the cylinder about forty five degrees."

Cooper and Ethan turned the cylinder. Sara held the light. And there it was. *WORD IS* reflected on the ceiling.

"Word is," Cooper said.

"I see you passed remedial reading," said Billy.

"Once again boys," Kendall said.

As the cylinder turned, *CENTER*, reflected above. They turned the cylinder again to see the word, *KEY*, once more. The turning continued several rotations until they were sure they had seen it all. The words were a revelation, one more supernatural event to cap off the day. But the words were also a riddle still needing a solution. *KEY WORD IS CENTER.*

* * *

It was 9:30 PM Tuesday and Carson had managed to snub Alex's verbal sexual advances, at least for now. He didn't need any more on his plate because Dante wanted him at Kendall's, and Spencer wanted him at the charity event. Somehow he would have to do both. He had not seen Alex since he left her sitting in the truck but he knew she was lurking around somewhere.

Carson found a large bedroom upstairs, changed his clothes, but he felt a little foolish as he looked at himself in the mirror. He looked like a cat burglar. He wore a black sweatshirt, black jeans, black tennis shoes, and even had a black knit cap in his back pocket. The gun was in his hand. He pondered how to conceal it in his sleek outfit. He also wondered should he carry it at all.

Carson had pulled the trigger on Rob and Bob but somehow that was different. Maybe deep inside he knew they weren't going to die. The question upset him again, was he really capable of shooting someone? He strapped the holster under the sweatshirt, slid the nine millimeter into place deciding, yes. He could kill if he had to.

Carson left the bedroom, walked down the stairs to find Alex sitting in a large pillowed chair with one leg hung over the arm.

"I'm going to Kendall's," he said as he kept moving toward the door.

Alex waved. "Have a good day at work honey."

"And where will the defender of evil be this evening?" Carson said, opening the front door and looking back at Alex.

"I'll be as close to you as I can without being detected. The two angels guarding the cylinder know my scent. We had a run in before. But if you need me, call my name and I'll be there. Be careful Carson and I don't mean just from the Christian gang."

Alex's last remark sounded sincere. Carson knew the warning was about Dante. He was the most dangerous and unstable player in the game.

"You take care too," and he walked out.

Carson left the house driving down the winding road thinking about what he would do when he got to Kendall's. He guessed there were a relative handful of people around the world feeling that life or death hung on their next decision. Carson was one of them and he didn't like it. He trusted his judgment most of his life, but maybe that was the cause of his unsettled mind; that one bad call twenty years ago with Dante, which had him in Clear Lake tonight. Let it go, he thought. And he rolled down the window, hoping the cool wind would wash away the fear.

The drive to Maple Street where Kendall lived would take twenty minutes. Twenty minutes for Carson to try and think of something other than where he was or what he was doing. The last lingering look from Alex leaped into his head. It was a look a mother would give her child leaving for the first day of school. She was so likable and it wasn't just her looks. It was something inside her that drew him.

Alex had really put the hook in him. It was her specialty. There were hundreds of men before Carson who had felt the same way. Some had resisted and some had not. Alex was a temptress and the worst kind, a temptress with a heart. She really cared about most of the men she eventually brought to ruin. But that was her job. And another reason Carson was thinking about her, she was sitting undetectable in the backseat of the Hummer.

* * *

In Kendall's basement the lights were back on. He had broken up the group into teams of two. He wanted each pair to come up with a theory as to what KEY WORD IS CENTER could mean. He had given each team a piece of paper with the phrase and thirty minutes to form an opinion, all except for Billy. Billy was doing a microscopic examination of the cylinder for any clues to the mysterious refection trick.

The professor and Sara stayed in the basement, not knowing they were in the presence of their two invisible guardian angels. The two winged warriors were allowed to help the group with predetermined instructions at precise times. This was not one of the times.

Ethan and Kate sat at the kitchen table starring at the piece of paper as Ethan spun it in a circle.

Cooper and Rachel had gone outside to the backyard. They were sitting in lawn chairs gazing up at the stars with the paper in Rachel's lap. Cooper's mind was not on the code. He was thinking about Rachel.

"We haven't had much time to be alone," Cooper said. He leaned over and kissed her on the lips.

She did not protest. She kissed him back. After the long kiss was over she took a breath trying to focus on something beyond the urge to jump into his lap and submit to his charm.

"We have a job to do here Cooper."

"I have to say something first. I love you Rachel."

"Cooper I don't think we should do this now. We need to be concentrating on this phrase."

"So you're not going to say you love me?"

"We've been through this. I take those words very serious."

"So do I Rachel."

"There is no one else in the world I would like to say those words to. But I have to be sure. There are too many unknown factors in my life to make a commitment now."

"You know Rachel my mother had a saying about love. If you give love, it will always come back to you."

"Always huh?"

"In your case Rachel, I'm counting on it."

"I had a dog I loved once. She ran away and never came back."

"Escaped did she?"

"In the wind."

"But that's a dog. I'm not going to run away."

"Yeah Cooper, this is much bigger than dog love. We're talking about a sacred union between a man and a woman that is supposed to last a lifetime. Don't give up on me Cooper. Just give me some time."

"I can give you time. But its love I'm giving and I expect it to come back." He leaned over and kissed her again. Cooper settled back into his chair. "I needed that to keep me going."

Rachel exhaled and looked at her watch. "We better get to work. We have twenty minutes before we rejoin the group. Have any ideas other than love coming back to you?"

"The key thing huh? Well, looking at this beautiful sky makes me think of Star Wars. If Yoda said this line it would be, word center key is."

"That's the best you can do?"

"Really, maybe the words are not in the correct order."

"And what order do you suggest, Obi-Wan?"

"Word is center key, center is key word, word is key center, are you writing this down Rachel?"

"As a matter of fact I am. Maybe it's an anagram. Too many possibilities to work out now. I'll just write down anagram. What facts do we have about the cylinder?"

"Besides the miraculous healing of the professor?"

"Yeah, during that. It glowed a blue light and remember, there was a melody."

"I have a song in my heart for you."

"Knock it off Cooper. Light music and the order of the words. Let's focus on that."

Kate and Ethan were concentrating on the music angle. The word key stuck out as a musical key. Ethan assumed the words of the phrase were in the correct order.

"Looking at, key word is center, from a letter positioning perspective," Ethan said, "key is the only word that has an exact center. That would be E. The key of E."

"But what in the key of E. Can you remember the melody from earlier?"

"I have a pretty good ear but I couldn't tell you if it was ZZ Top or Nelly Furtado."

"I doubt it was either. It could be an E chord or an E note at a certain octave. At least we have something to take to the group."

"Are you writing this down Kate?"

"Everything but the ZZ Top, Nelly Furtado remark."

Professor Kendall and Sara worked on the light theory. Sara was intrigued that it took darkness and then a light in the darkness to reveal the message. To her this suggested a biblical slant.

"Okay dad, we don't know much about this Dante guy except he's different."

"So I've heard."

"Still can't remember."

"Not the morning. I'm taking your word on the dude flying."

"Okay so he flew. That means nothing in scientific records. Let's think outside the box or the cylinder if you will."

"Outside the box?" Kendall said. "I've been inside the box so long I don't know what the outside looks like."

"Allow me dad. The guy flew, no doubt about it. Too many people saw it. First conclusion, he's not human."

"That's outside the box."

"Second if he's not human what is he?"

"The next David Copperfield?"

"Don't think so dad, and will you concentrate?"

"It's hard to concentrate on something I do not remember."

"Then stow it and let me talk."

"Yes ma'am."

"He could be an alien. He could be a demon. He could be an angel."

"Aren't angels supposed to do good?"

"All but the fallen ones. I feel the cylinder is of spiritual significance. I think Dante is a fallen angel."

"So where does that bring us with the phrase?"

"I'm thinking light. Dante is definitely from the dark side of the street and for some reason he could not take the cylinder this morning. It took light to bring out the code. It may take light to open it."

"Alright Sara, let's say you are correct. What can we equate key is center of word to the spectrum of light?"

"Glad to see you're back inside the box. But wait. That could be good." Sara said, with a look of expectancy on her face. She sat down in front of Billy's laptop to look up spectrum of light. Sara's crash course into light would answer some questions. That's one thing the humans had in common. Questions. The guardian angels had answers they were not allowed to reveal. Dante and Alex had answers they were not willing to reveal. But before the night was over, the answers would only bring more questions.

* * *

Carson had plenty of questions as he approached Maple Street. His questions did not address whether the cylinder would open but would he loose his life finding out. He turned on to the street then clicked off his headlights. When he rounded the corner Dante was standing next to the curb. Dante simply motioned Carson to drive on but his presence gave Carson a sense of urgency.

Alex floated out of the truck seat, going straight through the rear glass without a sound. She stood next to Dante as they both watched Carson stop a few houses down from Kendall's.

"What do you say Alex. How's he doing?"

"He's still on course, but he is getting inquisitive."

"About what?"

"About the big picture. What he's supposed to do next, that kind of thing."

"I don't suspect his human pea brain will figure that out until it's too late."

"Roger that. At least he seems to trust me. I'm going to get a little closer. See you around," and Alex drifted off in the direction of Carson.

Carson got out of the truck staying on the opposite side of the street from Kendall's. He was crouched down walking slow, looking for anyone who might be outside. As he got closer he could see a light on in the basement. He made his move across the street, and the lights suddenly went out. He turned back, diving into some evergreen shrubs by the curb. After he removed the prickly branch from his ear, he looked up thinking someone may have seen him. For a second he thought he saw a flashlight through the basement windows, and then the lights came back on again.

Alex was standing behind him knowing he had gone undetected. "Checking out the foliage, hot stuff?"

Carson was startled and spun around sticking a branch in his other ear. "Yeah, the foliage I can see fine, but I may not be able to hear for a while with these branches attacking me."

Alex could not restrain from laughing as she reached down to help Carson up. He grabbed her hand and she jerked him up squeezing him tight against her chest. She looked down into his eyes. "I told you I would be here if you needed me. See anything down there you like?"

Carson's eyes rolled up to see Alex's smiling face. "Can't breathe," he said.

"Sorry," said Alex, and released her grip on his head.

"Although this does take my mind off my current situation, I would have to say, it is not a good idea."

Three words undetected and of relevance emerged from Carson's statement, his mind, his situation, and time. All three would have to come into harmony for him to complete his mission. There were two sides battling beyond what was happening on Maple Street, to assure victory for their respective side. But it all came down to mere mortals. And as Cooper had so eloquently put it earlier, the free will wild card God had given to man.

Chapter Ten

Spencer Bryant's evening was winding down and normal for a Tuesday. He had the remote in one hand and a cocktail in the other sitting on his overstuffed and overpriced sofa. Professional channel surfing progressed as the remote played like a fine instrument manipulating several high definition boxes. It obeyed each command and displayed the results on the nine LCD monitors strategically placed like family portraits across the wall. A 52-inch Mitsubishi honored the center spot, with eight 42-inch models framing the brilliant, liquid crystal HD picture.

Spencer not only channel surfed, he surfed TVs. He found a documentary on the history channel about World War II. He pushed a few buttons, and the picture came to life on the large center screen, while encasing him in audio from the 8.1 surround sound system. Spencer could relate to generals at war, as he fancied his life a battleground on a different level. At any rate, it was holding his interest for now.

"Amazing," he said out loud.

The documentary was at the point where it told how the American and Allied forces kept their communications secret. American Indians would do the major part of the code talking. They spoke to each other openly on radios and walkie-talkies, using their native languages. What a simple solution and the code was never broken.

Spencer had people in his employment writing to him in code. They would send him a proposal with unreadable notes in the margin and he would let Donna decipher them. She had years of practice because Spencer never wasted his thoughts on what he considered the little things. That is not to say he never got his hands dirty. He would go head to head with any CEO, and even leaders of government in other countries. It was the small stuff he didn't like.

The charity event in Clear Lake was small stuff to Spencer. He just didn't want to deal with it, and that's why he sent Carson. Spencer had no idea Carson's mind was miles away from charity.

* * *

Carson was not giving charity to anyone. He was ready to shoot the evergreen for attacking him, but after thinking about it, the bush acted in self-defense. Carson drew first sap when he used the defenseless shrub as camouflage, and a branch to the face was a minor pay back.

He stood silent, catching his breath, with Alex still laughing at him. Alex made another attempt to get grabby with him when she leaned in, and dusted him off.

"I got it," Carson said and took a step backwards. He straightened his sweatshirt, checking his gun was still holstered, as he brushed away the remnants of evergreen.

Alex looked at Kendall's house across the street. "It's over there," she said, pointing.

"I know where I'm supposed to be. I thought someone saw me."

"They didn't see you. They're busy with the cylinder."

Carson looked both ways, and then walked across Maple Street in a huff, talking to himself. "Women," he said. "And women angels no less. I don't deserve this abuse."

Unexpectedly the light in the basement went out again, and Carson found himself diving behind the Oak tree at the edge of Kendall's yard. As soon as he hit the ground a look of regret covered his face. Why did I do that, he thought. He rolled over and Alex was kneeling beside him.

"Cat like reflexes," said Alex. "That's a good quality to have."

Carson scrambled to his feet, pushed Alex aside, and he again walked toward Kendall's. He was about halfway there, and the light came back on. He ran across the lawn, sliding into the flowerbed at the corner of the basement. This time when he hit the ground, although he knew Alex was laughing from somewhere, he had a perfect view of the basements interior. He breathed a sigh of relief, having reached his destination, and seeing the cylinder was not open. He didn't know why the light kept going on and off, but he understood it had nothing to do with him, as he checked out the group's behavior.

Three of them were in the basement, and the rest were coming down the stairs. They formed a semi-circle around the table holding the cylinder. Carson could not hear what they were saying, but Dante never said anything about taking notes. He could tell which one was Kendall, the older guy doing all the talking.

* * *

"Glad to see everyone back on time," Kendall said. "I separated you to try and come up with some different options as to the meaning of our hidden message. Sara and I decided on a direction we could go, but let's hear from Cooper and Rachel first."

Rachel held the paper up and looked at Cooper. He nodded for her to go ahead.

"We came up with four possibilities. We thought about..." She stopped to choose her words carefully. She started to say, Professor Kendall's death and coming back, but she thought better of it. "We considered this morning, and what the cylinder showed us. It glowed a bluish purple color, so light may have something to do with opening it. It played a melody, so music may be the key.

"That's it," Ethan said. "And more specific the key of E."

"Hang on Ethan," said Kendall. "Let Rachel finish and you can go next. Rachel?"

"Thank you Professor. Next we puzzled the placement of the words in the phrase. Would it make more sense in another order? We wrote down some alternatives to the original."

Kate and Ethan leaned over to see Rachel's paper. Rachel laid it on the table and continued, "Last was an anagram. But we wanted to check the computer for anagrams. And that's it"

"Very good guys," Kendall said. "I'm glad you spent your time on the problem."

Cooper wanted to turn his head, look up at the ceiling and start whistling, as if he didn't hear the last remark. Cooper knew he had spent more time thinking about Rachel than the problem. But they had received an at-a-boy from the professor. Cooper just smiled and acknowledged Kendall's compliment.

"Okay Ethan," said the professor. You seem pretty anxious. What do you have?"

"First off, excuse me Rachel for interrupting."

Rachel half curtsied, "No problem."

"But I was serious about the key of E," Ethan continued. "Key is the only word in the phrase with an exact center, and that's the letter E. Our theory is music in the key of E. And that's all I have to say about that."

"Very concise and to the point," Kendall said. "I like the key of E probability. Good job."

Ethan raised his eyebrows looking at Cooper. Cooper smirked back and they both focused their attention on the professor, who still had the floor.

"Sara and I, well, more specifically Sara, honed in on light as an answer. If you would Sara, share with us what you found out about light."

"Okay here goes. I couldn't find the Light Spectrum For Dummies Book, so I'm forced to remember science 101 and what I found on the computer. I went with the color of light the cylinder gave off earlier. I'm sure most of you remember," then she looked at her dad, "was a violet blue. Going with a light in the blue spectrum, I found a light that blocks the harmful UV-B and UV-C light, allowing only the benign long wave UV-A, and blue violet visible light to pass through. Again, most of you remember the light I'm talking about," glancing at her dad once more. "It's the black light from the sixties. We may have one in the house."

The group smiled and looked at the professor.

"Yes, there could be one here," said Kendall, "but for scientific purposes only."

"Of course it is," Sara said. "I know it's not to enhance that Jimi Hendrix poster in your bedroom."

"That's not a poster. It's an actual billboard, advertising Hendrix playing at the Fillmore Auditorium, February 1, 1968. I was there and it's a collectable."

"I'm not putting down your poster dad, but maybe I can borrow the scientific black light?"

"Be my guest. Okay everyone, you did good."

Billy, who had been quiet and had no specific assignment as to a cylinder opening theory, raised his hand.

"Yes Billy, what information do you have?"

"First off I would like to say, however unpopular it may be, I don't think we should continue. I believe the cylinder could be dangerous. Someone more qualified should do the research."

"So you haven't dealt with it," said Sara. We had this discussion before."

"Not formally," Billy said.

Professor Kendall held out his arms. "Hold on a second. Billy, your protest is noted. But, we may be, and I can't believe I'm saying this, the ones who were meant to find it. And honestly, I wouldn't know whom to call. From what I hear, the cylinder has not posed a threat but exactly the opposite. Apparently I would not be standing here, if it weren't for the cylinder.

"But on the other hand," said Billy, "you would not have needed the cylinder to bring you back, if we had not found it in the first place. Did that make sense?"

"It did," said the professor. "Your saying if we had not found the cylinder, I would not have been struck by lightning."

"Exactly."

"I see what you mean Billy but we did find the cylinder. We did," and Kendall moved his arms in a circular motion. "And for whatever reason, some I'm still processing, we have a duty to see this through."

"You're the boss Professor."

"Let's get something straight Billy. Whatever this thing is we are all part of it, and it's going to take each individual's special talent, to find the answers. Can I count on you?"

Kendall watched as Billy leaned back in the barstool and shook his head yes.

Kate reached out and touched Billy on the shoulder, "It's all right, God will watch over us."

"It's not God I'm worried about."

The professor thought it time to move on. "Cooper and Rachel, why don't you work on the order of the words and the anagram theory. Ethan and Kate, see if you can find out how the musical key of E might help us. Sara you know where the black light is and Billy, if you would, please finish your inspection of the cylinder. I'm going upstairs, does anyone want a sandwich?"

Kendall saw hands go up and heard, "Yes, I do, and I'm down with that."

He was going to be making sandwiches for everyone. He went upstairs leaving a small cloud of tension, but they all went straight to their work. At least it looked that way. Billy was looking through the microscope at the surface of the cylinder, but he was thinking about something he had done. Was it right or was it wrong.

* * *

Carson was outside, still on the ground peaking in the basement window. At least he was comfortable. He was lying on his side with his head propped up on the knit cap. He prepared for a long night. He hadn't heard a word of the group's conversation, but made out there was some kind of disagreement.

The man he identified as Kendall had gone upstairs immediately followed by one of the girls and one of the boys. Of the four left in the basement three of them were busy with some type of task. A boy and a girl were looking at the computer, and one girl was writing on what looked like music composition paper. From what Carson could see, the guy sitting in front of the cylinder just looked busy.

The guy would look at the cylinder, then at the others in the room, and then down at his watch. He seemed nervous, but Carson couldn't be sure. After all, this guy was the one speaking when things got tense in the room. Carson didn't know and he didn't care. He was having fun with his voyeurism---a good thing because Carson had nowhere else to go, for now.

* * *

Back in the basement, Billy had nowhere else to go either but you couldn't tell by looking at him. He finished his microscopic examination of the cylinder, looked at Cooper and Rachel on the computer, then to Kate writing something in the key of E, then down at his watch. "I'm done and I've got nothing," he said. "No runs, no hits, and no sign of an opening."

Billy lifted his arms behind his head and stretched. "Man what time is it," he said, glancing at his watch again. "11:15. I'm going out to get some air."

"Hey, on your way out tell the professor no mayo on my sandwich," said Cooper.

Billy held up his hand signaling he would relay the message, and then walked up the stairs. Sara was on her way down. She paused when Billy got close stopping him.

"You've made it clear how you feel," she said, "but we need you. It's like I told dad earlier, try and think outside the box."

"Outside the basement is what I need. I'm going to the back yard."

"Come back for sandwiches."

"I will, thanks," and Billy continued up the stairs.

He made it to the mudroom and was almost to the back door when Ethan came out of the kitchen. Ethan was carrying a guitar, and a mini-keyboard. "Hey Billy, where you going?"

"Out back for some air."

"The food will be ready in a minute."

"I'll be back," and Billy opened the door to a lovely night---where people wouldn't be bugging him about sandwiches, or silver cylinders.

He went over to the lawn chair, plopped down, and let every muscle go trying to force the tension out his fingertips. It seemed to be working as he noticed his wrinkled forehead straighten out and relax. What he didn't notice was a man, barely visible, about twenty feet away.

* * *

Carson however, had noticed Billy. Carson tried to make himself small, as he changed focus from the basement, to the man sitting way to close. Hey it's the nervous guy, Carson thought, and remained still. He could see the man very well from his prone position in the dirt, but the man could also see him if he only looked. Carson hoped for the best.

He got worried as the man jumped up from his seeming catatonic state, walking around and talking to himself. Carson put a hand on his gun and tried to listen. He could make out a few things the man said like, doubt or no doubt, but he defiantly heard the words, Professor Kendall and mad in the same sentence. Carson was ready to pull the weapon when his backyard companion went back to the chair and resumed his tranquil position.

Carson removed his hand from the gun, but kept his eyes on the man. That's when the lights in the basement went out. It took Carson by surprise. So much, his legs jerked kicking the side of the house, making a thud sound. Carson got small again. He could see the man in the chair and the kids in the basement just by moving his eyes.

The man in the chair sat up and scanned the area for the source of the noise. He could see the lights were again out in the basement. He studied the darkened windows a few seconds, and then sat back in the chair.

A different light came on in the basement, and this time Carson was able to remain still. It wasn't so bright as the overhead light and it was moving. Someone had a black light in hand moving it around the cylinder. Carson glanced away from the purple light, and wished the sedate stranger would go back in the house.

Kendall was putting the finishing touch on his platter of sandwiches, hoping it would energize the group for at least a couple of hours. He decided to go get everyone, bring them to the kitchen, and have an actual break before the long night ahead. The professor left the kitchen, opened the basement door, and stepped inside on the top step letting the door close behind him. It took a moment for his eyes adjust to the dim light of the basement. He could see his daughter and the dark glow on a couple of the kids. The scene had him somewhat bewildered.

Sara had the black light holding it over the cylinder, looking hard at the surface. Ethan held the guitar playing E notes at different octaves, checking for a reaction from the cylinder after each one. Kate was sitting in front of the keyboard hitting E chords with reckless abandon, not noticing any effect they might have. Rachel was yelling out stupid anagrams for the code, and Cooper was topping it all off by singing the theme from Close Encounters.

Professor Kendall went quietly down the stairs, and stopped about three steps from the bottom taking in the confused, uncoordinated efforts of his team. He was going to stand there until someone saw him.

* * *

Carson felt relieved he hadn't been seen, but the guy in the chair was still there. Carson saw him sit up again, and this time, slowly raise his head to look at the night sky.

* * *

As Billy sat up, he felt like a warm blanket had been placed around him. He wasn't even thinking of the cylinders code, as a matter of fact he was trying not to. But there it was. It just fell into his head. He knew what the code meant, and how to open the cylinder. Billy got up, and walked to the house savoring each stride he took. He went into the kitchen and starred at the Bible sitting on the table next to the platter of sandwiches. He picked up the Bible, holding it close to his chest as he silently thanked God. Billy knew where the answer had come from, and he again rejoiced in each step as he made his way downstairs.

* * *

Carson breathed easier now that the anonymous dude had gone back inside. The frozen position Carson was forced to assume, left his limbs tingling and numb. He moved his arms and legs a little to get the blood flowing, and settled down to view the proceedings. He could see Kendall standing on the stairs, but no one saw him. They were all doing their thing and all at the same time. Carson saw the guy from outside, come down the steps with something in his hands and stop behind Kendall. From Carson's vantage point, he could not see what the guy was holding. Carson could tell Kendall had not seen the man behind him, and the rest of the group had not seen either of them.

* * *

Billy was clutching the Bible, standing to the left and one step behind the professor. He lowered the Bible and started to open it. Kendall felt movement and turned to see Billy. Billy smiled at the professor, and then focused back to the scripture he was trying to find. It was Psalms 118:8.

As Billy turned the pages, he remembered an amazing fact about the Psalm, and God's deliberate construction of his book. Psalm 118 was carefully placed between the shortest chapter in the Bible, Psalm 117, and the longest chapter in the Bible, Psalm 119. There are 594 chapters before the 118th Psalm, and 594 chapters after it. If you add those two numbers together, you get 1,188 chapters. The exact center of the Bible---Psalm 118:8. Billy thought, God must have a sense of humor, and He's probably pretty good at math.

There was no mistake about it. God had put it on Billy's heart that, *KEY WORD IS CENTER* meant, the key is the word of God, and specifically the precise center of the word.

Billy scanned the room, and the faces of his friends, who were still in their own world, unaware of what was about to happen. Billy read the scripture aloud. *It is better to trust in the Lord than to put confidence in man.*

As soon as the words were spoken, it sounded like a large bank vault opened, and released gale force winds swirling through the basement. It was followed by a light so bright everyone instinctively closed their eyes. The brightness of the light pressed against them like it was trying to get out and they were in the way. At the same time the group felt they were being held in place by the ultra-white light, otherwise they all would have fallen to the floor.

For better or worse the cylinder was opening. As the light and wind pounded his body, Billy thought; why me, and of all the times, why now.

Chapter Eleven

The light coming out of the cylinder shot through the basement windows, lighting the area around Kendall's house like it was high noon. Dante, gliding a half-mile above the house with his wings stretched riding a wind current saw the light. Alex, with her legs propped up sitting twenty feet up on a limb in a Sycamore tree saw the light. The brilliant burst of light lasted no more than ten seconds then retreated, leaving a normal August night by the lake. They both knew it must have been the cylinder opening, but they patiently held their positions. Carson would be their eyes to what happened next.

Carson's nose was almost pressed up against the basement window, and his eyes were wide open when the light from the cylinder escaped into the midnight air. He felt the same pressure on his face as the basement dwellers, before he rolled over on his back to dodge the radiant energy. Carson stayed on his back, wedged between the house and the shrubs, blinking his eyes then opening them slightly to look. He blinked again, only harder this time, then held his eyes open trying to see something. He closed his eyes, and rubbed them with his fingers waiting for the brightness to dissipate. Only now it wasn't bright.

It wasn't like when he was a kid, having his aunt sneak up on him and take his picture from three feet away. The light from the camera flash would have him seeing white, and then white dots wherever he looked. This was different. Carson was not seeing anything but darkness.

He couldn't see his hand when he raised it, and held it in the air before rubbing his eyes again. He couldn't see the streetlight at the corner he passed earlier, where Dante was standing motioning him on. And he couldn't see into the basement, when he turned his head to the side and tears from his throbbing eyes trickled down his cheek. He lay still now. No blinking or rubbing. He tried to steady his breathing, relax what muscles he could, and most of all not think about the developing possibility.

Carson was blind. His eyes would do Dante and Alex no good because the eyes were not working. Carson thought a minute about what to do, and used his ears to listen. He could hear a cricket down the street, he hadn't noticed before, and water on the lake lapping up against the boat dock. He didn't hear signs that anyone came outside or he was in danger of being discovered. He realized what he had to do. Using his inside church on a Sunday morning voice he whispered, "Alex."

He waited a few seconds, then softly again, "Alex."

Alex heard Carson's first distress call and she rose up out of the tree. She heard her name the second time then blasted up to meet Dante in the air.

"Your boy is calling me," she said.

"I know, I heard. What is the problem now?"

"Alex," they both heard Carson whisper a third time.

"You better go get him Alex. Bring him over to his truck."

"He's pretty close to the other angels in the basement. I'm going to have to do a swoop and grab."

"Try not to give him a heart attack," said Dante.

"Ghost rider requesting to do a flyby sir."

"Just go get him."

Alex reared up, and with her wings pinned back she took off. Like a bullet she rocketed toward Carson, extending her wings for an instant to slow down as she got close to the ground. She pulled her wings back again flying between the house and shrubs. While grabbing Carson under both arms and picking him up out of the dirt she knocked the wind out of him. He was gasping for air when she put him on the ground by the truck at Dante's feet.

"You okay," said Alex, leaning over him.

Carson was still sucking wind. "Can't breathe."

"Yeah, I've heard that before," she said.

Carson caught his breath a little. "I can't see."

"Well, that's a new one," and Alex waved her hand in front of Carson's bugged out eyes.

Alex looked up at Dante, pointed to her eyes, and shook her head no. Dante looked calm, but he wanted to take his boot and stomp Carson's head. Instead he bent down and brushed away some dirt on the side of Carson's face. "Take it easy son; we are here to help you."

Dante then turned to Alex speaking in their native angelic tongue so Carson could not understand, "Give him thirty minutes," he said. "If he is still blind, kill him."

Alex was not comfortable with Dante's command. She liked the guy. Alex got the truck keys from Carson's pocket, and put him in the backseat of the Hummer. "There you go, just rest. I'll take care of you."

Dante was sitting on the grass, leaned up against the rear tire of the truck, "Carson, did you see anything when the cylinder opened?"

"Light. The last and only thing I saw was light."

Dante's head fell into his hands, as he mumbled some derogatory remarks in some unknown language. Then in a language you could understand he said, "Light, I saw the light. They probably saw the light in Texas."

* * *

Kendall and his team saw the light, but more specifically experienced the light. Even after they all closed their eyes they could still see it and even smell it. Some had detected an odor of fresh cut grass, others a spring rain and Kendall noted a fragrance of baby powder. The light also contained emotions, flowing through each witness in the basement, one to the other. They seemed to be able to tell what each other was feeling, and for the most part, knowing themselves and their companions were safe.

The light was gone now, but everyone stood with eyes closed in their original positions. The sense of the light holding them up had also left, and they were standing, however precariously, on their own. The professor was first to open his eyes, and he stood in awe of the presence before him. One by one each member of the team opened their eyes to behold, yet another unbelievable sight, on a day filled with things before unseen.

Sara was standing about two feet in front of the table, and the black light she held before was broken on the floor beside her. She had the best view of the opened cylinder, but only caught a glimpse, before starring to the right and left at who illuminated the room. The lights in the basement were still out.

On each side of the cylinder stood one of the guardian angels, with their heads almost touching the eight-foot ceiling. Their wings were massive, tucked in close behind them, and the long robes they wore glowed a warm, pinkish light. The angel on the left spoke first.

"Fear not. We have come in the name of the most High God and your savior Jesus Christ. We have come to summon you and to bless you. The Word says; for unto whomsoever much is given, of him shall be much required. You are all a whomsoever. We will offer to give you much. You must choose to receive. After you have seen the unseen, known the unknown, and given new power to challenge the darkness, your decision will be binding. To accept is to commit. To commit would mean for life. And congratulations on opening the cylinder."

The angel on the left went over and turned the basement light on, and both angels took a moment letting their presence sink in. They studied the ones God had chosen to fulfill his plan.

The group was handling the angel's manifestation in a calm, collected manner. It was almost as if two old friends dropped by, unannounced, with some exciting news. Hundreds of questions could have been asked but the team felt weak and drained from the experience. Everyone waited for the angels to talk again.

The angel on the right put his hand in his pocket and pulled out a handful of what looked like grapes, only they were blue. He walked to Kendall first with his outstretched hand. "Take one and eat. It will strengthen you," he said.

He went to each of the depleted members saying the same thing, as he offered them the heavenly food. He came to Cooper last. "Take on and eat. It will..."

"Yeah I know, strengthen..." Cooper said and his head started spinning. He was headed to the floor, beginning to pass out.

The angel grabbed him at the shoulder and held him upright. "Open your mouth."

Cooper opened his mouth just wide enough for the angel to deposit the fruit on his tongue.

"Eat before you talk," said the angel.

Cooper bit down to a flavor explosion that woke up more than his taste buds. He had never tasted anything so satisfying, plus the burst of flavor was followed by a burst of energy. He likened it to drinking a triple espresso, without the jitters. He smiled at the angel with a thank you expression on his face.

Kendall leaned into the room to better see Cooper. "Are you okay?"

"I'm great, Professor. But I don't think we'll need those sandwiches. I'm full."

The blue food had the same effect on everyone. Making them alert and putting them all in a good spirits.

The angel stepped back beside the cylinder as the other angel spoke. "We have been protectors of the cylinder and it's destiny for many centuries. The two of us have been with you for a long time now, and feel like we know your hearts. We have come to know you very well. I think introductions are in order. Our original names were given to us in the angelic language and would be difficult for you to pronounce. You may call me Bert." Bert held his hand toward the other angel. "Please call him Ernie."

Cooper opened his mouth to speak. Rachel pulled on his shirt, and with a pleading look, shook her head, trying to tell him to be quiet. Cooper could not let it pass and out it came. "Like the Sesame Street, Bert and Ernie?"

Bert and Ernie having a sense of humor took Cooper's comment in stride. They knew someone would make the Muppet connection, and they figured it would be Cooper. But they had not picked their names from Sesame Street.

"Sara," said Bert. "Perhaps you could enlighten us to another Bert and Ernie in twentieth century media."

Sara was surprised the angels called on her with a chance to use her movie trivia knowledge. She was glad she had an answer. "The first time I remember Bert and Ernie being used together for characters was in a Frank Capra movie. Bert was the policeman. Ernie was the cab driver. It was that Christmas movie 'It's a Wonderful Life'. The one where every time a bell rings an angel gets his wings. I wonder if that's where Jim Henson got the names for his characters."

"Thank you Sara," Ernie said, and turned to Cooper. "I hope you won't think of us as Muppets."

Cooper straightened up almost at military attention. "No sir. No Muppets sir."

Ernie laughed, but Bert only smiled and looked down to gather his thoughts. Comparing their personalities, Ernie was the less serious of the two, and more like Cooper than he cared to admit. Ernie had long blonde hair and looked like a surfer from the north shore of Hawaii. But at heart he was a warrior with thousands of years of battle experience, and the one who had etched the scar on Dante's face. Now he was called to teach a bunch of kids---a task where he would need his sense of humor.

Bert enjoyed a good laugh like most angels, but his dedication and absorption in the job at hand made him seem a little curt. Bert had an olive complexion and long black hair. He looked like a Greek movie star, with a silky voice, and brown eyes. But when he spoke, he sometimes sounded like a lawyer.

"In view of us standing here together, and the amount of information which must be imparted on our behalf, we must proceed in as orderly a method as possible," said Bert. "I will start with some basic facts. Feel free to ask any pertinent questions you deem necessary."

It was day one of cylinder orientation and just after midnight. The group had been up for eighteen hours, but the magical fruit had them ready to go. Everyone was anticipating answers to unasked questions, and what role they would play in this unfathomable act of fate. In the midst of eager expectancy, Billy looked at his watch.

Ernie and Bert knew of Billy's double mindedness and concerns. But the simple knowledge of the earlier phone call he made, gave them no clue as to the outcome of his actions. They would press on with their work and deal with the consequences later.

Bert raised his head and viewed his awaiting pupils.

"First off, congratulations on opening the cylinder. Other men have tried and failed. We will start with the light you experienced when the cylinder opened. This was but a thousandth of a portion from the light of the glory of God. It was put inside to discourage anyone, other than yourselves, and especially any evil forces. We shielded you from a degree of the light; otherwise you may have gone blind or worse. It is written, for there shall no man see Me, and live."

* * *

Carson did not know where the light came from, but he had a full taste of what it could do. He was about fifteen minutes into Dante's thirty-minute time limit, and it didn't look good. The light not only blinded him but also zapped his strength. He fell asleep in the back of the Hummer.

Dante was flying around keeping watch over Kendall's basement, but not close enough to see in the window, and just far enough away to go undetected.

Alex, who was agonizing over what she must do if his sight did not return in time, was attending to Carson. It wasn't like Carson would be the first man she ever killed, but from what she knew of the plan, they still needed him. At least giving him more time to heal was better than ending his life. Reasoning with Dante to let Carson live was not an option. She would try something else. Lying.

She checked to make sure Dante's attention was not on her and slipped into the backseat with Carson.

"Carson. Carson wake up."

Carson jumped and was grabbing at air, not knowing for a second where he was.

Alex held down his arms. "Be still now, it's only me."

"Alex is that you?"

"Yes. How do you feel?"

"Like crap."

"I'm going to turn on the overhead light," Alex said, flipping the switch. "Can you see anything?"

Carson opened his eyes, straining to see, but quickly closed them. "No."

"Try again," said Alex turning his head to look directly at the light.

Carson opened his eyes again, and the throbbing was down to a dull ache. Once again he closed them in frustration.

"I can't see anything," he said. "I feel like I've been run over by a train."

"Listen, Dante will be back shortly and when he gets here I want you to tell him you can see a little. Tell him you can't make out much, but that you can see something."

"Why do you want me to do that?"

"Believe me; it's for your own good."

"I'll do it," said Carson, hearing urgency in Alex's voice. "Now, I just want to sleep."

"Carson stay awake and listen. If I have to, I'm going to ask you how many fingers I'm holding up. I'll tap you on the arm to give you the answer. Understand?"

"Yes. Can I go to sleep now?"

"Go to sleep," and Alex put her hand over Carson's eyes. She had no special recuperative powers and there was no one to pray too. Her master was not known for healing people---exactly the opposite. She hoped Carson's sight would come back, or at least her plan to deceive Dante would work. If not, there could be blood on somebody's sword tonight. She kept her fingers crossed the blood would not be her own.

* * *

Professor Kendall accepted his role as student, deferring his position as teacher. He could see the opened cylinder, but it didn't open like you would cut a watermelon and have it open, with two halves side by side. It opened ninety degrees like a laptop computer. In fact it looked similar to a laptop, but a laptop from the future. From what Kendall could tell, the top portion held a large wide screen monitor in the center, surrounded by four smaller screens, two on each side. Above and below the large display were two long skinny screens, making a total of seven monitors. He would not venture a guess as to their use, but instead, checked out the bottom part of the cylinder.

There was definitely a keyboard with the English alphabet. On either side of the keyboard stuff was going on that gave him eyestrain trying to get a better look. On the right was a hole or a port about the size of a baseball. To it's immediate right, several sliding bars like you would see on a sound mixing board. Switches, and buttons, and lights, oh my. Kendall got hung up analyzing the cylinders insides when maybe he should have been listening.

"Fancy rig, huh, Professor?" Ernie said.

Now Kendall knew first-hand how his students felt when he caught them daydreaming in class. "Ah, yes it is."

"I know you are all anxious, but I'm getting to that," said Bert. "I cannot stress how big a responsibility, comes with what we are about to give you. If you choose to accept this challenge, there is no going back. You do have the option to refuse. Such is the free will gift you are blessed with. But make no mistake..."

"Come on Bert," said Ernie. "You'll have to forgive him folks. He's been waiting centuries to give this speech." Ernie looked at Bert apologetically. "I know this is serious stuff, but let's get to the punch line, Bert."

Bert smiled knowing Ernie was as anxious as the rest of the team. "Ernie, why don't you do the honors?"

"Thanks Bert. There has been some discussion among you, which asks, should the cylinder be opened or not. To clear that up, yes. You and the cylinder have come together at this pre-destined time and place."

Bert cleared his throat and looked at Ernie. Ernie was doing a speech of his own.

Ernie continued. "We can get into that later. Now, to what is in the cylinder. The contents are two-fold. Each designed for a specific use and purpose. As you can see, the cylinder has a keyboard I'm sure you are familiar with and it does function as a computer. But more like a super computer, that has an inexhaustible power supply."

Billy's eyes lit up.

"But the computer supports what is hidden beneath. Below the keyboard and monitor sections of the cylinder, are stored rules and equipment for a game. A game called Battle Ball."

The group starred around the room at one another.

"A game?" Sara said.

"Yes. A game that once the playing field has been constructed, you learn the rules, and you are familiar with the equipment; will be a test of your character, and more simply, an exciting sport."

Cooper held up his hand. "Hold on guys, you went through all this to give us a game?"

"This is not just any game," said Bert. "But the game of angels. A game played since time began, and God himself enjoyed seeing the angels compete in the sport He created. The game unfortunately transcended itself over the centuries. But that's a tale for another time. Begging your pardon there is so much to tell it is hard to keep a perspective."

Ernie reached over to the cylinder as he spoke. "I told you the purpose was two-fold. Surely we did not come to give you just a game. Yes it is a game, we know will bless you. But Bert told you we came not only to bless you but to challenge you---now for the challenge part."

Ernie was about to reveal what was under the keyboard portion of the cylinder, when the doorbell rang.

"It's almost one in the morning," said Kendall. "Who could that be?"

The doorbell rang again, followed by a loud knock. Billy hung his head, and the angels disappeared without a word. The cylinder clanked and started closing on its own, marked by a loud click as it shut.

Sara glared at Billy. "What did you do?" she said.

Billy kept his head down so his eyes did not meet Sara's, and neither could he talk, nor would he talk. It was going to be a long walk to the door for Billy.

Chapter Twelve

Dante watched the black Suburban drive down Maple Street, turn into Kendall's driveway, as five men got out and huddled near the front door. He dove out of the sky, slid across the top of the Hummer and landed in a crouching position outside the rear door. His eyes fixed on the new visitors. "Can Carson see yet?" he said.

"I don't know," Alex said, still in the backseat with Carson. "I haven't checked for a few minutes,"

Carson had been asleep until Dante crashed into the roof. "What is it? What's going on?" Carson said.

Dante stuck his head inside the truck. "Carson, can you see?"

Alex turned on the inside light again waiting for Carson's answer.

"Hey, I can see a little," said Carson. "Things are kind of fuzzy, but yeah."

Dante thrust his hand at Carson stopping about a foot from his face. "How many fingers am I holding up?"

Dante held up no fingers but a fist, which Carson would surely feel if the answer was wrong. Alex attempted to make a zero on the palm of Carson's hand. Carson gently closed his hand around Alex's finger.

"Zero sir," he said. "You're holding up zero fingers."

"How about now?" Dante said, holding up six fingers this time and all on one hand?

"Wow, good trick sir. I count six fingers. Do you play piano?"

Dante pulled his arm back. "Glad your back Carson. Get him up and back at his post Alex. There is something happening at Kendall's," and Dante disappeared into the sky.

"You really can see," Alex said pulling her finger from Carson's feeble grip.

"How about that. I'm going to sleep now." Carson closed his eyes, turned his head, and in seconds went back to sleep.

Alex noted the time. "I'll give you five minutes. You better enjoy."

* * *

There was no joy in Kendall's voice when he ordered everyone to keep quiet about the cylinder and stay in the basement. Billy was the exception. He was going upstairs with the professor. The knocking and doorbell ringing persisted as they made their way thru the kitchen.

Kendall stopped a few feet from the door but did not look at Billy as he asked, "Did you have anything to do with this late night visit?"

Billy stared straight ahead at the door, "Maybe. Probably."

Four loud knocks broke the vagary of Billy's answer.

"Who is it?" said Kendall.

A voice with a heavy southern drawl spoke back. "I'm Major Henry. Are you Professor Jacob Kendall?"

"Yes."

"I'm with a special branch of the federal government. We need to speak to you please."

"He sounds like Forest Gump," Kendall said as he grasped the doorknob, turned it and paused, wanting an explanation from Billy.

"He's my ex-commanding officer from the Air Force," said Billy. "I called him earlier. But I didn't..."

Kendall opened the door. The Major wore blue jeans, sweatshirt, tennis shoes and a baseball cap with a John Deere logo. His shiny silver weapon was holstered at his side. Behind him were two men in haz-mat suits each with a metal briefcase and behind them two soldiers wearing fatigues, carrying automatic weapons.

"I'm Major Henry," he said and held up his ID. "Sorry for the late hour, Professor, but we could have a national security threat here. Hello Billy, it's been a long time."

"I was wrong to call you Major. There's nothing here that threatens the country."

"We have to be sure Billy. What you described to me over the phone sounds a lot like something we've dealt with before."

"I don't think so," said Billy. "This was a big mistake."

The Major handed Kendall a piece of paper. "We have a search warrant."

"This is crazy," Kendall said. "What makes you think there is anything illegal going on here?"

"I didn't say illegal sir, I said national security. Now please step back, Professor," and Major Henry divided Billy and Kendall stepping into the house, followed by the two haz-mat guys. The armed soldiers stood at the door warning it was Kendall's move.

"Which way please?" said the Major.

Kendall shook his head and glanced at Billy. "This is your doing. You take them."

Billy knew he messed up. But he held out hope there was something he could change, while leading the way to the basement. "Major, I called you, just to get an opinion about this cylinder thing. How did it come to you barging in armed, with a search warrant?"

"As chance would have it, I'm in charge of this small elite group here. ARC is the name of the unit. It stands for Archeological Related Contamination. But it has to rank pretty high on the weird meter for us to get involved. My superior thought it was."

"We go way back Major, please..."

"It's out of my hands now, Billy. You'd be surprised what these book types find digging around the world. But no matter what your professor might think, you did the right thing by calling us."

Billy did not take solace in the hollow praise as he entered the mudroom. He was on his way to more ridicule in the basement, and wished Bert and Ernie could help him.

Ernie and Bert had flown outside after disappearing, just after the first knock on the door. They were in a holding pattern flying around the back of the house. They could still see through the walls inside, but blocked Dante or Alex from any visual access.

Kendall had walked into the kitchen and stood by the table with the machine gun toting soldier behind him. The professor noticed the bible Billy laid down on their way to the door. The Key, he thought, placing his hand on the bible, and said a silent prayer. *Lord, I'm really new at this. As a matter of fact this is the first one of these things I've said, actually expecting an answer. We need your help God. I guess that's it, Amen.*

Kendall looked up out of the corner of his eye, waiting for an answer. After a second or two he said out loud, "I'm just standing here looking at the ceiling."

"What?" the soldier said.

The professor jumped and spun, forgetting his armed guard was there. Kendall said nothing and walked to the stairs. The soldier went with him.

God heard the prayer. So did Ernie and Bert. There would be no answer for now.

At the top of the stairs Billy gave it another shot to convince the Major they were not in harm's way. He said what he could without revealing the cylinder opened, and the appearance of the angels. It was too little, too late.

Major Henry walked downstairs alone, telling the others to stay put. He stopped on the bottom step looking around the room. The four kids stood shoulder to shoulder in a not so subtle attempt to hide the cylinder. Sara stood out front. The Major seemed not to notice the group's formation as he pulled a strange item from his pocket. It looked like a half pair of broken tinted goggles from a pilot's helmet. He held it up to his right eye while closing his left, and scanned the room again.

"Come on down," he yelled, putting the looking glass back in his pocket. "Now, if I could get you all to stand over here, out of the way."

"And who are you?" said Sara.

Just then, the two white suited gentlemen came down with Billy and the professor.

"They have a search warrant," Kendall said.

"On what grounds?" said Sara. "No crime has been committed here."

Kendall held up his hand. "Please Sara, do what they say. They also have guns."

As the scowling group broke ranks to reveal the cylinder, the haz-mat boys opened up their cases, exposing equipment a little more sophisticated than the Majors broken sunglasses.

* * *

Dante had taken a sheltered position where he could see the lone soldier standing guard at the front door. Who are these guys? Dante thought, while kneeling down to prevent hitting his head on the low ceiling. To the fallen angel filled with hate, and carte blanche orders to dispose of anyone who got in his way---the tree house in the yard next to Kendall's seemed an unlikely place. The tiny estate was built for newcomers to the earth, filled with things defining the hopes and dreams of a child.

The place sickened Dante. Each wall was painted a bright primary color. Dante was a basic black kind of guy, but now the reds, blues, and yellows soaked his vision with distasteful vibrations hurting his eyes. Books of wonder, triumph, and discovery, all the things he fought to keep dormant in man lay sprawled on the floor.

Watercolor paintings and artistically done coloring book pages hung on the walls, with the deadly implements of imagination on a table across the room. They were deadly to Dante's cause for sure. These tools would give him more trouble than the most battle-seasoned warrior of God. Pencils, crayons, paint, and blank paper, were a few of the weapons that could lead to his worst nightmare. Creativity. God had given man the power to create. Which Dante knew, at its deepest level, was driven by the capacity to love.

But this love, the mortals were able to give to one another was but a drop in the ocean compared to the love God had toward man. Even a fallen angel knew the unbridled love God felt for man, because Dante had experienced it firsthand before the fall. Sure, he had tricks and lies to combat the love force, although when it was strong and in operation, evil could not prevail.

Dante had had enough of this happy place and was ready to leave, when he felt his knee on something other than the floorboards of the tree house. He lifted his knee to look and fell back across the small room. Of all the summarizing, of all the gifts he hated, there on the floor was the thing he hated most. The bible. "God's raggedy word," he said out loud. He continued letting his mind go and getting madder with each new thought.

Why couldn't God create this mess and leave it alone. No, he had to give them a book and an instruction book no less. Dante was beyond angry now, and oddly enough, he thought of a bible scripture, Psalms 8:4. What is man, that thou art mindful of him?

Dante was seething with contempt for every human on the planet, and focused his attention across the moon lit lawn, at the sentry, now lurking in the shadows. The moon had just come up over the mountains, causing the soldier to hide in the veil of the oak tree. The well-armed silhouette could not conceal himself from Dante's angelic vision. Dante could read the serial number on the AK47, and see the man's blue eyes darting from the lake to the street.

Dante sighed at his predicament, being able to see for a hundred miles but he couldn't see a hundred feet into the basement. This simply added to his frustration and he began to seek an outlet for his rage. That know-it-all smirk eased back on his face. The same smirk he lost somewhere on the road to Clear Lake, and he knew exactly how to feel better. He picked up the bible and threw it under the couch, while fluttering his wings, as pencils and paint scattered on the floor. He felt a little better, but he was just warming up.

He checked outside again, trying to decide his best course of action, and saw a man walking down the block. It was Carson. Dante could only watch as the imminent blunder took place.

Carson was feeling better after the nap. His vision was back, and he strolled with confidence in the middle of the street. There would be no diving into shrubs or behind trees this time. He hopped the curb with a spring in his step, when a man came out from behind a tree in Kendall's yard. The man was pointing a gun.

"Who goes there?" the soldier said.

Carson froze and almost wet his pants. "I'm a... I live down the street. I'm just out for a walk."

"Well keep it moving" and the gunman disappeared behind the tree.

Carson lowered his head, briskly walking off down the street, passing the crowded basement without looking.

Dante again let his face fall to his hands.

* * *

The basement was in total silence and Major Henry stood with his arms folded, while the plastic covered men poked and prodded the cylinder. Sara was as nervous as a cat, and broke the deafening stillness by tapping Major Henry on the back. "Where's your protective outerwear?"

Major Henry smiled with his southern charm, and spoke slowly with a heavy Georgia accent. "If you will notice ma'am, I'm not standing any closer to that thing than I have too. And besides, Mr. Smith and Mr. Jones know what they're doing. If anyone is in need of medical attention, we'll make sure you get it."

The Major went back to observing his men, leaving Sara with a new, uneasy thought. Medical attention? It only lasted a moment before the spirit rose up in her saying; you have come from being captured in a chokehold by a depraved angel, to standing in the light of God. No weapon formed against you shall prosper. She smirked at Major Henry, and heard the unmistakable sound of a Geiger counter going off above the cylinder.

"We have some radiation here Major."

"That's not right," said Sara. We checked that earlier with a negative reading."

"Hold your horses' now young lady," the Major said. "How much Mr. Smith?" Now talking to the man wielding the instrument.

"That would depend on the length of exposure. Not bad for us, but..." He then nodded at the group.

Major Henry unclasped his arms and put them on his hips. "Professor Kendall. How long would you estimate you and yours," again a nod to the group, "were close to the cylinder today? Oh, let's say, within a ten-foot radius."

Kendall thought, but knew he couldn't give a number. The memory cells were still on the fritz. "I'm going to let my daughter Sara answer that one."

Major Henry folded his arms again. "If you would ma'am?"

Sara computed the numbers pretty quick, but she didn't like talking to the sweet southern military man. She answered anyway. "Billy, Cooper, and Ethan, had the most time but probably no more than three hours. Kate, Rachel, and myself, less than an hour." The memory of her dad with his hand inside the cylinder came to mind. She wondered how that changed the equation, if radiation existed to start with. "My dad had about the same amount as the guys."

The Major unfolded his arms once more. "And where does that put us Mr. Smith?"

Mr. Smith studied the bobbing needle on the meter. "About the same as a couple of dental X-Rays. They should be all right."

Major Henry looked pleased. "We'll, that is some good news now isn't it?" Now with a grimaced look, the Major sucked wind through his teeth. "I am sorry, but here is some news you won't like. We need to take the cylinder."

Sara took a giant step forward. "Over my dead..."

Before Sara could blink, the Major's American Eagle Colt was held to the side of her head. Major Henry never lost his southern boyish charm, as he threatened Sara's life. "Over your dead body can be arranged. And we can do this the easy way, or the hard way. But, your United States Government respectfully requests the accompaniment of the cylinder, to our location for a thorough examination. And on the completion of said examination, you may get the cylinder back. But with that radioactive thing, I wouldn't count on it."

Kendall could have cared less about the cylinder at that moment. "Take it. Take it and just go."

The Major kept his eyes on Sara. "Your dad has the right idea. Now what do you say Sara?" Then he pressed the gun a little harder to her temple.

"You can have it," Sara said.

"Thank you," said Major Henry. Then he gently raised and holstered his gun. "Okay boys, we can go now."

Mr. Smith and Mr. Jones pulled out a padded, zippered bag for the cylinder, and began packing their stuff. Major Henry handed Professor Kendall a business card, and yelled up the stairs to the soldier standing at the top. "Mr. Brown, we are almost ready down here, are you and Mr. White all right?"

"Mr. White is outside sir, everything is shipshape."

The Major focused back on Kendall. "We really did not want to cause trouble here tonight, but this is the best for everyone. You can reach my superior at that number. We will be out of your way shortly."

The professor looked at the card. N.S.A., ARC Unit it read Major Benjamin Henry commanding officer. Kendall looked at the cylinder thinking, now it will be lost forever.

* * *

Dante had no idea he had competition terrorizing the Christian gang, still studying Mr. White in the shadows. Dante was hunched in the tree house and felt something wasn't right with these military types. The earlier reading of their nametags fueled his suspicions. Mr. Brown, White, Smith, and Jones are not a coincidence, and the AK47 the soldiers carried were not Government Issue. If these guys were covert they were way under, he thought. It is time for action.

Leaving the tree house, he was invisibly gliding through the air, on his way to surprise the guard. As he approached, Dante sensed this was not a good man. Mr. White killed for money, not for country, and Dante almost hated to mess with such a bad guy. But the ego needed to be served. It only took seconds for Dante to land behind the soldier, materialize, pull a six-inch knife and cut Mr. White's throat. Mr. White fell dead in pool of his own blood.

"I never get tired of that," said Dante, and he took off to meet Alex and Carson.

* * *

In the basement Mr. Smith and Jones had finished gathering their equipment, the cylinder was ready to travel a second time, and Major Henry was still as nice as could be. "Thank you Professor Kendall, ladies and gentlemen. I suggest you all stay right down here until we're gone. Goodnight," and he followed Jones and Smith up the stairs.

Billy wanted to say something but had never seen this side of his old commander. The weight of the world was on Billy's shoulders, and he was about to feel the wrath of Sara. He sat down on the steps thinking, he was the one who opened the cylinder, but he also was the one who gave it away.

Upstairs the ARC Unit exited the house and saw their companion on the ground. Major Henry pulled his gun. "Mr. Brown, please check Mr. White."

Mr. Brown bent down over his buddy. "He's dead sir."

The Major double checked the soldiers pulse, then stood and brandished his weapon from side to side. "Could Kendall have had something to do with this?"

"No sir. I was with him the whole time before he went downstairs."

"Let's get Mr. White in the truck boys. I don't know who the new player is, but we may have smoked a fox out of the henhouse."

They loaded the truck, screeched out of the driveway and sped off. One soul less than they came.

* * *

The black Suburban hurried by Alex, Dante fell out of the sky standing next to her, and Carson came around the corner.

"That's what I call timing," she said. "I saw what you did to that soldier."

"Yeah, the highlight of my day, but they have the cylinder," and Dante turned and pointed at the empty street.

Carson just walked up and saw Dante point. Carson spun around, "What, where."

Alex laughed. "There's those cat like reflexes again."

Dante glared. "Get over here Carson."

Carson scurried over to join them, and Dante slapped him across the forehead.

"We need to go to plan B," Dante said.

Alex put her finger to the side of her head. "I think we have gone past plan B. This could be plan C, no wait, this would be plan D."

Again, Dante was not amused. "Alex, find and follow the suburban before it gets too far. Keep track till I get there."

"Will do. Where are you going?"

"Believe it or not, I'm going to talk to Bert and Ernie."

"The Muppets?" said Carson.

"Are you still here?" Dante said. "Carson, I don't think your services are needed any more tonight. Go get some sleep."

Goodnight," Carson said, opening the truck door.

"Hey Carson," said Alex. "You did okay. Things don't always go as planned. Rest up. We'll go at it again tomorrow."

Carson half smiled, waved, and drove off.

"Wasn't that sweet," Dante said.

"I think he's doing the best he can, plus you ride him a little hard."

"Leave," said Dante.

"Yes boss" and Alex shot off into the sky.

* * *

The aggravation in the basement was spilling over with accusations, as Ernie and Bert appeared. Sara was in the middle of a rant flogging Billy with whys, and how comes.

"Sara," Bert said, stopping her in mid-sentence. "Billy did not intentionally hurt anyone. He did not know what the phone call would do. Tell me Sara, what does the bible say about love?"

"A lot of things," she said.

"It does," Bert said. "Paul started 1st Corinthians 13 by saying: Though I speak with the tongues of men and of angels, but have not love, I become sounding brass or a clanging cymbal."

Sara realized her voice could have sounded like a clanging cymbal to Bill's ears.

Bert continued. "In verse 13 Paul ends the chapter. And now abide in faith, hope, and love, these three; but the greatest of these is love. I think a little love would go a long way."

"Or come back to you," said Cooper looking at Rachel.

Bert let the remark slide. "Billy had no way of knowing when he called the Major; he would be the one to open the cylinder."

The group was shocked.

"I thought I did, with the guitar," said Ethan.

"I thought it was me on the keyboard," Kate added.

"It wasn't the black light?" said Sara.

Rachel and Cooper's eyes met and knew, her calling out anagrams, or him singing the theme from Close Encounters had done nothing. But they were surprised to hear it was Billy.

"How did you do it man?" Cooper said.

"The bible," said Billy. "The key was the bible, or the word, and center was the center of the bible. Psalm 118:8. I read it out loud and it opened."

"A lot of good that will do us now," Sara said.

Bert and Ernie starred at Sara.

"Okay, okay," she said as she went over and hugged Billy. She whispered in his ear. "I love you, but let's try to work together from now on."

"Point taken," said Billy. "What do we do now?"

"We," Ernie said, as he pointed to Bert and back at himself, "go after them."

"How will you find them and what about us?" Sara said.

"Bert can answer that," said Ernie.

"I had a word from God. He said we would get help to find the cylinder, from an unusual source. To answer part two of your question, go to bed. Do not worry and sleep. You are going to need it."

Bert held out his hand. "Can I see the card the Major gave you, Professor?"

Bert studied the card. "If this team is who we think they are, we've been after them for some time."

Bert showed the card to Ernie.

"ARC Unit huh," Ernie said. "What did the Major say it meant? Yeah, Archeological Related Contamination, pretty elegant handle. Bert would you like to tell them what ARC really stands for?"

"I guess it won't matter much now. We suspect ARC means, Angel Retrieval and Containment. These guys are angel hunters."

Angel hunters.

Chapter Thirteen

Options were limited for Kendall at this point, and he was in delay and pray mode. Prayer was an outlet still foreign to him but he knew it was the right thing to do. The angels were saying their goodbyes as they bolstered the team with words of faith, when Kendall thought of something he could do in the natural. Call the man with unlimited resources, his old friend Spencer Bryant.

Kendall found the number in his cell phone directory and pushed talk. He knew if Spencer was home he would be disturbing his sleep, but he also knew of Spencer's adventuresome spirit. He would count on the adventure part to offset the late hour.

Spencer was in the middle of a recurring dream. He stood at the top of Mount Everest, after having assaulted the summit alone, and planted a flag with the Spin-Corp logo. The ringing phone interrupted the victorious moment. Spencer opened his eyes to find he was only in bed, and leaned over to see what idiot was calling him in the middle of the night. He was surprised to see Jacob Kendall's name on the readout, and grabbed the phone.

"Hello, is that you Jacob?"

"Hey Spence, sorry for the late hour."

"That's okay, I know what happens in the dream I was having."

"The hot tub on Mount Everest dream?"

"Yeah, but I hadn't made it to the hot tub part yet. You remember that?"

"How could I forget? You used to wake me up shouting, more ice, more ice for my drink."

"Truth be known Jacob, it was the waitress who brought the ice, I was interested in."

Kendall laughed. "The more things change, the more they stay the same." His voice quickly turned serious. "I need your help Spencer." Kendall went on to tell Spencer about the cylinder, leaving out the lighting incident, and the angels. He did get specific about the ARC Unit and the gun to his daughters head. "I don't know what you can do Spence, but I thought I'd call."

"Any other names besides Major Benjamin Henry?" Spencer said.

"Only aliases I suppose. Mr. Brown, Mr. White, Mr. Jones, and Mr. Smith. All tough looking dudes accept the Major. And his demeanor gave us no hint of how deadly he was. Until he pulled his gun."

"Okay Jacob, let me get on this and I'll call you back in the morning."

"Thanks Spencer."

"Goodnight Jacob" and he hung up the phone.

Spencer called and woke up the head of his research department, giving him the names ARC Unit, and Major Benjamin Henry. He was instructed to find out all he could, as quickly as he could about the subjects, but not to call Spencer back till after seven.

Then Spencer made another phone call; this time to Carson. Carson had turned his phone off while sneaking around the basement and neglected to turn it back on. Spencer heard Carson's phone go to voice mail, for the third time in twenty-four hours, and slammed the phone down. He rolled over to go back to sleep, maybe to return to Mount Everest once again.

* * *

Bert and Ernie had no qualms leaving Kendall and the group without their angelic protection. With the theft of the cylinder, Dante's attention would shift from the Christians to the thieves. The two angels had an idea where the unusual help would come from. They found their suspicions correct, when they flew through Kendall's roof, to the outside. Dante was comfortably sitting on the chimney, like he was waiting for the school bus to come by.

"Good evening gentlemen," he said. "Did you lose something?"

"Look," said Ernie, "our unusual source."

Dante threw up both hands, "I'm unarmed guys. I suggest we call a truce, at least for the time being."

Ernie and Bert drifted closer to Dante. "And what would be the conditions of the truce?" Bert said.

Dante lowered his hands. "Terms I'm sure you can live with. But before I get to terms, do you know who the guys were who took the cylinder?"

"Yeah," said Bert, "the ARC Unit."

"I thought so," Dante said. "The angel hunters. I've heard stories about them but I never really believed they were real."

"They probably thought the same thing about you," said Ernie.

"This certainly adds a new wrinkle in our personal agendas, huh boys?"

"The terms?" Bert said.

Dante was in full smirk. "Of course the terms. I propose we work together. We find them; we kill them, and take back the cylinder. Simple."

"And after we have the cylinder back?" said Ernie.

"Well, that point does kind of catch in my craw," Dante said. "What to do with the cylinder?" He paused. "We give it back to Kendall and let the mortals go where their will leads them. I happen to think they will screw up and I will get my chance."

"You don't know how to open it, do you?" said Bert.

"If I knew how to open it, Bert, our showdown would have come at our earlier reunion."

Bert and Ernie nodded to one another in acceptance of Dante's plan. "We agree," Bert said, "all but the killing part. We are not allowed to kill a human. That would be against our laws."

"We can cross that bridge when we come to it," said Dante. "First things first."

"Exactly," Ernie said. "If we're here, shooting the breeze on Kendall's roof, how do we know where the ARC Unit went?"

"My partner, Alexandra, is following them."

"Alex is here?" said Ernie, with a surprised look. "The same Alex from the old days?"

"Yes," Dante said. "That's right; you and her had a thing back before the fall, huh Ernie?'

"Alexandra," said Ernie, and his mind filled with memories.

* * *

The night air combined with the freedom of flying put Alex in a good mood. She was having fun trailing the suburban through the countryside going north from Clear Lake. Occasionally she took the liberty to do a loop-de-loop expressing herself as she flew through the night. Her mind traveled back to a simpler time, back before man was created.

There wasn't any of this materializing in human form hiding your wings, or showing yourself as you really were, an angel and proud of the wings. You just were what you were; God's chosen race, the race of angels. She knew him by a different name then, but she thought of Ernie. They were a couple before the heavenly choosing of sides, in a utopia they thought would never end. But never was a long time.

How would she act when she saw him again, she wondered, and where did it all go wrong. Then she remembered. She cheated on Ernie with another angel. Then he found out and the fight began---what a fight that was, she recalled. The two of them argued for hours and when it was over they never spoke again. Of course this all happened one week before the third of the angels, including Alex, were expelled from heaven and banished to the earth. It would have ended anyway, she thought.

Alex did another loop-de-loop to clear her head, leveled out, and saw the black suburban turn off the main road, to a dirt road leading into the hills. She flew down for a closer look.

* * *

The ride was a somber one for the ARC Unit. They had what they came for, but they lost one of their own in the process. As difficult as it was to let go of a friend, this was war. A war they had all volunteered for, and were paid very well to fight. It was a fight in the shadows and the unseen, bordered by heaven and hell.

The ARC Unit's opponent had wings, flew close to the speed of light, and then there was the ability to be invisible to the naked eye. Plus they could see and walk through walls, and a third of them were just plain mean. The enemy wasn't fighting for political power or natural resources, but for souls. But the guys in the unit only partially looked at its prey as an enemy, but more like specimens for a zoo. Another species to be tested and studied by the men in white coats. And like any animal, when it was cornered, it fought back.

This would not be the first phone call Major Henry would make to surviving family members. Nor he guessed would it be the last. The Suburban neared the end of the journey, at the end of the dirt road.

"Mr. Brown," said the Major, "let's get the phone number for Mr. White's next of kin. I'll call them in the morning. And maybe we should break out the special weapons. We don't want to get caught with our pants down again."

The truck stopped at what looked like a dead end, with the headlights shinning on thick underbrush below the trees. Mr. Brown reached under the dashboard and pulled out a remote control. He pushed in three numbers and the thicket of vines and limbs parted, to reveal a concrete driveway. Mr. Brown steered the truck up the drive toward a small frame house. The old farm house looked run down and empty but for a faint light shining through one of the windows. There were no concrete barriers, barbed wire fences, or guard towers outside. The ARC unit defended against a special enemy.

Major Henry looked in the backseat. "Could you check the security field Mr. Smith? We could have visitors later. And if we're lucky, we could have guests.

* * *

The alliance between Bert, Ernie, and Dante, was superficial at best. Bert and Dante were openly mistrusting of each other, but Ernie thought more about seeing Alex. The improbable trio was high above the lake, as Dante tried to communicate with Alex. He spoke in a normal voice. "Alex where are you?"

He waited but there was no response. "Alex can you hear me?" Again there was no response. Dante flew higher with Ernie and Bert right beside him. "Alex, this is Dante. If you can hear me, tell me where you are." They all waited but heard nothing.

"Is this some kind of trick?" Bert said. "You let her get the cylinder and then rendezvous later."

"No trick Bert. I'm concerned."

"Do you know which way she went?" said Ernie.

"Give me a minute," Dante said, rising higher. He leaned his head back, closed his eyes, and inhaled long and slow, searching for Alex's scent. "She went this way," and pointed to the north.

"This better not be a game you're playing here," said Bert. "We were in guardian mode when you surprised us yesterday. I guarantee the outcome will be different this time."

Ernie grabbed Bert by the shoulder. "No, I smell her too."

* * *

Alex liked the fragrance and feel of the pine trees, and she settled in the branches next to the ARC unit's house. She had been trying to call Dante with no answer, and she sensed there was something different about this place. She watched the Suburban pull around the circular drive and stop by the front door.

* * *

Inside the truck Major Henry was a little skittish. "Hang on a second men. I should check it out before we embark."

The Major pulled out the broken piece of glass he had used in the basement, followed by an elastic headband, which he carefully clipped to the sides of the unusual eyepiece. He took off his John Deere cap, slipped the eyepiece over his head and adjusted it. He put his cap back on only backwards this time. He looked like a pirate going to a tractor pull. The Major reached into the back seat. "Hand me one of those A-T guns, if you would Mr. Smith?"

Mr. Smith handed him a weapon that resembled a single barreled sawed off shotgun. Only the barrel was large enough to stick your fist inside, and there were wings painted on the wooden stock.

"Let me have a look see boys," said the Major. "Stay put."

Major Henry cradled the gun like a newborn, and got out of the truck. He pretended to stretch as he scanned the perimeter. His lens-covered eye caught something in the trees. He stuck his head back in the suburban. "We may have a bogie in the compound gentlemen. Let's be casual, take Mr. White into the house, and I want everyone to go inside. And please leave the cargo hatch open where the cylinder will be visible. Let's go now."

Mr. Jones and Mr. Smith unloaded Mr. White and took him into the house, with the Major and Mr. Brown walking behind.

* * *

Alex saw the unit unload Dante's victim and she waited. She could see the moonlight reflecting off the silver cylinder, inside the clear plastic case, at the rear edge of the truck. She looked around for Dante with the cavalry and then back to the cylinder. It couldn't be this easy, she thought. I may never get another chance like this. "I'm going for it," she said out loud, and she blasted out of the tree planning not to slow down, while she grabbed the handle on the bag and hoped it didn't break.

The Major saw her all the way. He peeked through the slightly opened front door and he could see her get ready to lunge. He stepped out on the front porch just as she left the tree. She never saw him. Boom! He fired the gun and a large net with the consistency of a super thick spider web came out the end. It hit Alex only a few feet from the cylinder. When the net hit her, it wrapped around her several times and tiny sparks jumped across the glowing fibers. The Angel Tamer had done its job.

Alex didn't know what hit her as she crashed and rolled across the driveway. She lay there paralyzed being stung by the electrical impulses of the net. She fell in a position where she could still see the cylinder, unattainable in the back of the truck. Then she beheld her captors, coming in for the kill she imagined. Just let it be quick.

"Good shot Major."

"Thank you Mr. Brown, and what do we have here."

The Major bent down with his face inches from Alex. He smiled and stood up. "We have caught us a female angel boys and she's a big one. Let's get her inside. The Doc will be glad to see you, miss."

Alex fought to talk. "Alexandra. My name is Alexandra. Now back off and let me go."

"Boy howdy," said the Major, "she's a feisty one too. Alexandra is it? We don't plan to hurt you, so don't give us a reason."

Alex could only look to the skies for the help she anticipated would come.

* * *

The tops of the trees were like a rolling carpet to the angels cruising only a few feet above. The angels mission was about to change from retrieval of the cylinder, to the rescue of Alex. Dante and Ernie were correct in identifying the scent of Alex and they were close enough to hear her say, "Alexandra. My name is Alexandra."

They gauged about one mile straight ahead Alex would be found, plus whomever she introduced herself too. Ernie, Bert, and Dante were about a hundred yards out when Bert stuck his wings out, stopping the other two.

"I see a clearing ahead," Bert said. "There's some kind of high frequency sound waves coming from the ground. Do you hear it?"

"I hear it now," said Ernie. "Proceed with caution."

They flew up to the edge of the clearing and saw the objective of their new mission. Alex was being carried through the front door, and Major Henry stepped to the lip of the porch, surveying the trees.

"Get down," Dante said. "He can probably see us. I think that eye patch looking thing he's wearing is a piece of our mask."

They slid down behind the covering of the trees, and heard the front door close and lock.

Bert rose up to check. "All clear."

"I'm going in after her," said Ernie.

"Hold it Ernie," Bert said. "We don't know what this sound field does; it could be a warning system. If I can focus... Yeah, I can see it. It goes all the way around the house and straight up, about..." Bert looked up. "Wow, a long way. It's also preventing me from seeing inside the house. We need a plan."

"That would be plan E," said Dante.

"What?" Bert said.

"Nothing. We should split up and do some reconnaissance. If we could find their power source and shut it down, that would give us the advantage."

"They would surely have a backup system," said Ernie.

"We might have a few seconds," Dante said. "We would have to coordinate our efforts."

"So what's your plan?" said Bert.

Dante thought a moment. "Bert, you fly up and over this sound screen, it has to dissipate somewhere. Come back down over the house and maybe you can see in, or get in."

Ernie had another plan. "I want to go in."

"Not a good idea," Bert said. "I'll do it."

"But Bert..."

"Stop Ernie. I know you well my friend and your history with Alex might cloud your judgment."

Dante wanted to smart off, but refrained. "Ernie, why don't you search about a mile radius around the house, for a power source, or guards, or whatever."

"And where will you be?" said Bert.

This time Dante did smart off. "I'm going out for a cappuccino. May I bring you one? Don't forget I have a history with Alex too, Bert. But it was more a working relationship, unlike your friend Ernie here."

Ernie moved with his hand on the sword hidden inside his robe. Bert stopped him.

"Now as for me," Dante continued, "I should get as close to the house as I can and try to communicate with her."

"Fine," Bert said.

"And what if the plan goes bad?" said Ernie.

Dante bobbed his head from side to side. "Well, we fly in, kill every human in sight, and rescue Alex. We could pick up the cylinder while we're inside."

Bert did not respond to Dante's remark, but instead looked at the sound field extending to the heavens. "I'll meet you both by the house later," and he flew away.

"Be there or be square," Ernie said, and left to scour the perimeter.

Dante was left alone with one final thought, which he spoke out loud. "Wet work. We could get bloody on this one."

* * *

Inside the house, Alex lay on a striped French Country rug next to the cylinder. The cylinder was as neatly packaged as she was. To her the room seemed normal---too normal for the situation. There was a sofa, lamps, and pictures on the wall. It was like any minute, Ma and Pa Kettle would walk out of the kitchen. In reality Major Henry walked out of the kitchen.

"And how are you doing Alexandra?"

Alex could not move, but she could talk. "I've been better. And what is this thing you have me wrapped in? I have never been bound by anything man made before."

"That's because it is not man made. Well, the net was but not the material. That was one of the Doc's biggest breakthroughs, which led to us being able to continue our work. In your current position, I suppose it would be okay to tell you of what material it's made. The net is woven from the robe of an angel. It still has that warm pinkish glow, don't you think?"

Alex recognized the light emanating from the fabric and she knew she was in trouble. "Major, I'm going to tell you one more time," and then she shouted, "Let me go."

Knick-knacks vibrated of the shelves by the power of Alex's voice, and Mr. Brown pointed his weapon at the source of his ringing ears. Major Henry closed his eyes until his eardrums quit pounding. "We better get this one downstairs and mental note; we need to work on silencing these creatures."

* * *

Dante was silent when he snuck up on the side of the house. He heard Alex yell but it sounded like she was ten feet under water. Then he spoke, "We're coming baby. Just hold on till we get there."

Chapter Fourteen

The sound field around the house kept Alex from hearing or seeing anything that was happening outside. She had not seen the security screen being deactivated, so the ARC Unit could carry her into the house, and then switched back on after she was inside. The field was angel sensitive. The Unit's years of trial and error had the angel warning system tuned to perfection. A bird or a squirrel could cross it with no consequences, but if an angel broke the beam, sirens and flashing lights would have everyone in the complex on alert.

Arc had never had a breach of security during their seven-year history, because they were very good at hiding. They did have one limitation they worked to correct, but so far with no success, the ability to see invisible angels or to detect an angel posing as a human. The restriction was in the form of two pieces of tinted glass, allowing the wearer to see the angels in stealth mode. One piece stayed in the laboratory and was required to be worn twenty-four hours a day, by an on duty guard patrolling the work area. The other glass stayed with Major Henry.

He used it for fieldwork and no one was allowed to wear his angel spotter, but him. He had given up too much to get it. The Major was wearing it as he opened two sliding closet doors in the hallway of the house, revealing a pair of stainless steel doors leading to the elevator. The living quarters were three floors down, and four floors down the lab. The house above ground was just a front.

He pushed the button for the elevator. "Help me get our girl inside. I want to get her settled, and get some shut eye."

Alex heard him and again she yelled. "Don't touch me you pervert."

"Pervert," said the Major. "I have a feeling that would be a case of the pot calling the kettle black."

Mr. Brown came out of the kitchen holding his ears and a roll of duct tape. "I don't think we've tried this before Major." He tore off a foot of tape, pulled down the net to expose Alex's face, and slapped the tape across her mouth. He jerked the net back over her head, and jumped back out of the way.

"Very inventive Mr. Brown."

"Just a field test Major. If it works we'll tell the Doc."

Alex was fit to be tied, but she already was. She still could not move, so she inhaled as deep as possible through her nose, and out her mouth she blew. The tape shot off her face, through the net, and flew across the room to wrap around Mr. Brown's neck. He fell to the floor unable to breath. Major Henry ran over and ripped off the tape. "You okay son?"

Mr. Brown signaled yes, with thumbs up.

"Let me help you up," the Major said. "Well, we can take angel muting off the 1001 uses for duct tape. And let's get her in a cell before she hurts someone."

* * *

Three hundred yards from the house, Ernie was flying a circular grid and getting closer with each pass. About a mile out he had come across some Army vehicles hidden under camouflage netting. There was a Halftrack, a Six-by, a green fire truck and an old Jeep. All with keys, good batteries and full of gas. Ernie had inspected the trucks before moving on. He hadn't seen much else on his rounds, besides a few deer, but he continued the search.

In the distance he saw a ten by ten galvanized steel building, with no security. He went inside. There were large and small, steel and copper pipes coming out of and going back in the ground. Some were labeled coolant, water, and propane. The large twelve-inch diameter pipe was void of any marking. He considered the possibility where the pipe might lead and if he could squeeze inside. Ernie decided to try and slid inside the pipe.

* * *

Dante was checking for any breaks in the force field that would allow entry and found none. His next course of action was something he truly disliked. Flying through the earth. Not all angels had mastered the art of terra firma diving and Dante understood why. He had to see what was under the house, but all those rocks and roots, plus he was going to get his clothes dirty. Only for you Alex, he thought, and let himself go, to sink into the ground. The structure extended several floors below, but so did the sound energy field. A quick pass was made and he came back up. Bert was standing there as he popped up.

Dante raised his eyebrows. "Bert what are you doing back?"

"There was no way in. The signal came to a cone shape about eight miles up. Have you been looking for friends down there?"

Dante was swatting away the dirt from his coat. "No entry below the surface. The field goes all the way around the structure, but I did count four floors below."

"That could be helpful. Have you seen Ernie?"

"Not since he left," said Dante. "Let's go back in the trees until he shows up."

* * *

Major Henry and Mr. Brown carried Alex into sub level four, the containment and testing facility. She was laid on a gurney to be wheeled past armed guards with strange weapons and one with that glass eyepiece---the same one the Major wore. Alex's inability to move and the netting impaired her view. But when the gurney stopped she feared she saw her fate, an angel in a cage. The captive stood up and looked at her. "Your one of the fallen ones," he said.

"I see no reason to name names," said Alex.

"Believe me, they have ways of finding out," and he sat back down.

Alex did not like the sound of that. As she was being rolled into a room marked, 'Examination', she spoke to the angel. "I don't care what side you're on. In here there are only two sides, us and them."

* * *

The pipe going underground was tight, but Ernie managed to slide down without much thought of how he would get back up. There was nothing flowing through the pipe, but Ernie could see a purple colored liquid clinging to the sides. He exited the pipe into a large steel tank with a foot of the purple liquid on the bottom. Ernie was standing calf deep in the unknown substance. His wings were coated with the stuff, but there was plenty of room in the tank to flap a few times and clean them.

He put pressure on his muscles to move the feathered covered limbs but nothing happened. Again he strained to dislodge his frozen wings but they were not responding. The purple liquid covering was soaking deeper into the white feathers and growing heavier as it went. Ernie had made a terrible mistake. He could not fly, and he could not communicate with Bert through the sound field. However he could see through the tank into sub-level four.

When he focused to look into the room a man wearing a white coat walked straight at him. The lab tech stopped at the tank, tapping a gauge and pulling out his two-way radio. "Henderson, are you in the control room?"

"Go ahead Frank, what do you need?"

"Yeah, the A.F.A. is down to forty gallons, and with the Doc doing treatments every two hours, we have a five or six day supply. Better have the center send a shipment."

"Will do Frank. Order Anti Flying Agent. Wouldn't want these folks mobile, would we?"

"Roger that Henderson." And the lab tech walked away.

Ernie realized what he had gotten himself into. He was on the right level, but in the wrong place. Anti Flying Agent at two-hour intervals, he thought. It must wear off after two hours---maybe a bright spot in my otherwise purple existence. He would wait two hours and see. Meanwhile he would have ample time to scrutinize the ARC Units sub level four.

* * *

Dante was impatiently waiting in the forest passing the time stargazing. He would point to a star and out loud, spoke of whether or not it had been graced by his presence. "Been there. Been there. Don't want to go there. Got kicked out of there. Hey Bert, where's your friend Ernie?"

Bert was standing behind a tree watching the house, "I don't know universal traveler. But I'm going to give him some time before I panic."

"No panic here Bert. Just ready to do this." Dante continued his study of the stars, "What time do you think it is, five, five thirty?"

"Five thirty AM sounds right. I'll give Ernie till sun up. If he's not back, I'll go find him."

"Just as well," said Dante. "Maybe him and Alex will come flying out carrying the cylinder."

Bert could not believe Dante's optimism. "You think it will be that easy?"

"As a matter of fact I am counting on the opposite to be true. I am in the mood, for a fight."

* * *

Alex's first stop in ARC's orientation was a sterile place. The exam room was bright and smelled like disinfectant. Six men in white coats lifted her off the gurney and onto a steel table to the side of the room. She was placed face up, cinched in the net, with the overhead lights glaring down on her. Alex closed her eyes and heard several people walk out of the room. Then the unmistakable voice of Major Henry pierced the air. "Where is the Doc, Mr. Brown? I don't want to leave..."

"Good morning gentlemen."

"Doc. You need to quit sneaking up on me."

"You look tired Major," said the Doc as he peered into the room. "Is that a female?"

"One hundred percent," the Major said. "And a worse attitude I have never seen."

The Doc walked into the room, picked up a clipboard, and started writing. He had his back to Alex as he tried to calm her. "The first few days are the worst madam. We will do our best to make you comfortable."

Alex opened her eyes and closed them seeing only the overhead light as she tried to get a look at this Doc. His voice sounded familiar. She hoped it was someone she had no prior history with. Most men who came in contact with her got the short end of the deal.

The Doc was still writing. "Do you have a name miss?"

His voice bugged Alex and she knew she had heard it before. With all her strength she pulled against the net, turning her head, and viewed the Doc with his back facing her. "Wings," she said. "The Doc is an angel?"

The Doc turned. "Alexandra?"

Alex closed her eyes and sighed. "Bishop. You working for these guys?"

"I'm in charge of the lab."

"Is that your name Doc, Bishop?" the Major said.

"It was Bishop in another life," said the Doc.

Major Henry tilted his John Deere cap. "And you two know each other?"

"In the old days we did," the Doc said. "We were on the same side."

The Doc walked over to Alex and pulled on the net checking the tension. "This is my robe you're wrapped in. Not the first time for that, huh?"

"I have two words for you Bishop, piss and off."

"Oh Alexandra. What a way to reunite. We are going to check you out now, but first I must take some security measures. Help me turn her over Major."

They turned her over, wings up. The Doc took a spray bottle and saturated her wings with the purple fluid.

"Sorry Alexandra, this has to be done."

Alex felt the weight of the extract soaking her normally repellent wings. "What is this stuff?" she said.

"Remember what it was like during the big war in heaven, Alexandra; after hours of battle. How hard it was to fly with other angel's blood coating your wings. This is a synthetic compound of my blood. You won't be able to fly."

Alex lay there mad, tied up, and now she was wet. She didn't see Ernie inside the tank, a couple of hundred feet away. She could have seen him, if she knew to look, and concentrated her vision on the steel vat. None of the angels in the room were aware, they were being observed by one of their own.

* * *

Ernie took in the surreal scene of sub level four with sorrow in his heart. Besides Alex, there were two other angels being held in silver mesh screened containers about the size of a large outdoor storage building. The silver screen covered the walls, ceiling, and floor. One angel sat quietly looking into the exam room holding Alex. The other angel paced from corner to corner of his cell, and whipped his head to glare at anyone who walked by. And then there was this other angel, walking around like he owned the place and spraying Alex with Anti Flying Agent. Ernie did not know him and could only imagine how he came to be partners with the ARC Unit.

I will go down fighting, Ernie thought, and sensed he better check the tank to make certain he could get out. A trip back up the pipe was not a good idea because there could be more purple residue on the walls. He turned facing a side where no one could see him and put his finger through the tank wall, then drew it back. He felt better knowing the tank was not made of the same material as the cells.

Waiting to fly was the hard part, but when and if he could all hell was going to break loose. Ernie began to formulate a plan and he prayed. He didn't pray for rescue, but for wisdom, to discern the proper method to stop this insanity.

* * *

Doc wasn't a real doctor, but he knew more about angels than anyone in the unit. He was part of the third kicked out of heaven. The two veteran angels being held by ARC were captured three years ago and were on the side of the Lord. Before them were four others who had managed to escape, because Doc had not perfected the containment part of the operation. Since then the silver screen material was redesigned and has held ever since.

Doc was getting ready to release Alex from the net but other forms of restraint were necessary. Alex refused to call him Doc and called him Bishop, his given angel name.

"What are you doing Bishop?"

"Call me Doc, Alexandra. Would you help me flip her over Major?"

They flipped Alex face side up.

"I'm going to lift the net over your feet," the Doc said. "You will be more comfortable after I tie your feet and hands and remove the net."

"That sounds comfy Bishop. Tied to the table instead of trapped in a cocoon."

"Alexandra, you haven't changed."

"You have," she said.

"Yes and it was out of necessity," said the Doc. "I almost ceased to exist eight years ago. That's when I met the Major."

"The boy was in pretty bad shape all right," the Major said.

"I was beyond bad. I couldn't move, I could barely see, and I could not make myself invisible. My wings were hanging out for the world to see."

"Strangest thing I'd ever seen," said the Major, "to that point anyway. I thought he was a dead animal. I was coming out of Mexico about fifteen miles west of El Paso, and pulled over to check a rattle under the hood. That's when I saw the Doc lying face down in the dirt. He looked like he had been run over by a herd of cattle. But it wasn't cattle, was it Doc?"

"No, I was on a mission similar to you, Alexandra," the Doc said. "Three of us were in a battle with five angels of light, when the two I was with decided it was a losing cause. They abandoned me. I kept fighting as long as I could. I finally took a defensive posture; lying there letting them beat me. But after a while, they just left. I guess their side has more compassion, huh Alexandra?"

Alex didn't care about the trip down memory lane and tried to kick as her feet were being tied. She couldn't. The net was too tight. But she could move her mouth. "So, the only good the Major ever did in his life was to save a scum angel. I'm impressed."

The Doc was finished tying her feet and moved beside her touching her arm; then looked at her face. "Take it easy Alexandra. I'll have you lose in a minute." He worked to free her left arm, only to tie it to the table.

She jerked her arm up a few inches, but that's all. Seeing the binding around her wrist was the same as the net, she dropped her arm to the table. "They wouldn't be much without you, Bishop. Your robe made into a net for capture. Blood compound so we can't fly and leg and arm restraints to hold us. What happens next?"

"Next, you go into the cage," said the Doc.

"I figured that one out, Bishop---after that? What's the purpose of all this?"

Major Henry put his hands on the table, on either side of Alex's head. He leaned over to look her in the eyes. "We have enemies in this world just like you do," he said. "With your powers, did you not consider the complete and total victories we could have, and with no loss of American lives? We could take out terrorist organizations from the top down and they wouldn't know what hit em. If we could just get one of your kind to cooperate."

Alex felt the Major separate the net and pull it down exposing her face. She moved her jaw around working the taught muscles before looking at Major Henry. "Why didn't you just ask," said Alex. "Sounds like fun to me."

The Major straightened up, walked across the room, and leaned on the wall.

Doc was pulling the net out from under her. "Come on Alexandra, we're not hardwired that way. It's taken years for me to come close to that kind of mind alteration, but I am." He looked through the glass in the exam room door to the angel sitting in the adjacent cell. "That one's close. I haven't yet been able to convince him that killing a human, even a terrorist, is best for the world. He's an angel of light. The terrorists have declared Jihad against all the people in his charge. All the Christians are targets for death and he still resists."

"He's sticking to our law, Bishop," Alex said. "We're not allowed to interfere to that extent."

"Time is ticking down on this world," said the Doc. "The lines between the natural and the supernatural blur a little more every day. Some angels and demons are crossing those lines. And it sounds like you've been doing some line crossing on your own---you know, trying to steal the cylinder."

"I wasn't interfering. It was just trying to set things straight."

"Semantics," the Doc said. "That reminds me Major, where is the cylinder?"

"On the first level Doc, in a blast proof room."

"As soon as I take care of my old friend here, I'll do an inspection."

"We were never friends Bishop," she said.

"Maybe not, but we were lovers."

"Once, kind of, anyway it meant nothing. But tell me, why don't you go do the Majors bidding? Fly around the world and kill everyone on the Major's list."

The Doc slid a chair over and sat down next to Alex. "Ever since that day eight years ago in the desert when the Major found me, I can only stay invisible for thirty seconds. I can fly about two miles then I have to rest. I can't walk through walls, and my vision has been reduced to that of a human. I owe the Major my life. That's why I work with the ARC Unit, and that's why you'll never leave. I want my powers back. You can help me achieve that goal, Alexandra."

"Touching," Alex said. "I almost cried. A boy meets boy story of how one fights insurmountable odds to regain his health, with the other at his side. But if Bishop gets his powers back, how does that help you Major."

"Yes ma'am, he could just fly off and leave us. But the Doc is also working on making one of us, like one of you."

"Impossible. You're really into this mad scientist thing, aren't you Bishop?"

"At first it seemed impossible," said the Doc. "But a few hand selected humans have responded to skin graphs and blood additives. That's the ultimate goal. Take a human solider that already has the will to kill the enemy and give him the powers on an angel. I have only scratched the surface on what the angel blood can do. You also underestimated the power of the blood, didn't you Alexandra?"

Alex knew he was talking about the blood of Jesus. It was a defeat for all the evil ones, but a personal defeat for her. She had a part in hardening the hearts of the Pharisees two thousand years ago. She stood in the courtyard with the chief priests as Pilate decreed 'I can find no wrong with this Man;' and when the time came, she yelled the loudest, 'crucify Him, release Barabbas,' with victory in her heart. There was victory that day for the fallen ones. But three days later their plan fell apart and mankind had a Savior. Jesus was resurrected.

Alex let go of her bad memory and hoped someone outside the ARC house had a plan to free her. She was helpless, but could still verbally spar with her captors. "It sounds like you two deserve each other," she said. "Am I to believe you two just thought this up and did it?"

The Doc stood up, pushing the chair backwards, and yielding the floor to the Major. "No," said the Major. "There are other people involved who don't want to be involved, if you know what I mean? It takes a lot of money to fund this operation. And we wouldn't want to skimp when it comes to making your stay as pleasant as possible."

Alex only starred at the light overhead letting it fill her line of sight.

"What, no snappy come back Alexandra?" the Doc said. "That's not the girl I know." Doc looked at the Major and back to Alex. "Rest Alex. Major, I'll call Frank and let him put her in a cell; she's in good shape. But you look tired Major."

"You said that already." The Major starred down at Alex and said. "Before I go Miss, that day when I found the Doc, the biggest surprise came when I rolled him over. He was clutching a cylinder just like yours." The Major smiled and went to his room.

"I'll be back later Alexandra." And the Doc left the exam room for the stairs. For Doc to negotiate the three flights up to the first level and the cylinder, this angel would have to walk.

Chapter Fifteen

At 7:01 AM, Spencer's phone rang waking him from a sound sleep. "Hello."

"Mr. Bryant, this is Stan from research."

"Yeah Stan."

"I've been up since you called sir, but I have the information you requested. I sent you an e-mail containing everything I could find on this Major Henry."

"Thanks Stan. Get some sleep. Call the office and tell them I said it's okay for you to come in late."

Spencer hung up and dialed Jacob Kendall. Kendall was half way through his second cup of coffee, alone in the kitchen. Everyone else was asleep when the phone rang.

"Hello," said Kendall.

"Morning Jacob, you awake?"

"Hey Spencer, yeah, I've been up since six."

"I have information on Major Henry. I don't know what exactly, but I was coming to Clear Lake this week anyway. How about I see you in an hour."

"I'll be here buddy. Do you need my address?"

"I can get it Jacob. I'm about half awake, and I need a shower."

"See you soon," Kendall said, hanging up the phone.

Kendall sat sipping his coffee, and debated what he should and shouldn't tell his old friend Spencer.

* * *

Bert's position hadn't changed much. He stood invisible outside the ARC house still using the trees as cover. Dante flew in from taking a birds eye view of the area. "Hey Bert, the suns up."

"Yeah I know," said Bert. "Did you see Ernie?"

Dante shook his head. "Not a feather."

"I hope he's okay. I can track him. Stay here Dante, I'll be back."

"I'll be back," Dante said out loud. "Take your time Bert. I've been here so long, I'm thinking about building a little cabin over here in this clearing."

Bert retraced Ernie's flight around the property. Bert saw the military vehicles, the same deer, and finally came to the small steel building. He went inside and could tell Ernie had been there. Pipes in the ground are all he saw. But the large pipe stuck out as being so much bigger than the others, he touched it and thought, Ernie you didn't. After a few seconds of holding the pipe, Bert realized Ernie had gone inside. Bert was not going to follow, but instead, stuck his head through the pipe wall.

"Ernie, are you in there?"

"I'm in here Bert. Do not come inside the pipe."

"I'm not," said Bert.

"Good. There's some nasty stuff in here. Once you get it on you, you can't fly."

"You can't fly?"

"Not yet Bert. But I can move my wings, and in another hour, I think I could fly."

"So where are you Ernie?"

"I'm inside a tank, inside the building."

"Do you see the cylinder?"

"No, the cylinder is on the first sub-level. I'm on the forth. But I do see Alex."

"Look Ernie, we're not going to be able to get through this force field without tripping some kind of alarm. Do you have a plan?"

As a matter of fact I do, Bert. Did you see the trucks about a mile from here?"

"Yes."

"How about this," Ernie said. "Wait an hour and a half before you act. Then..." Ernie laid out the plan for Bert. And although Bert wasn't sure the plan would work, it was the only plan they had.

* * *

The old Coke clock above Professor Kendall's kitchen sink read eight A.M. The professor was sitting at the table, now on his fourth cup of coffee, and reading the Bible. His daughter Sara walked in. "Morning dad."

She kissed him on the back of the head, and went straight for the coffee pot. "Where is everyone?"

"Cooper, Ethan, Kate, and Rachel went down to the lake. Billy's in the basement. I think he wants to be alone."

"I'm glad to see you reading the book," Sara said. "Where are you reading?"

"It's funny Sara; I was sitting here worrying about what's going to happen next. I picked up the Bible, opened it, and let my eyes fall on a passage. It was Matthew 6:31-34. It says, 'Therefore take no thought, saying, what shall we eat? Or, What shall we drink? Or, Wherewithal shall we be clothed? For after all these things do the Gentiles seek: for your heavenly Father knoweth that ye have need of all these things. But seek ye first the kingdom of God, and His righteousness; and all these things shall be added unto you. Take therefore no thought for the morrow; for the morrow shall take thought for the things of itself. Sufficient unto the day is the evil thereof.'"

"Jesus is telling you not to worry, but to seek Him. Get your mind off the problem and onto the solution. It's amazing isn't it? I think God does that for new Christians. Allows them to open the Bible to a random scripture that turns out to be the specific word they need."

"It got my attention."

"I'm so proud of you Dad."

She kissed him on the head again.

"Spencer's on the way here. He has some info on Major Henry."

"It's been a while since you've seen him."

"Six or seven years."

"I better go change out of my pajamas," said Sara.

down below the Major's picture. "It says he was highly decorated in Desert Storm, and wrote a couple of papers for the military academy as to why the U.S. should have taken Baghdad and Kendall was flipping through the Bible when he heard a vehicle out front. He opened the front door as Spencer walked up with a laptop under his arm. The two men shook hands, a quick hug, and settled at the kitchen table.

"It's good to see you Spencer."

"You too Jacob. I guess we can catch up later. You probably want to hear what I've found."

"Show me."

Spencer opened up the notebook computer and brought up the attachment on his e-mail. "First the ARC Unit. It shows them to be a small group under the E.P.A. titled Archeological Related Contamination. They received about one million dollars last year in government funds, relatively small in comparison. Digging deeper, they got twelve million from two undisclosed private sources. A lot of money but not much about what they do. That's it on ARC, but look here. Is this the guy?"

Kendall saw a picture of Major Henry pop up. The Major was wearing his full dress Army greens. "That's him. What does it say?"

Spencer scrolled Saddam in 1980. He served twenty five years in the Army and took an honorable discharge in 1998."

"He's not in the military anymore?"

"According to this, no. He went into the private sector. Check this out. This is from the El Paso Times, dated March 1999. It reads, while working for private contractor ARC-LITE, Janice Meyer Henry was killed in an explosion Friday at the company's local facility. The cause of the blast is still under investigation.

"His wife was killed in an explosion?"

"Yeah. There's a photo of the aftermath."

Kendall looked at the photo of a distraught Major Henry, standing in the rubble. "There's two things in this picture that stand out Spencer. First, the cone shaped piece of metal at his feet. It's a small piece, but I think I know what it is. And what do you make of the object he's holding in his hand?"

Spencer turned the computer. "It looks like a round piece of something, maybe plastic or tinted glass."

"That's it Spence. The first thing he did when he went in to the basement was pull that glass out and look around the room."

"Very strange Jacob. What do you think he was looking for?"

Kendall thought a moment and decided what the heck. If the level of Spencer's involvement were to deepen, he would need to know the whole story.

"Spencer, he was looking for angels."

"Angels? Like little angels with bows and arrows on Valentine's Day?"

"No. Like eight foot tall warrior angels with swords and a mandate from God to do..." Kendall paused. "Well, I don't know what they're going to do but it's something big."

"I'm afraid you've lost me old friend," Spencer said.

"Join the crowd. We're all trying to digest what happened yesterday. Do you remember Sara?"

"Sure, daughter Sara?"

"Yes. I'll get her to help me with the explanation. Man, the Major was a phony. That means the search warrant was bogus too. It's up to Bert and Ernie now."

Spencer slowly turned his head toward Kendall, to stare.

"Hold that thought Spence. Let me get Sara."

The professor went for help.

* * *

Doc came back down the stairs to sub-level four and went to check on Alex. He stood in front of her cage, but he couldn't see her. "Hey Alexandra, I know you're in there."

Alex remained invisible and did not speak.

"Come on Alex, how would you like to be spray painted with some special purple paint I've developed?"

Alex made herself visible standing inches from the Doc. Only the thin, silver mesh screen separated them. Alex hit the screen with her fist. "Why can't I break through this stuff, Bishop?"

"Works well, doesn't it?"

"If it didn't, you wouldn't be standing," she said.

The Doc smiled. "The Major told you we had a cylinder. The screen material is the same molecular structure as the metal in the cylinder. We finally came up with a manufacturing process that would work, but not before four of our subjects escaped."

"You had four angels get away?" Why didn't they come back and kick you're..."

"Didn't give them a chance. When they escaped we moved locations the same day."

"So where's your cylinder now?"

"My new cylinder is on the first level, upstairs."

"Not that cylinder," said Alex. "The one you had years ago."

"It's gone," the Doc said. "Opening the cylinder proved to be a difficult chore. It was tragic from a human standpoint. Major Henry's wife was our lead scientist trying to open the cylinder. She used some volatile substances and there was an explosion. She died in the blast and the cylinder was destroyed; all but a couple of pieces from a mask. By the way Alexandra, do you know how to open my new cylinder?"

"I don't, but if I did, I would not tell you."

"Good enough. There will be time to find if that's true. There's food if you want to eat. Frank is the supervisor on the floor. Tell him if you need anything."

"Like a hacksaw?" she said.

Doc smiled again and waved, as he walked away, back to the stairs to the first level.

Alex had calmed down some, and now her efforts were concentrated on how to get out. She heard someone speak her name.

"Alex. Over here Alex, it's Ernie."

Alex looked in the direction of the voice to the steel tank in the corner. She focused and saw Ernie inside, waving his arms. She checked the floor, seeing no one could hear her and sat down on the bed, speaking softly. "Whatcha doing Ernie?"

"Planning a jail break, want to go?"

"I thought you would never ask."

"Listen Alex. Bert and Dante are outside, and in about five minutes, they'll be coming through the ceiling. I'm going to get the keys to the cells. You follow my lead."

"I can't fly," Alex said.

"I know the feeling," said Ernie. "I just got my wings back myself. Just be ready."

I'm ready. But what about my two cellmates?"

The other angels heard the question and waited for Ernie's response.

"We're not enough to take them both," Ernie said.

"Take the one in the first cell, Ernie. He seems to be close to breaking."

The angel in the first cage perked up. The second angel spoke directly to Ernie. "Just open my door. I'll do the rest."

"You got it," said Ernie. "Everyone keep your eyes on the guards. You'll know when it begins."

Ernie planed his moves and waited.

* * *

Bert told Dante the plan for extracting Alex and the cylinder. The rescuers had their game faces on.

"It's time, Bert said. "You ready to do this?"

"Giddy-up," said Dante.

From the stash of vehicles hidden on the property, the two of them sat in the biggest Army truck they could find. Bert was behind the wheel and turned the ignition key. The truck roared and black smoke blew out of the tailpipe.

"Do you know how to drive Bert?"

"It has been a while, but you know what they say, it's like riding a bicycle."

"Do you know how to ride a bicycle?"

"No, but I'll manage."

Bert pushed in the clutch and ground the gears trying to find first. He eased down on the gas, let out the clutch, and the truck jolted forward. They were rolling down the road toward the house.

"We're moving," Dante said.

Bert shifted to second, grinding more gears as he did. "Yeah we're moving all right. I just hope I can stop where I need to."

The truck lumbered through the forest in second gear. "Hey Bert, I think it's time to shift."

"Don't worry about it. I like this gear. Just worry about keeping them off me, once we get inside."

"No problemo. After myself, you will be my first concern," said Dante.

Bert mowed down the chain link fence around the backyard of the house, took out the Mimosa tree in his way, and stopped with the trucks engine over the sound field.

"I hope this works," Dante said.

"If it doesn't," said Bert, "we're going to wake up the natives."

Dante nodded. "Let's go!"

Bert went first, flying through the engine block and Dante followed. They were inside the house and paused. No alarms and nobody upstairs. The engine block shielded them from the alarm system.

"Okay Dante, we are going to level four, then back up to one."

"Ten four. Level four ladies lingerie, to level one silver cylinders."

They flew through the hall closet doors and down the elevator shaft.

Ernie waited in the tank. The other angels watched the two guards standing by the elevator doors. They saw Bert and Dante fly out of the ceiling, knocking down the guards. Their special angel weapons slid across the floor. Dante and Bert each picked up a gun, turned, and fired. The two guards were wrapped up like Christmas hams.

Ernie shot out of the tank, grabbing Frank, the guy with the keys. He picked Frank up and deposited him on top of the fifteen-foot high tank.

"I'll take these," Ernie said, and relieved him of the keys.

Ernie flew back down and unlocked the cells to find Bert and Dante tying up a couple of lab techs. Henderson in the control room saw the guards bound in their own angel netting, and Frank was screaming over the radio, "We have a breech! Hit the alarm! Hit the alarm!"

Henderson pushed the red alarm button.

The complex was filled with sirens and flashing red lights, as eight guards on the third level hit the floor running. Major Henry slipped on his eyepiece running behind them. They were all coming down the stairs as Dante and Bert flew through the building to the first level.

Ernie was carrying Alex. The other two angels stood outside their cages, unable to fly, and not knowing where to run.

"Hide inside the wall by the elevator," said Ernie. "I gotta go."

Ernie flew up through the floors clearing the house with Alex hanging on just when the guards and Major Henry ran out of the stairwell downstairs. The Major was the only one who saw the invisible angels dive behind the wall.

"Over there," the Major said. "Two of them are inside the wall. I don't see any more of them. Three of you come with me. The rest of you guard that wall."

Dante and Bert were already on the first level and Bert had hit the button to summon the elevator from the fourth floor. When the two angels downstairs heard the elevator move, they jumped inside.

From inside the blast proof room that housed the cylinder, Dante saw the Doc pick up the cylinder and run to a steel mesh lock up, like the cells below. Once inside, the cylinder would be secure.

"No need for that," Dante said, and he head butted the Doc knocking him unconscious. He threw the cylinder to Bert, just as the elevator doors opened containing the other angels.

"Get out of here Bert. I've got it."

"I have to go up the stairs. I can't take the cylinder through the concrete walls"

"Go Bert!"

Bert ran up the stairs and busted through the front wall of the frame house, flying away with the cylinder.

Dante heaved one angel over his shoulder and grabbed the other by his collar. Dante was half way through the ceiling when Major Henry bolted out of the stairway firing his weapon. The net spewed out of the gun, hitting the ceiling, and wrapped around Dante's leg. Dante could not move. He was carrying too much weight.

He sat one angel down inside the farmhouse. "You're on your own."

The angel got to his feet running out the hole in the wall Ernie had made, and in to the woods. Dante flapped his wings like he was working out with Jack La Lanne, recognizing this as the first time he felt fear from a mortal. He jerked his leg and freed himself from the netting below. He flew off with one angel over his shoulder.

Major Henry watched as the net, which was magically clinging to the ceiling, fell at his feet. "Okay boys, we probably have two angels in the air and at least one in the bush. Unwrap the guard downstairs and get the eyepiece. Get the vehicles up here, and somebody check on the Doc. Tell Henderson to call the center. We need to relocate. Come on, let's go get em."

Chapter Sixteen

Spencer slumped at the kitchen table with his mouth half-way open, and in total disbelief of the story Sara and Kendall were telling. What's happened to Jacob, he thought, thinking back to college remembering their long nights of discussing what was wrong and right with the world, and how they were going to change it. Back then, they both believed in the science.

There was at least some proof for evolution according to what they were taught, but an all-powerful God creating everything, it just didn't sound feasible. And now Kendall sounded like an evangelical preacher, with stories of angels appearing, a mysterious silver cylinder, and there were no maybes or I think so's in the language. Sara and Kendall were laying this out like it was what they did on summer vacation.

Sara finished up with the tale of Major Henry and the gold eagle wing inlayed on the chrome barrel of the Colt 45 held to her head. This Spencer could believe because there was physical evidence the Major was real. But the angel encounters as truth, no way, no how, and not in this lifetime. Spencer eased back in his chair, not sure what to say, and wondering if his old college buddy expected him to believe this unbelievable story. His wondering was answered as Kendall spoke. "For now, I don't expect you to believe anything we've told you Spencer, but as Sara said to me yesterday, I will ask you to keep an open mind."

"An open mind is one thing Jacob. What you're asking is a total reprogramming of what I believe."

Sara saw this as an opportunity to enlighten Spencer with some scripture. "The Bible calls it, putting on the new man." She opened the Bible to Colossians 3:9-10 and read. "Lie not to one another, seeing that you have put off the old man and his deeds; and have put on the new man, which is renewed in knowledge after the image of him that created him."

Spencer was not accustomed to having scripture forced on him, especially when it was used as a reason to why he should believe or disbelieve something he thought impossible. "There is no reason I can think of for you to lie about this," Spencer said. "But to believe it; let's say for now I have an open mind."

"Billy printed some photos this morning dad."

"You went down and saw Billy? How is he?"

"Depressed," said Sara. "We talked and I told him I harbored no bad feelings toward him, and that God can turn our mistakes into something positive for our lives."

Kendall stood up. "Come on Spencer. Let's go downstairs and look at the photographs."

Cooper, Rachel, Ethan, and Kate were out back of the house, sitting on the end of the pier with their legs hanging off, wishing for recreation.

"I want to go swimming," said Kate.

"Swimming and a picnic," Rachel added.

"The professor has a boat doesn't he? We could go water skiing," Ethan said.

"I could take a nap," said Cooper. "What I really need is some practice for my tennis match Saturday."

Rachel patted him on the leg. "You still have three days. And with the cylinder missing, what else are we going to do?"

Cooper leaned back on the gray decking behind Rachel, making a heart shape on her back with his finger.

She slapped at his hand. "Quit it. That tickles."

"Come away with me Rachel," Cooper said. "We can leave all this behind."

Rachel smiled and shook her head as Ethan and Kate gave Cooper a look.

"Maybe we should go find out what the professor wants us to do," said Ethan.

"That would be a better plan," Rachel said.

They all stood up to go inside, but when they turned, they stopped seeing an obstacle now standing before them. Dante hovered a foot off the uncut grass at the edge of the pier with a body draped over his shoulder and blocking the only exit. He drifted down to the ground unloading his passenger leaning him against the railing. Dante watched the four students, frozen in stride, trapped on the end of the pier, and thought. How can these be the chosen ones? "How's the Christian gang doing this morning?" he said.

Cooper spoke under his breath. "Everyone stay still. Don't give him a reason."

Dante stepped on the pier walking toward the kids, when Ernie flew down in his path carrying Alex.

"Maybe you should take her and leave," said Ernie. "Our partnership is over."

"Good to see you again Ernie," Alex said, "and thanks."

Dante took Alex and lifted off, but not before one last remark. "I know you opened the cylinder and you know what? Good for you. Now we must let things play out in the natural. And Ernie, be sure and take care of your players." Dante and Alex were gone.

Ernie pulled the dazed and confused angel to his feet. "You'll be safe now, and as soon as this purple junk wears off you can fly again. Help me get him inside guys. Bert should be here shortly, and I have to go back for the other angel."

"There's more?" Cooper said.

"One more," said Ernie. "When you see Bert, tell him where I am."

Ernie flew away, and the kids escorted the new angel to the house.

Kendall, Sara, and Spencer were downstairs in the basement with Billy. Billy sat in front of the table where the cylinder used to be, with a kind of hangdog expression on his face. Spencer held the photos from the previous day, showing the cylinder at different stages of discovery. They varied from earlier shots with only a small portion breaking the ground, to pictures of Billy doing his cleaning and holding the Popsicle stick.

Spencer saw no Kodak moment of the opened cylinder, or of any angels. His doubts were still intact. "You have found something unusual here Jacob. But I don't see any..."

The upstairs door to the basement slammed, and someone came running down the stairs. Bert emerged from the stairway, ducked his wings to get under the doorframe, and straightened his eight-foot frame, smiling as he held out the cylinder. "I got it."

Spencer's mouth was open again but this time all the way.

"Good job Bert," said the professor. "Check it out Billy."

Billy walked over and held out his hand. "Thank you Bert."

Bert shook his hand when the door upstairs opened again. The kids came down with everyone talking as they ushered in the new angel, like they had found a lost puppy. They grew silent as Cooper spoke. "Look what we have, Professor."

Amazingly Spencer's mouth would open further and it did.

Kendall was also surprised. "Where did..."

"It's okay, Professor," Bert said. "He's with me. Where's Ernie?"

"He said to tell you he went back for the other angel," said Rachel.

"Good. He should be back soon. But for now, we need somewhere else to stay. Any thoughts
Professor?"

Kendall looked at Spencer seeing he was stunned, and by the look on his face possibly waiting for a dental exam. "Close your mouth Spencer," Kendall said. "Where's my manners? Spencer this is Bert, Bert this is Spencer." Kendall stepped back laughing.

Bert went over to Spencer, with the cylinder under his left arm and his right stuck out to greet him. Spencer grabbed his large hand and hung on as Bert did the shaking.

"He looks like he's in shock," said Bert.

"I bet you get that reaction all the time," Sara said.

"Honestly, through the centuries very few humans have seen me. And if we are to keep that streak alive I must say again, we need to go elsewhere, and go now."

Kendall tapped Spencer on the back. "You okay man?"

"Yeah, okay," Spencer said.

"Spencer look at me," said Kendall. "Is there somewhere we can take everyone, where we'll be safe?"

"Hey, sorry Jacob. Yeah, open mind. Yes, the home I grew up in is twenty miles away, and the only person there is an employee of mine."

"You heard the man," Cooper said. "Road trip."

Everyone packed once more and Cooper made sure he loaded the tennis equipment. There was ample room for the expanding team with Spencer's Escalade, the Cherokee, and Kendall's GMC. When they were ready to leave two more passengers showed up. Ernie and the other emancipated angel from the ARC house landed in the driveway.

"Thanks for the lift Ernie," said the hitchhiking angel.

"You'll be able to fly soon," Ernie said. "Where are we going?"

"Hopefully somewhere we can't be found," said Bert. "A house owned by the professor's friend, Spencer."

Bert went to the Escalade, with Spencer behind the wheel and Kendall riding shotgun, literally. The shotgun was propped on the seat between them. Bert knocked on the glass. Spencer still unsure opened the window. "Yes sir," Spencer said.

"Ernie and I, and by the way that's Ernie."

Spencer looked to see two more angels, with Ernie waving, and made a conscious effort not to let his mouth fly open again.

Bert continued. "We're going to follow you from the air. Two of these angels can't fly just yet and they need to ride with you."

"Let me unlock the door," Kendall said.

"No need Professor," said Bert.

Spencer and Kendall turned to find the two angels already in the backseat. Kendall laughed, and Spencer's mouth fell open again. Spencer turned back around to a smiling Bert. "It's okay Spencer," Bert said. "You'll get accustomed to our habits. If you don't need to open a door to enter, why bother."

Spencer closed his mouth. "If you say so."

"I need an address where we're going," said Bert. "In case Ernie and I get separated."

Spencer knew it from memory. "1187 Hunterwasseur, Potter Valley."

The caravan left Clear Lake for their new safe house.

* * *

The ARC Unit helicopter with Major Henry and Mr. Brown as passengers rose above the trees surrounding their clandestine homestead for the last time. Two, fifty three-foot tractor-trailers were out front, with everything but the plumbing fixtures being loaded for transport to a new unknown location. Being mobile was part of being ARC.

The Major sat looking out the helicopter window and spied the Suburban filled with armed guards, which had left ten minutes earlier. It was following its previous path to Clear Lake, and Professor Kendall's. This was the Major's first major setback in three years. His cells at ARC were empty, the Doc was hurt, and the chances of finding the escapees grew slimmer by the minute.

"Gentleman," said the Major, "these birds have flown the coop. We don't have a chance in thunder of catching them."

The pilot clicked his mic. "You want to go back Major?"

"Head on to Kendall's lieutenant. Maybe they left us a clue."

* * *

After a shower and five hours sleep, Carson came downstairs at the house in Potter Valley, to find Alex stretched out on the sofa and Dante pacing the length of the grand room. Carson sat down next to Alex. "You okay?"

"She's all right," said Dante. "Now we not only have the Bert, the Ernie, and the Christian gang to deal with, we have the angel hunters."

Carson stood. "Angel hunters?"

"Never mind Carson. Alex cannot fly just yet, but we need to stay with Kendall and his group."

Carson's phone rang. "This is Carson."

Dante stopped pacing and listened to Carson's end of the conversation. He heard three yes sirs; one I can do that, and a no problem. Carson hung up with an I know something you don't look on his face.

"Well," Dante said.

"It's your lucky day sir. That was my boss on the phone. He's on the way here with Kendall and his team. Then he said something about, no matter what I saw, keep an open mind."

Dante's juices started flowing again. "So the sheep are coming to the wolves, how appropriate. And the open mind remark, there are probably a couple of wayward angels with them in the same shape as Alex. I guess he did not want to scare you. You are not scared of angels, are you Carson?"

"Most of the time, no sir."

Dante walked over and put his arm around Carson. "It is time for duty again son. Are you ready?"

"Yes sir."

"Good," said Dante. "Ernie and Bert do not have a clue you have an allegiance to us. So be friendly, volunteer to help, and keep your eyes and ears open. I saw a guesthouse about two hundred yards east in the woods. Alex and I will be there. If we don't come to you, come find us later."

Dante picked up Alex and left, leaving Carson alone with his thoughts. One more turn of the screw, one more blow to the nail head, and a little tighter pulls the lid on my life.

* * *

Major Henry was on the radio with the guards exiting the Suburban in Professor Kendall's driveway.

"Bravo one, anybody home down there?"

"No one's answering Major, and the doors locked."

"Kick it in Sergeant."

The Sergeant's foot made contact and the door crashed open. The motion pulled off part of the doorjamb and it sailed across the living room smashing into a lamp. With guns drawn, five guards entered turning over furniture, slamming drawers on the floor, and generally tearing up the place looking for anything as to where the group may have gone.

The Major looked through his eyepiece out the window. "Bravo one, did you find anything yet?"

"Nothing so far Major."

"Keep looking Bravo. I don't see any bogies in the area, but you can never..." Something flashed by the Major's window. "What the heck was that? Did you see that Mr. Brown?"

"No sir. What was it?"

"It could be a new customer. Wait, about a half mile out and coming this way."

The Major's head whipped to the other side of the aircraft. "Holy Moses, that sucker is moving. It just did a flyby. On your side Mr. Brown, he's coming back again."

Mr. Brown readied his weapon, and prepared to slide the door open, but the object flew up and stopped about fifteen feet away. "It's the Doc."

"Doc? What in the Sam Hill is going on here?"

The Doc flew over and popped inside the helicopter. "Greetings Major."

"I see you're feeling better Doc."

"More than that Major. I got most of my powers back. I can disappear, I can fly, and my hearing and sight are about eighty percent recovered. It must have been that blow to the head I took back in lab. When I woke up, I was fixed."

The Doc was excited after eight years without powers, and he rambled, as the Major relaxed in the seat with his hand on the gun in his lap. "Bang!"

The Doc fell trapped in his own net, rolling on the floor trying to get loose.

"Sorry Doc. But since you've had a miraculous turn in health, I need to talk to the center."

"You will regret this Major," the Doc said.

"I already do Doc. I already do."

* * *

Carson welcomed the Kendall caravan with opened arms and an open mind. "Come on in everyone. There are drinks in the fridge and I just ordered groceries. They should be here in about an hour. Hey Spencer."

"Sorry to bust in on you Carson. We had no choice. Everyone this is Carson, Carson this is everyone, and don't mind these two, they're with us."

Carson stepped back as the two angels walked through the door and took a seat on the sofa in the foyer. Carson trying to be the gracious host approached them. "Something to drink for you?"

"We require no nourishment at this time. We will be leaving shortly," the angel said.

"Fine," said Carson, "If everyone else will come this way, have a seat and relax."

They all picked a spot in one of the three seating areas of the fifty by hundred foot room, all except Billy. He held the case with the cylinder. "What do you want to do with this, Professor?"

"I'm not sure," Kendall said. "Spencer, I don't suppose one of these rooms has a large safe?"

"Well, not a safe, but we have a vault. My father had the over grown piggy bank, as my mother called it, installed sometime in the late Forties. I think I can remember the combination. It was based on American historical events. Let's see, the big stock market crash, 29, the bombing of Pearl Harbor, 41, when women got the vote, 20, my mom added that one, and the first production Model T Ford, 08. That's it, 29, 41, 20, 08. I'll go try it."

Spencer stopped in his tracks. Ernie and Bert had entered the house through the large picture window overlooking the backyard, and the clear water in the large swimming pool glistened in the sunlight. A cabana with two bathrooms stood at one end. Across the plush Bermuda grass lawn was a tennis court in disrepair with no net and the lines withered and faded.

Pleasantries were not on Bert's mind as he went directly to Billy and held out his hand. "May I?"

Billy looked at the case, then back into the room with a surprised look.

"Hear me Billy," Bert said. "This has nothing to do with what happened back in Clear Lake. Ernie and I have a mission."

Billy handed over the case. Bert turned to address the group. "I want to take up where we left off before the interruption in the basement. Professor Kendall, you and your team are part of a plan, all with varying degrees of participation. I'm going to have to ask your patience at this juncture."

It was clear to Bert everyone in the room was part of the bigger plan, including Spencer and Carson, but now he had to deal with the principle players. Bert's voice relayed the gravity of the situation, but he also spoke with compassion realizing the unpredictable emotions the humans possessed. Bert too had emotions. But through the centuries he had somewhat learned to keep them in check. Not all angels had mastered this fete.

Bert continued. "Some of you are aware there is an unseen spiritual, supernatural war taking place on the earth and in the heavens that has been raging for centuries. If you so decide, you are about to become directly involved in that battle. I cannot force you to do anything beyond your will. With that said, I need to see Cooper, Rachel, Ethan, and Kate. I have special instructions for you. I saw a place above the garage. What is that Spencer?"

"It's the old servant's quarters. It's a self-sustained unit with two bedrooms, kitchen, bath, and a living area. About fifteen hundred square feet."

"That is perfect," said Bert. "If you four will come with me, Ernie and I will tell you why we are here. The rest of you do not fret. You will find out the mission shortly, and I suggest you keep a look out for the ARC Unit. The Major seemed a determined man and is not likely to give up easily. That's it. We will see you later."

Two angels and four students walked together, to begin a new era in angelic warfare.

* * *

A little ways back on the six-acre property the guesthouse was now occupied by Dante and Alex. Alex walked around the living room shaking her wings and forced her muscles to attention as they fluttered, hitting the ceiling and floor with the movement. Her body rose off the floor. "Hey, I can fly."

Dante sat uninterested in Alex's accomplishment, starring out the window at the big house where all the action was. "Great Alex, why don't you fly out for some Chinese? I'm hungry."

Alex flew to the window and put her arm around him. "What's the matter boss?"

"Waiting, waiting, and more waiting, that's the matter. It goes against ever notion of evil in my nature to let this thing play out. The actions of the Christian gang, the guardian angels, Carson, and now Spencer must line up with our plan if we are to have victory."

Alex tried to sooth him. "You're all too aware," she said, "how fallible these humans are; and the extent they go to protect their precious egos and beliefs."

"Yes, correct Alex. Wars have been started with less cause. Once they find out their mission that should put some doubt in their hearts. But if we just had a way to stir the pot a little."

"Let me think on it sir. Between us both I'm sure we can come up with something nasty to do. But now, there is something I would like to do. If you're game that is."

"Game," Dante said. "I love games."

* * *

Major Henry's attempt to reach the center had gone unsuccessful. The center was the hub for ARC. It consisted of ten men on alternating shifts in a communications bunker that network throughout the world. They controlled a vast amount of resources with very little manpower. Manpower like the truck drivers loading their trailers back at the ARC house. They had no idea who, or what, they were moving only where to pick up and where to drop off. There were a total of two hundred and fifteen people around the globe, and one angel, who worked for and knew what ARC really did. But the Major was concerned with the one angel.

Major Henry considered long and hard the decision that led to detaining the Doc. On the one hand, Doc had been loyal and the source of all their knowledge in angel capture and containment. On the other hand he was still one of them, an angel; and prior to the security breech at the house, a disabled angel. Now he was mobile.

The Major had to entertain the possibility that the Doc might turn his wings on the whole project, and what to do if he did. That's why Major Henry had to reach the center; he did not want to make that decision alone. The helicopter circled over the lake while the guards finished their search of Kendall's house.

"Bravo One here. Are you there Major?"

"I'm here sergeant."

"We've done everything short of ripping open the walls and we didn't find much."

"What did you find Bravo One?"

"Kendall has one uncle and two aunts in Texas according to his Christmas cards from last year and some other ties to the state; looks like a couple of savings accounts in Dallas banks. I think he's from there."

"Texas boy huh. Bag up some of the personal stuff Bravo, and let's go home."

"This is Bravo one. Where's home Major?"

"Ah, good question Bravo. I'll get back to you."

Major Henry saw the co-pilot turn and shake his head signifying no communications yet. The Major turned his attention to his friend and prisoner on the floor. "Doc, you need to think about the corporate position on this. I can tell you there has been a deal in place, which ARC is prepared to offer you in the event you regained your powers."

"A deal?" said the Doc. "I don't know of any deal."

"I don't know the details either," the Major said. "Only if this situation presented itself, I was to detain you until we could sweeten the pot."

"You guys are all about mistrust, aren't you?"

"More about self-preservation Doc. Too much is at stake to leave any room for doubt about where you stand. I trust you, Doc, but I don't answer to you."

Chapter Seventeen

The uneasy feeling in the great room rising from the Kendall's and Billy being left behind, had Spencer excusing himself and leaving Carson to be host. It seemed like forever to Spencer since he had been in the home of his childhood. He strolled through the rooms taking time to reacquaint himself and conjure up some memories.

His earliest memory began at six years old when the house was full of people he didn't recognize enjoying a dinner party. He had escaped from the nanny and rode his big wheel in and around the furniture of the great room when he found his way to the dining room.

He remembered pedaling as hard as he could toward the long table encompassed by tuxedo-clad men and gown-draped women. He crashed into the chair of the Junior Senator from California, sitting at the head of the table. The man stood up laughing, turned him around, and gave him a shove saying, "There goes the future, gentlemen."

Spencer found out years later it was Richard M. Nixon he had broadsided, and the party was in his honor. Nixon was preparing to run for the vice presidency of the United States. Spencer's father indulged himself in political clout. A lesson Spencer had retained over the years. He moved into the commercial style kitchen recalling the hustle and bustle of Christmas in the room, and sitting in a metal Cosco chair eating cherries while his aunt made fruit salad. The kitchen window had a good view of the backyard and the fifty-year-old swimming pool lounged in immaculate condition.

Spencer became aware as he stood soaking in the scene of so much of his juvenile summer fun; he had been paying for cleaning, maintenance, and annual draining and filling of the concrete pond, for no telling how long. He vowed to go swimming as he rejoined the professor.

Carson sat across from Kendall asking subtle questions about the cylinder and the angels, while Carson pretended to be amazed by the unheard of events. Little information came forthwith that Carson was not already privy to. The method in which the cylinder finally opened became Carson's goal but that fact eluded him for now.

Spencer came in. "Hey Jacob, I have an idea. Let's go swimming. I know we have some swimsuits around here, if you didn't bring one."

"I brought one," Sara said.

"You did? Kendall said.

"It's summer dad. I don't travel anywhere without my bathing suit."

"Not even when you're running from a rouge military group?"

"I packed it when we left for the dig and I never unpacked."

"I have a suit," said Billy.

"Me too," Carson said.

"It's settled Jacob. Last one in is a Democrat."

Kendall had not heard that line since college. Spencer was famous for his last whatever is a democrat line, which he used only to get a rise from certain people. He used it this time to get a smile from Kendall. But swimming sounded good to Kendall, and since the angels had taken charge, that's what he would do, swim.

* * *

The living room in the servant's quarters above the garage had been set up like a small classroom. The cylinder rested on the table brought in from the kitchen, and the six chairs were arranged in two rows of three facing the table. Ernie and Bert quietly talked, standing alongside the cylinder.

Cooper sat in the front row with Ethan sitting behind him. Rachel was in the other front chair with Kate behind her. Two empty chairs were behind them all. Cooper turned his head and whispered to Ethan. "This feels like we've been called to the Dean's office for toilet papering the girl's workout room."

"Hey, all your idea man," said Ethan. "We're lucky we didn't get expelled."

"You guys did that?" Rachel said.

Cooper smiled and pointed to the angels breaking their pow-wow. Bert sat on the edge of the table. "We told you the cylinder contained a game played by angels, from the beginning of time up until the great banishing of the third from heaven. God can work instantly in some matters, but more times than not, things take time to allow people to grow and mature. We have no time. We will ask you to grow up very fast."

The two girls and Ethan looked at Cooper. Cooper responded. "What?"

"I suppose you are a little like Peter Pan from Neverland," said Ernie.

"I think holding on to some of your inner child is important," Cooper said.

Bert stood up. "We are not here to change anyone's personality. What things will change because of this mission will change on their own. One thing you need to understand is that you have been chosen. Chosen to be part of something no human being has ever been graced to do. It is time to open the cylinder. Would someone read the scripture?"

Kate reached into her bag and opened the Bible to Psalm 118:8. She read the passage and the cylinder opened again, but this time without the light.

"Cool," said Ethan.

"Where's the bright light?" Kate said.

"The light was depleted during the original opening and cannot be replenished," said Bert. "From this point on, all of us will have to guard the cylinder. And never speak, to anyone who does not already know, as to how it is opened."

Ernie flipped up the bottom or keyboard section of the cylinder to reveal a storage compartment. "Several pieces of equipment will be given to you that will become solely your possession. The first piece is the mask."

Ernie held up four masks. Each consisted of a pair of goggles, which looked like a pair protective eyewear used in racquetball, but extending down from the tinted glass was a faceplate. The faceplate was made to hang down below the wearers chin and curved around to the ears, protecting the users face. The masks were black, but each had a splash of a different color in the form of a stripe or symbol for identification.

"I want the red one," said Cooper.

"Blue for me," Ethan said.

"I'll take yellow," said Kate.

Rachel rubbed her chin, thinking. "I've never been picky about color. The purple one will do."

"Yeah, like that hour you spent picking out shoes," Cooper said.

"It wasn't just color, Cooper."

Ernie passed out the masks. "We want you to try them on, but before you do, look around the room and familiarize yourself with the contents."

They all looked, and wondered if something special lay within the walls they were supposed to notice. A large photograph of the house hung on the wall behind them, with what could have been Spencer as a toddler standing on the porch with his family. That and the two empty chairs stood out.

"Put on your masks," said Bert.

They slipped on the masks adjusting the elastic type band and securing the protective covering to their faces.

"Whoa dude," said Cooper looking to the back of the room.

The two angels rescued from the ARC Unit sat in the seemingly empty chairs behind them. Kate flipped up her mask and could not see the angels. She pulled it back down to find one of the angels waving at her. "Are you all seeing what I'm seeing?" Kate said. She could tell by the silence, they were.

Bert spoke to the angels. "Thank you for your help in demonstrating one of the powers of the mask. Do you feel like traveling yet?"

"We're ready to go Bert. But first, thanks to you and Ernie for springing us. If you had not come along... Well, if we can do anything for you, just call."

Bert signaled with a fist held over his heart, and the other two returned the gesture as they left through the back wall.

"We can see invisible angels guys," Ethan said.

"Do you notice anything else in the room you did not see before?"

Rachel got out of her chair and went to the old photo of the house. "Hello," she said. "Standing on the roof in this picture is an angel I didn't see before."

"Very good Rachel," said Ernie. "You get the most observant award."

"But..." Rachel checked, and she could only see the figure on the roof through the mask. "How is that possible?"

"The angel was there and captured on film when the camera shutter opened. You just needed the mask to see him. Do you have any family photos with you Rachel?"

Rachel opened her billfold finding a picture from her family vacation a year ago, showing her and her sister standing at the edge of the Grand Canyon. As she gazed through the mask she viewed the image in a whole new light. She saw an angel standing between them and the drop off into the canyon.

The other three masked covered faces groped and grasped to find their own personal photos, and the before unseen angels. They shared their newly discovered protectors with astonishment but tempered with a youthful zeal.

"Hey, my angel is taller than yours Ethan," Cooper said.

"Yeah, but mine is better looking. And besides Cooper, I bet your angel had to put in for overtime to keep up with you."

"I always believed angels were real," said Kate, "But to see *my* angel with me in a photograph, I can't put it into words."

Bert interrupted. "Here is our paradox. We are seldom thought of, but first to respond. We are everywhere, and nowhere. We are always with you, but never seen---until now. You four have been allowed to see into the spiritual realm, but as you will find out, not for your own enjoyment. Believe this; a great gift has been bestowed upon you."

The kids listened as Bert spoke, but as soon as he finished, they were more interested in comparing their newly found angels, than really hearing what he said. Bert considered they were not ready for the mission.

* * *

Down at the pool splashing and floating was in full swing, and Carson managed to keep the conversation centered on the cylinder. He figured anyone hearing the Kendall's story for the first time would have a hundred questions. He had a hundred and one.

Carson stood chin deep at the five-foot mark in the pool and hammered away, still acting shocked, and trying a little sympathy for good measure. "Sounds like you folks have been through a lot. I don't envy you."

The professor sunbathed in a lounge chair. "We didn't have much of a choice once we found the thing. It kind of snowballed from there."

Carson used his dogpaddled stroke to reach the pools edge. "And this Major guy, you were acquainted with him before?"

Kendall opened his eyes a little, seeing that Billy floated on a blow up raft in the deep end. "I'm not sure we want to go there," Kendall said. "Billy didn't know..."

"Don't worry Professor," said Billy. "I've come to terms with that mistake. The cylinder is back, two angels were set free who otherwise would still be imprisoned, and no one got hurt."

Sara, who was swimming laps across the width of the pool, stopped. "Thank God we are all fine now, but when the Major stuck that gun to my head, I did come critically close to needing a change of drawers."

Everyone laughed.

"Oh I see," Sara said. "In the it's serious now but we'll laugh about it later equation, this is the laugh about it part."

"You'll have to excuse my daughter. She has a habit of speaking her mind."

"I don't understand how you all are still going," said Carson. "You have to be exhausted."

Billy slid off the raft and swam to the shallow end. "Not really. Must have been the blue food."

"Blue food?" Carson questioned.

"That was a totally freaky experience," Billy said. "After the cylinder opened, a light so bright I can't describe zapped us. Then the angels gave us some blue fruit and we all perked back up."

Carson could describe the light. To him it was blinding. But the words 'cylinder opened' reverberated in his head, and he had to control himself. He felt he was close to finding out how. "So the cylinder opens, huh? What is there a latch or a..."

"Carson why don't you give it a rest," Spencer said looking at his watch. "I think they may want to think about something other than the cylinder. And besides, it's 1:15. You need to go lay out the site for the charity event. The trucks will be arriving in the morning."

Carson wanted to sink to the bottom of the pool and not come up. He was so close to finding the cylinder opening technique he could taste it, or maybe it was the chlorine he tasted. He decided he could not force his hand for fear of seeming over anxious. He would do as his boss asked. "Good call Spencer, check the site. But I do want to hear more of your adventures later."

"Sure thing," said Kendall.

Billy nodded and Sara flashed a peace sign as she went under water, swimming past Carson.

Spencer looked at his watch again. "And Carson, check on the groceries. It's been over two hours now."

Carson would change hats again, from cylinder informant to charity giver, and now grocery procurer. As he walked to the house, he could not help but turn an eye to the rooms over the garage and ponder the things taking place upstairs.

$* * *$

There were not angels in every picture the group found but enough to excite them. Ernie let the newness of the kids secret protectors subside, before he got back to business. "Okay everyone, please take off your masks and be seated."

Cooper checked the room again before removing his mask. "Where's my angel now?"

"We have been assigned to you for now," Bert said. "If you will sit down and listen you will find out why."

Cooper sat down.

Ernie reached into the cylinder. "This is your ball holster. The balls inside are your ammunition."

He gave the red holster to Cooper, blue to Ethan, yellow to Kate, and purple to Rachel. They held them looking perplexed. The holster was made of a leather like substance, only they guessed it was some heavenly product, and the balls looked like tennis balls, but the colors were different.

The holster had two compartments, an upper and lower. The upper was accessed from the top and held three balls, all white. Balls were pulled from the lower compartment by reaching in from the back, and held two balls, one blue and one red. They continued to study the holsters, while waiting for Ernie to explain.

Ernie threw them each a belt and a leg tie. "Go ahead and put them on. But do not play with the balls."

Cooper slid the belt through the loop in the holster and buckled it to his waist, then tied the bottom of the holster to his leg. "Man, I feel like a futuristic Marshall Dillon."

Rachel looked puzzled. "Excuse me?"

"You know Gunsmoke, the old western. How about Palladin, ever heard of him. This one you'll know, Rowdy Yates."

No one gave recognition.

"Man, Clint Eastwood was Rowdy Yates on Rawhide. I dig those old westerns."

"I tell you what Cooper," said Ernie. "We're close to an angel who looked after Clint when he was young. We will introduce you, if you will please sit down."

Cooper sat down again.

Ernie reached into the cylinder again. "The last part of your arsenal is the racket."

Ernie held up a racket that could have been manufactured by Ferrari. In fact, the Archangel Michael was in charge of some of these earlier designs. It was similar to a tennis racket, but the lines and shape looked something like a distant future prototype. The racket had a head and strings, and below the head was a round opening. The body of the frame consisted of two thin bars extending down from the head, to a wrapped handle with three strands of the wrapping hanging loose on the end.

Cooper held up his hand and smiled big. The racket was red. A lightning bolt emblazoned the strings.

"Yes, this one's for you Cooper," Ernie said, and he handed out rackets. Each one with a slightly different shaped head, a different shape embossed across the strings, and of course color coordinated to match their other equipment.

They were all standing getting a feel of their new toys. Cooper was swinging at the air pretending he had just served an ace. He pulled a white ball from his holster and started to throw it up, when Ernie grabbed his arm. "Give me that."

Ernie walked to the cylinder, pulled down the keyboard section, and pushed the on button. The cylinder beeped twice as seven screens lit up, and Ernie typed on the keyboard. "You want to see what this ball can do? Line up next to the wall."

The kids somewhat reluctantly moved against the back wall facing Ernie, who had his back to them. He put a white ball in the receptacle to the right of the keyboard and closed the cover. The ball was encased inside its own special holder. Ernie made keystrokes with his left hand and held out his right behind him. "Cooper, your racket please."

Cooper threw the racket up in the air toward Ernie who still had his back turned. Ernie snatched the racket in mid-flight without looking. A collective "Whoa" was heard from the cheap seats.

Ernie finished his data entry, flipped the ball cover back, picked the ball up and hit it as hard as he could at Cooper's face. The ball streaked across the space instantaneously. No one saw it leave the racket and no one saw it fulfill its course. But they did see the ball stop one inch from Cooper's nose and hover, spinning wildly.

Cooper's head was as tight to the wall as it would go as his eyes crossed to focus on the revolving sphere. He grew dizzy from his gaze, and to his surprise, the ball suddenly shifted to hang in front of Ethan's face. Straight down the line it went stopping at each one and coming to Rachel last. She started to swat it but the ball jumped back to Cooper, this time touching his nose. And with each vertiginous motion he could feel his skin starting to weaken.

Ernie held up the racket and placed his thumb to the side of the grip. A light came on around the outside of the round hole under the racket head, and the ball retreated back across the room, fitting snuggly in the hole. Cooper felt the end of his nose and was relieved to find it still intact. "What was that?" Cooper said.

Ernie pressed the side of the grip once more and the ball popped out into his hand. "Some of the balls are programmable for motion and destruction rate. To a point, they will do whatever you want them to do."

Kate had a mini-revelation and shared it with a calm and quiet tone. "Has anyone else noticed he used the words destruction rate, arsenal, weapon, and ammunition?"

Ernie smiled and looked at Bert, who stepped forward. "Expanding on what I said earlier, you have been invited to see into the darkest corners of the spiritual plane. You have been chosen to fight every evil avenging angel, along with every disturbed demented demon from the pits of hell. They are all going to want your blood on their hands. You will be so unique; they will be sitting around thinking up ways to destroy you."

Cooper looked down the row at his wide-eyed friends, and could not resist an attempt to defuse Bert's sobering remark. "You didn't have to sugar coat it like that Bert. Why didn't you just tell us straight out?"

Bert wanted to smile, but held back. "The truth is you all were picked not in spite of, but because of your personalities and abilities. The ability to joke in the face of death may come in handy."

Cooper raised his hand. "Bert, do you know the meaning of sugar coat?"

Bert unleashed a broad smile. "I know this is a lot to grasp. What hasn't been in the last two days? I want you to think seriously about this because we all have to be sure. There can be no weak link. Think about it overnight, and if you accept the chosen status, be in this room at 6:00 AM tomorrow morning. Remember, there will be no bad feelings or repercussions if I do not see you sitting here in the morning. If you show up tomorrow, we will begin the equipment acclimation phase, which allows your gear to operate in the higher functions."

Cooper scratched his head. "What did he say?"

Rachel slapped his arm. "He said, the equipment will do stuff beyond what we've seen."

"Thank you Rachel," said Bert. "If you will all give your gear to Ernie he will store it in the cylinder. The cylinder will be placed in Spencer's vault. Have some fun tonight. Get some rest. I hope to see you in the morning."

Among the four, a marked difference in their mood was noted going down the stairs, as when they came up. The next decision they made would change their lives forever. It didn't matter whether they answered yes or no. They would never be the same.

Chapter Eighteen

The co-pilot in the Arc helicopter tapped on his headphones signaling to Major Henry he had The Center on the radio.

"Patch it through lieutenant," said the Major. "Good to know you're still in business there Center, two things: any decision on the relocation site and somebody needs to get the head honcho on the horn. The Doc has his powers back."

"Ten four on the Doc," the radio operator said. "It's going to take some time on the new site. We can't just put you up at the Hilton"

"Roger that Center, Major out." The Major looked out the window. "Come in Bravo One."

"Go Major."

"We're still on hold about the new site. Are you boys ready to go?"

"Ten four Major."

"I sure didn't want to Bravo, but I guess we better high tail it back to the old house and help pack some of that equipment."

"See you there. Bravo One is looking for highway."

Major Henry flipped down the microphone from his face. "Man I hate to move. Fly slow lieutenant. Maybe they'll be done when we get back."

"We're about ten minutes out. Do you want me to take the scenic route Major?"

"The scenic route," Major Henry said as he thought back to a different time. "That's what my wife used to call it if her and our daughter ever got lost. I always admired that woman's patience. Never upset her and she always kept her cool, because she was only taking the scenic route. Negative on the re-route lieutenant, let's get on back."

"Nine minutes out now sir."

The Major's eyes caught the Doc's who at least rested on the seat now instead of the floor. The net was still tight around his body.

"How are you Doc?"

"I forgot what this felt like," the Doc said. "I haven't been wrapped up like this since the testing phase."

"I hope to have you out soon Doc. If they don't come on with it, I may release you myself."

The pilot sat up in his seat. "Looks like we've got trouble Major."

The major could see through the windshield of the aircraft, a black plume of smoke billowing into the sky from the ARC property. "Great Granny's cornbread, get us in there lieutenant."

The nose of the helicopter dipped and the pilot hit the gas slinging the Doc onto the floor again. The Major adjusted his eyepiece, checked his gun, and as they topped the trees into the clearing, he saw the raging fire. The army green fire truck had two leads out and men were spraying the fully engulfed house, in vain.

"Henderson, this is the Major. Are you down there?"

"I'm here Major. What a mess."

"What happened?"

"We didn't hear or see a thing until stuff started blowing up. I don't think it was an equipment malfunction."

"Angels?"

"That would be my guess Major."

"Anyone hurt?"

"Just a few minor burns and Frank broke his leg when he slipped off the top of the tank. No casualties."

"Were the trucks loaded?"

"A little over half the equipment was secured. The rest is toast."

"We're going stay up here and give you air support Henderson. Round up everyone and get them in a vehicle. We need to move before the county Mounties show up curios about what's burning."

"Will do. Where are we headed Major?"

The Major sighed. "You'll know as soon as I do. Have em drive north Henderson. Major out."

The Major slapped the mic from his face this time, and starred out the window. "Doc, a lot of our hard work is drifting toward the east in that black cloud of smoke."

From the floor, the Doc twisted his head to see through the netting. "I guess my stock just went up, huh Major?"

"Yep, we need you more than ever now. Let's hope they offer you a deal you can live with."

* * *

The sun had subsided, the groceries were delivered, and Spencer cooked steaks and fresh corn on the grill by the pool. Bert and Ernie were stealthily around somewhere, and everyone else hunkered down for a pool party and some good food. Carson returned from Clear Lake pulling in the driveway out front, turned off the ignition, and taking a moment to figure out his next move.

Dante and Alex flew through the Hummer's roof, materializing as they hit the backseat. They were both laughing.

Carson put his hand over his heart. "Do you have to keep doing that? You're going to give me a heart attack."

Dante ignored Carson's request. "That was incredible Alex. Did you see that guys face when the propane tank exploded?"

"I never saw a human run that fast before," said Alex.

Dante laughed as he spoke. "And those guards, they didn't know what hit them. I think that was their Three Stooges impression as they were trying to get up the stairs."

"We surely struck a blow to the midsection of ARC today."

Carson turned in his seat. "You guys went up against that Major fellow?"

Alex stopped laughing. "That's the regrettable thing. Bishop and the Major were not there."

* * *

The four chosen students were all in their second year in college, coming to grips with what they wanted for their lives, and working on how to make it happen. The dreams they had and the goals they set were typical in most respects. Careers, marriage, kids, and maybe do some good along the way.

The option the angels gave them had really put a hitch in their get along. A reevaluation of things that seemed so basic a couple of days ago, was taking place as they huddled a few yards from the smoking barbeque grill and tempting waters of the pool. The others were honoring their request for privacy, and Ethan had the floor. "Did anybody think when you woke up yesterday you would be asked to become a defender of God?"

"As Christians, we're all supposed to be doers of the word and an example of a Christian lifestyle," said Kate.

"Does that include strapping on a holster and going toe to toe with villains from the underworld?" Cooper said.

"Maybe it does for us," said Rachel.

"And what about a chance at a normal life," Cooper added. "What are the odds we can do this and still... I don't know, go to our daughters dance recital or our sons baseball game?"

Ethan gave him a shove. "I think you're getting ahead of yourself. You're not married. But hey Cooper, you know who was, Superman. If he could do it, so could you."

Cooper cut his eyes. "Batman, single. Spiderman single."

Ethan rebutted. "Flash, married. Wonder Woman, married."

"Okay future superheroes give it a rest," Rachel said. "You want to know what concerns me. It's not if we say yes to the offer, but what if we say no. How could we live with ourselves?"

Rachel's comment hit home. You could tell by the silence. The decision to be made would not come from a rational mindset and a game of what if. They needed divine wisdom. That is exactly what they would seek, as Kate said a prayer to guide them to the right answer.

Billy saw his friends and the group he shared his life with join hands and bow their heads to pray without him. Billy prayed silently and alone. This was the third time he prayed for forgiveness for not telling the others about phoning the Major. God simply put on his heart, "What phone call? I wiped that slate clean the first time you asked."

Billy then prayed to become involved again. For God to use whatever talents he had, to what degree He saw fit, and let him be part of this thing that was about to unfold. He perceived no immediate answer to his last request, but made a decision. The best thing he could do was to seek peace, while taking one step at a time and running the race that had been set before him; or maybe that was the answer. Billy would find out as he took one step toward the four, who had finished their prayer and were now standing. "Hey Troopers, what gives," he said.

A light flashed in Cooper's mind. "When we do this, we're going to need a name."

"The Justice League is taken," Ethan said.

"Thanks for your input brother Ethan. We could be The Alpha State Troopers and their sidekick Billy."

Billy thought. "In the band I'm a full-fledged Trooper."

"Oh, that reminds me," said Kate. "Bert wanted me to tell you Billy, he would like you upstairs above the garage, tomorrow morning at six AM."

Cooper motioned with his head. "Get in here man. A fully-fledged Trooper it is. Hands in everybody."

They all stood in a circle and put one hand on top of the other in a sincere sign of unity.

"What happens at six AM?" Billy said.

"I don't know," said Cooper. "We are going to find out together. Now, one, two, three, Alpha State!" They all shouted.

"Alpha what?" Carson asked as he strolled through the French doors leading to the patio. Gregariousness flowed from Carson when he entered the aquatic sanctuary of the backyard, and made a beeline for Billy: the man who spoke of opening the cylinder. Spencer dodged smoke from the grill, turning the steaks one more time. "How'd it go Carson?"

"Good. But the lady who owns the country club, she's a handful."

"Mrs. Prescott?" said Spencer.

"The one and only," Carson said.

Spencer spun with an ear of corn hanging from the tongs. "Hey, when my father was alive she was a good friend to him, and remember, she has more money than I do. Be kind."

Carson acknowledged with a wave and motored toward the kids. "What are you cheering about?"

"Just the name of our band," said Ethan. "The Alpha State Troopers."

Cooper stuck out his hand. "Carson Taylor right?"

"Yes, and you?"

"Cooper Holt sir. I'm scheduled to play an exhibition tennis match Saturday morning at the charity deal."

"It's a small world, huh Cooper? I'll be looking forward to seeing you play. If I remember correctly you already know your opponent, Terry Green."

Cooper's thoughts of the last time the two met came and went as he pushed the loss from his mind. "Yeah, we've played a lot over the years, but I may not be there Saturday. I'll have to let you know tomorrow."

"Finding someone of your caliber will be very difficult at this late stage. Please inform me as soon as you can." Carson could have cared less if Cooper showed up or not and focused on Billy. "So, I hope you rested today. You are going to have to tell me more of this cylinder thing, and how..."

"Foods ready," Spencer yelled. "Come and get it while it's hot."

Carson found himself in the middle of a stampede for sustenance, surrounded by the hungriest creatures known to man. College students. He felt alone but that wasn't a new feeling considering his current condition. He was the outsider and at odds with the others. His despise of Kendall's clan, and all they stood for, grew every time he got near them. They talked like they knew God personally and could just converse with Him anytime, and about anything they wanted too.

Carson knew people like this when he was younger and forced to go to church, but they all creeped him out at the deepest level. Reflecting on how their paths might cross in the final hour, he embraced and fueled his contempt with the parting words Dante spoke. "Do not trust these Christians. They want your soul more than I do."

In Carson's hardened state, Dante's remark was taken in the same spirit it was given. Carson wanted no more to do with these holy rollers than he did with Dante. But Dante he owed. Owed his incredible success, when his abilities suggested there would be failure. Owed the love of a beautiful woman, when his plainness starred back at him in the mirror. And finally, owed the anointing to wield power, when his only jurisdiction was a one room apartment in the bad part of town.

His allegiance with evil had blinded him more severely than any light from any cylinder could impose. He was blind to the truth, but his hat hung on a fact. Dante was responsible for bringing about the desires he held close to his heart. Carson's loyalty would prove his gratitude.

Professor Kendall enjoyed his food and the good company, but he could not suppress the thought, what if anything would he gain from finding the cylinder? The cylinder was obviously heaven sent, found at his dig, and the ramifications of the find would be staggering if it went public.

After all Kendall's life was summed up in the moniker, archeologist. It's who he was and what he did, so naturally the outcome as to his long term participation in the find weighed on him. The professor may have found one of the oldest and most extraordinary pieces in history. But the realization it may have to remain secret was another pound tipping the scales of success toward another dry hole.

Kendall did have one thing he could cling too, however. The significance of the victory would not become evident for some time. His newly found faith and his born again status would be a more positive influence on his life, than a truckload of silver cylinders.

Sara's perceptions on the other hand flowed through a filter of knowledge of God's word, and what those promises meant to her personally. The mere fact she had been blessed to interact with angels had her enchanted. Over the years she learned and accepted the fact that she could hear God's directions in her heart. And even if her role was a cameo, the Almighty had already predestined her place in the drama of the cylinder. All she had to do is believe and receive.

In the downtime, which the evening seemed to envelop, Sara spent some resources on this Carson character. Since he was here, she assumed he had to be part of God's plan. Where he fell on the believer or nonbeliever divide she would find out by bluntness. "Are you a Christian, Mr. Taylor?" she said.

Carson almost choked on his steak before recovering with a smile. "Call me Carson, please. And to your question, I would have to say I have known for some time there are powers greater than us in the universe. But to pigeonhole it like that, I would have to say no. I like to keep my options open."

"But the angels, you did see the angels," Sara said.

"Of course I did, and it was quite impressive. But I will let time do its work on my reasoning. Any conclusions I form, I will ultimately have to live with."

Sara did not press him any farther, for now. The hidden meaning in what Carson said was, yes I know there is a God, because I worship his enemy. So back off and I'll be content with my decision.

After the food and a somewhat relaxing evening, they all retired for the night; all but the angels. Bert guarded the vault holding the cylinder, while Ernie flew around the outside of the house. Dante and Alex waited till deep in the night at four AM to hatch their next plan.

Ernie held steady on his circular pattern outside, when he saw an angel flash across the sky, and he followed. He only went about a mile from his post before deciding to go back, but that was enough time for Dante to sneak into first Rachel and Kate's, and then Cooper and Ethan's bedroom, finding them asleep.

Dante quickly made his way to each one of them planting doubt and seeds of lies in their heads, then exiting before Ernie returned. Dante had fulfilled his goal of stirring the pot by stirring the minds of the four. Whether or not the seeds would take hold was a chance he was willing to take.

* * *

In the pre-dawn hours Major Henry had been notified of their new location, and the trucks were rolling east for a site just north of Reno Nevada. Provided by a contact in Washington an abandoned missile silo in the mountains would be their new home. Details outlining a deal for the Doc had also been sent.

Part of the package to secure the Doc's freedom came in the form of an angelic tracking system. Something the Doc himself had suggested early on, but what they kept from him, was ARC worked feverishly to perfect the technology. The thinking was if they ever did get an angel to turn and fly missions, a method of tracking would have to be in place.

A chip designed to be placed in the spine of the subject held the most promise as the initial prototype. They succeeded in reducing the size of the chip equal to the tip of a pencil eraser, but failed to come up with a way to make the implant invisible. Even with the small size they surmised it could be detected, and therefore jeopardize the mission.

ARC's research came back to the blood, and the fact angel's blood was the source of their most potent weapons. They discovered adding a few radioactive particles, and a compound derived from and found exclusively in Doc's blood, would not only give them a means to track, but to retaliate.

From a series of satellites the particles could be distinguished anywhere in the world, and the compound encased in a protective shell, could be activated at a maximum range of fifty thousand miles. If the subject were to break protocol and try to leave the earth, a signal would be sent releasing the compound to be mixed with the blood, and rendering the angel powerless.

Doc never considered his original implant idea would come back to bite him. The immediate joy from regaining his powers dissolved, when Major Henry brokered the deal.

"It is what it is Doc," the Major said.

"But I never signed on to become a guinea pig, at least not like this. Is there an upside?"

"This part you'll like Doc. You will be given unlimited freedom to come and go as you please, plus a substantial expense account. If you are going to get out among the natives, you might as well enjoy some of our earthly comforts."

The Doc concluded what ARC asked him to do was a stab in the back, and had trouble believing they would turn on him like this. Then he remembered he dealt with ex-military and almost everyone was expendable, but not himself. He was their ace in the hole, their golden goose, and the source of all their power. And he should be more valuable with his powers, than without.

With the crossroads laid out in front of Doc, he could not be sure if he would be run over by a Sherman tank when he tried to cross, if he didn't try.

"I have made a decision Major. The answer to the deal is no, and I want you to let me go."

The Major pulled down his John Deere cap over his face. "No, don't ask that Doc. But somehow I knew you would."

"If you knew I'd ask, you must have thought about your answer."

"How long till Reno, lieutenant?"

"If we stay with the convoy, about two hours."

"Two hours. I've spent more time picking out a deer rifle. Two hours to decide not only your fate, but probably mine. Thanks a heap Doc."

Chapter Nineteen

Billy felt blessed for being asked to attend the morning meeting, even if he didn't know why. He rose early keeping to himself, and he entered the small house over the garage at five forty five a.m. He was the only one there. He took a seat in the back of the room, expecting to see the others soon, but a decision made in the comforting setting of last night's get together, might look different in the daylight.

For Billy, the minutes seemed to crawl by waiting for someone else to show up, and at five fifty five he was relieved to see Kate and Rachel enter.

"Morning Billy," they both said.

"Morning ladies. Where are Ethan and Cooper?"

"We left them alone this morning," said Rachel. "I did hear them through the door as we came down the hall."

The boys were not known for arriving before the appointed time and at five fifty nine and thirty seconds they held true to form, shuffling into the room and falling into their seats.

"It's still dark outside," Cooper said.

Rachel not agreeing with their halfhearted entrance responded with a bubbly sense of how to greet the day. "There they are," she said. "What a wonderful day. Trooper school is about to begin. Can't you feel it? I love the first day of school---the smell of new books and freshly pressed designer jeans. You guys better not let Bert catch you sleeping."

"I need some coffee," said Cooper.

"You got books," Ethan said. "And wait, don't tell me, Bert made you room monitor."

Bert walked in with the cylinder under his arm. "Bert needs no room monitor," he said. "You will learn to monitor yourselves. How did everyone sleep?"

"Great," said Kate and Rachel agreed.

"I slept good," Billy said.

"I'm still asleep," said Ethan.

Cooper rubbed his eyes and wiped some of the remaining crust out if the corners. "I woke up at four and could not go back to sleep. My mind would not stop working."

Bert knew of the angel spotted at that precise time and thought it might not be coincidence. But to give total angelic protection twenty-four seven was not possible, especially over their thoughts. Angels were not clairvoyant. They were given knowledge of some pertinent future events, but for the most part, quick thinking and the ability to move close to the speed of light served them best. When it came to the ones in their care, they relied upon God's word being alive in the group, and how those seeds affected their decisions.

Bert put the cylinder on the table, recited the scripture key, and powered on the unit while calling Billy to come forward. Billy jumped out of his seat just as the seven screens on the cylinder lit up.

Bert addressed the group. "I gather from your presence this morning you have all accepted the challenge of the cylinder. I commend you all on your decision. Despite my less than sugarcoated accounting of the general duties you will undertake, we are not going to throw you to the lions. But we may have to nudge you off a cliff and see who's standing."

Ethan raised his hand. "You need to work on your metaphors Bert."

"I'm saying you may have to do some things your mind and body will tell you, you're not ready for. But you will need to stretch your faith."

Bert held out his hand to Billy, and Billy shook it.

"Welcome aboard Billy. Because of your computer expertise, you will be in charge of the cylinder command post. It will be your responsibility to assist your friends when they are engaged with the enemy."

Billy was told of the mission to fight evil but as to how far they would go would be an eye opening experience. Bert explained the large center screen of the cylinder could be used for displaying data stored on the internal drive, detailing every fallen angel and demon that existed when the cylinder was sent to earth.

"Any background on who or what you are fighting will give you an advantage," Bert said.

He told how the screen could be divided, using one side for information and the other for a radar-like view of the battlefield. The masks they would wear gave off a GPS signal, picked up only by the cylinder, and showed up as a blue dot on the screen. The masks had other functions.

There were four other screens, two to the left and two to the right of the large screen, and each one was correlated to a specific mask. Billy could check the heart rate, respiration, body temperature, and because of a small camera between the goggle lenses, he could see what the wearer was seeing.

To demonstrate, Bert held up a mask and the image of Cooper sleeping in his chair projected on the right upper screen.

Kate tilted her head to better see the monitor. "This is where Professor Kendall would heave a blackboard eraser at you."

Bert opened the cylinder equipment compartment gathering a racket and a blue ball. "Let's try this, since we have no blackboard."

He put the ball in the ball receptacle next to the keyboard, programmed the ball, and lightly bounced it off Cooper's head. Cooper jerked upright in his seat awakening to everyone laughing. "I'm awake, Professor," he said.

Cooper had obviously been on the receiving end of a Kendall eraser toss. The group did not laugh at the ball striking his head, or for thinking he was in the professor's classroom. They laughed because Cooper's skin and clothes now glowed with a bright blue iridescence.

"It looks like Cooper has the blues," said Billy.

A resurgence of laughter followed.

Cooper stood up scrubbing himself with his hands. "What did you do to me?"

"Lesson number one," Bert said. "No sleeping in class. It could mean your death."

The laughter stopped and Cooper froze starring at Bert. "Relax Cooper," said Bert. "The blue color won't kill you but your inattention might. Plus this is a good way to demonstrate the advantage to having your opponent enhanced in a blue light."

Billy went over and with his index finger touched his new blue classmate. "This is cool. Will I be able to program balls Bert?"

"You will all learn the ball program. We will teach you first Billy, then you will be responsible for teaching the others."

Cooper started scratching his skin. "Make it go away Bert."

"Another thing," said Bert, "the colored balls can be programmed to do four different things, and can be changed by using the racket."

He placed the blue ball in the hole under the racket head, pushed a hidden roller knob to the right of the hole with his thumb, and four small lights lit up above the ball. He turned the knob until only the far right light was lit. Bert tapped the ball again as Cooper closed his eyes, and it bounced off his forehead returning him to his original color.

"I liked him better blue," Billy said walking back to his seat.

Cooper sat down and mimed locking his lips and throwing away the key.

"Excuse me while I change into something more appropriate," said Bert. "This robe just won't cut it on the court."

Bert closed his eyes and from his feet up a pink light engulfed him. When he reappeared he wore brown sweats and tennis shoes. His wings were gone and he had a whistle around his neck, resembling a football coach.

The group applauded.

"Thank you everyone. But we are going outside and I thought it best to appear human. Billy, you will be staying here for Ernie's training on how to operate the cylinder. As a surprise, we will have breakfast first, the most important meal of the day. Ernie should have everything ready downstairs."

Ethan took up the slack from Cooper's temporary vow of silence. "Angels can cook? What are we going to have, scrambled manna?"

"Some angels can cook, and some very well in fact. Check your Bible. 1st Kings 19:5-7."

* * *

Carson finished getting dressed and got ready to leave for the charity event, simply because Spencer was in the house. Carson had planned on sticking close to the Christians, but his cover must be maintained. From his last meeting with Dante the word had come down to wait and see. Wait for Carson to pry the secret for opening the cylinder from someone. And if that failed, see how the group reacted to their newfound destiny and would they embrace the calling.

* * *

Dante's overall goal meant keeping this new elite team of evil fighters from ever coming about. His main goal was to retrieve the red holster, mask, and racket given to him thousands of years ago when it was brand new. The red equipment that used to belong to Dante now belonged to Cooper.

* * *

The kids and angels finished their breakfast of eggs, bacon, biscuits, and cream gravy while toasting the new adventure with orange juice. "Troopers forever," Cooper said as they clinked glasses.

Ernie sat down his glass, also sporting a human form, and wiped the pulp from his upper lip. "What is this Trooper deal?"

"Well," said Ethan, "we figured if we're going to be superheroes of a sort, we should have a name. The Alpha State Troopers is the name of our musical group, and it sounds pretty good for fighting bad guys."

Bert held up his glass. "Raise a glass to the Alpha State Troopers. Let your knowledge grow quick, your aim be true, and your heart stay guarded."

As the Troopers strapped on their equipment preparing for the first day of training, it seemed strange these implements were once used by angels in heaven to play a game. The strange part centered on the news that angels played games at all. The fact man was created in God's image, and taking into account how many games man enjoyed, made the angels desire and passion to compete in a sport more practical. In heaven the game was known as Battle Ball.

* * *

The creation of Battle ball served as a way to interact and display one's angelic prowess in a controlled setting. Quickly becoming popular among the warrior angels the game took shape and grew. The silver cylinder came about as a means to keep track of play, compile statistics, and reprogram balls to keep the opponent guessing.

The battlefield stretched the length of a football field, but had an hourglass shape funneling down to a twenty-foot diameter circle in the middle. Poles extended up the sides and across the top of the center circle forming a goal.

Play started with a white game ball being served or launched as the angels called it, from the end line and kept in play like tennis. But the ultimate goal for the player was to reach the center circle of the battlefield, while keeping the ball in play. Once a player reached the circle the game changed.

The circle player became a goalie defending the goal above the circle, but also became the hunter allowed to hit colored balls at the competitor, all while keeping the game ball alive. If an opponent took a hit from a colored ball, the circle player was awarded points and play started over from the end line.

Play went on like this for centuries until three years before the rebellious angels fall. During those final years as angels picked sides and tensions were displayed openly on the field, the game took a turn for the worse. It became less like a game and more like warfare. An ever-increasing violence was introduced with the refinement of programming the balls.

The angels had to confront exploding balls, lightening balls, and balls of fire. Gashes on the skin and temporary blackouts became commonplace for the angels enduring the escalating game. The ball evolution came to a peak with the introduction of the Black Beauty by none other than Dante himself. Players started to loose limbs and become horribly incapacitated when merely grazed by the black ball. But a direct hit to the player's torso would extinguish the eternal life of these once immortal creatures.

From that day on, angels started dying by a new method and God turned his back on the game.

The day of the third falling became the last day for Battle Ball in heaven. Seeing the end was near, Lucifer and his minions struggled to steal anything they could from the heavenly kingdom. While the Evil One and the Archangel Michael fought over the possession of a silver cylinder, another fight raged between the lines of the Battle Ball field. Dante and a little known angel called Ernismatodis were two days into a nonstop match. Ernismatodis was now called Ernie.

Just as Dante appeared to be wearing the contender down, Ernie made it to the center circle and rocketed a black ball at Dante's head. Dante's evasive tactics were fast, but not enough. The very tips of the strands from the furry black covering on the ball touched Dante's left cheek as it sped by. Dante's scar would be forever etched on his face along with the memory of what happened next.

God had had enough. He ostracized the rebellious angels from their glorious home exiling them on the earth. The Archangels of God were then commanded to send four silver cylinders to earth for enforcement of His future plans.

* * *

That's where the Troopers were now, still finding out God's plan, but they were not going to be playing any games yet. Their mission was one filled with retribution and revival.

Bert waited till they were on the court to reveal the acclimation process for the equipment. The process of acclimation had been installed just for the humans, as a means of testing them and ultimately assuring no one else could use the equipment.

It began with speaking to your equipment, claiming it as yours, and signifying you accepted the challenge. The clock also started. An inherent time element to the process required the user to train with the equipment for two days, at a minimum of ten hours per day. The third day the equipment could not be used. On the fourth day the equipment would be acclimated to the user and unleash features related to battle.

This was accomplished by the racket and mask picking up the DNA of the user over the time period, and transforming into more weapon like functions. If after this period someone other than the original user tried to use the equipment, the racket would only be a racket and the mask just a mask. No special functions. If the acclimation rules were not strictly adhered to, the user must begin again.

The Troopers were three hours into the process when Bert blew his whistle signaling the first break. "You have ten minutes for bathroom and refreshments before we start again.

Bert had the four thinking much more seriously about what they had gotten into. But names and catch phrases were important in defining and labeling for the humans, as was evident by calling themselves the Alpha State Troopers. Plus, feeling invincible at that age came with the territory at that age. A motto quickly grew from their morning training session and they huddled to write it on poster board and hang it on the fence bordering the court.

VENGANCE IS MINE SAYETH THE LORD, UNLESS IT COMES BY A TROOPER.

The Clear Lake Country Club buzzed with activity getting ready for the Sports Expo starting tomorrow. Carpenters were building booths, day laborers unloaded trucks, while Carson jockeyed with unhappy vendors and of course Mrs. Prescott.

Two vendors demanded relocation of their booths, and Carson had something attached to his hip, the landowner Mrs. Prescott. "Tell those men to be careful on that grass," she said. "My grounds keeper will be quite upset if there is damage."

Carson tried to calm her. "I assure you Mrs. Prescott these men are professionals. Please don't worry because our own landscaper will be here after the event and if anything needs repair, we will fix it.

Mrs. Prescott depicted to gracefully grow old with her seventy five year old silver hair, done up in a bun, crowning her well maintained and active stature. She had an air of someone who knew how to get her way and promoting the tricks of her trade suggested *she* was the professional.

Mrs. Prescott fanned her face with her hand as to seem frail and foster sympathy from Carson. During the fanning, her fingernails caught the chain around her neck exposing an upside down cross at the end. She quickly stuffed it back in her blouse.

Carson wasn't sure what to make of her odd jewelry. He remembered seeing a news clip showing the inverted cross on a ceremonial chair in which the Pope sat, and decided there must be at least two schools of thought as to what it meant. He had always assumed it meant some kind of devil worship, but recalling the news report he could not be sure.

Mrs. Prescott a devil worshiper? The thought and image immediately evacuated his mind as she let out a yelp. She gazed at an overall clothed man standing on an eight foot ladder preparing to screw an eyebolt in her hundred year old Oak tree to hang lighting.

"Hold it a minute," Carson yelled at the worker. "Mrs. Prescott, I'll take care of this. Why don't you go inside where you will be more comfortable?"

She walked away talking to herself. "Tell me to go inside at my country club. Who does he think he is?" She settled on scolding a worker for dropping a paper cup on the ground.

Carson being freed from his shadow explained to the foreman the importance of protecting the greenery. Carson then walked briskly as far away from Mrs. Prescott as he could get, when his phone rang.

He answered. "This is Carson."

"Mr. Taylor. This is Cooper from the house."

"Yeah Cooper, how's it going?"

"I'm on a break, but I wanted to let you know I will be there Saturday for the tennis match."

"Great news Cooper."

"Well, thanks sir."

"Hang on Cooper." Carson saw a familiar face, jogged to him, and got back on the phone with Cooper. "There is someone here you might remember. He wants to talk to you." Carson handed the phone to the athletic young eighteen year old and whispered, "It's Cooper Holt."

The man smiled and took the phone. "Cooper is that you?"

"Yes. Who's this?"

This is Terry Green man. You ready to get your butt kicked Saturday?"

The utter beating and embarrassment Cooper felt from their last tennis match rushed back. He tried not to let it show. "I think the butts going to be on the other foot, this time." Cooper winced at his own remark.

"Whatever you say man. But you better come ready to play homeboy."

"I tell you what Terry; I'll let my racket do the talking."

Terry Green handed the phone back to Carson who quickly spoke in the mouthpiece. "Hey Cooper. Sorry. I didn't know you two had that kind of history."

"Break time is over Mr. Taylor. I have to go." Cooper hung up the phone.

Carson slipped the phone in the holder and addressed Terry. "You and Cooper don't like each other."

"I don't think I'd go that far. But we did come up on the amateur tennis circuit together---even if I'm two years younger than him. At first, competitively we were close, but when I hit my stride... Well, he hasn't beaten me in four years."

"Now remember son, this is all for charity," Carson said. "You would do well to keep that in mind."

"I'll do that Mr. Taylor; while I'm mopping up the court with his curly hair." Terry walked away.

* * *

Major Henry's chopper sat down at the new site forty miles north of Reno Nevada and two hours behind schedule. The pilot, copilot, and Mr. Brown were ordered inside, leaving the Major and Doc alone in the back. The Doc's own invention still kept him captive, but it was time for a decision.

"What's it going to be Major?"

"Are you going to play nice Doc?"

"I've always played nice," the Doc said. "This is my work now and I have nowhere else to go. Me being fully functional shouldn't change that."

"But it does Doc."

"Either let me go or lock me up, I'm tired of debating this."

The Major had to smile. "I like your spunk Doc, and I consider you an ally. I just hope you can fathom what would happen to yours truly if you go south on me."

"Major, believe me this work excites me. If we succeed, we could introduce a totally new species to walk the earth; half man, half angel."

"That would be a coop alright," said the Major. "But I've always wanted to ask you about a passage in Genesis. It says the sons of God, whom I took to mean you're kind, came unto the daughters of men and bore children and the children were giants. It sounds like you boys were less than discrete in the early days."

"You draw your own conclusions. I had nothing to do with that. In our experiments the subject wouldn't be a giant. And he could fly and become invisible. Think about it Major."

The Major looked off at the mountains, reached into his pocket, and came out with a device looking a lot like a garage door opener with one button. "This is sure pretty country Doc." The Major pushed the button.

Doc felt the net relax and he sat up, pulling it from his body coming face to face with the Major.

"You know Major; this could be the start of a beautiful friendship. But I gotta go." Whoosh! The Doc was gone.

The Major's head fell against the seat, and he closed his eyes as he said out loud. "Doc if you can hear me, you better be going sightseeing or I will hunt you down and you'll never see daylight again." He once more ushered the John Deere cap over his face, like an Ostrich with his head in the sand.

* * *

Dante viewed the concrete slab of the dilapidated tennis court where the Christians were training, from the confines of the guesthouse in the woods. His red holster, racket, and mask were being flaunted in the daylight like new toys on Christmas morning. He thought about his last time playing the game, only it went beyond a game at that point, and his own infamous black ball coming back to mark him just before the whole show crashed down.

But there his stuff was; in sight but out of reach. The end to his centuries old wait danced before him, but he took no action. Alex wondered why he hesitated, and sat down next to him by the window. "Tell me boss, is there a reason we don't just fly over there, kick the stuffing out of those punks and take back the equipment?"

Dante thought a few seconds. "I would draw the parallel as to why the Big Man didn't just start over after Adam and Eve messed up. He had a plan. He needed an actual flesh and blood representative to do what Adam couldn't. His Son. Sure we could surprise them and take everything they have, but what would happen next? I'll tell you. Every angel in the northern hemisphere would be on us like white on rice."

Alex stroked the scar on her cheek. "I've always thought of you as a golden brown."

Dante grabbed her hand. "Seriously Alex. If we gain control through one of these earthly vessels, who can argue with that? The weapons have been given to these kids and if one of them decides to give it to me, I call that a natural occurrence. No harm, no foul."

"And how do you intend to make that happen?"

Dante starred out the window considering the free will uncertainty and decided if he told Alex anything, it would only be a guess. His gaze still fixed, he answered by shrugging his shoulders.

Chapter Twenty

The silver cylinder that became Billy's new plaything sat unlocked before him, opening his eyes and mind to a realm and society he had barely thought about before: the world of angels and demons. The database of the supercomputer housed in the cylinder held a treasure trove of information detailing the strengths and tendencies of these clandestine creatures. He now understood why there were forces that would kill to possess it.

The computer could also hook up directly to the Internet without a hard line connection or the aid of a wireless router. Billy could download the picture of an attacking demon, and order a pizza at the same time. He immersed himself, satisfied in his element at the keyboard, and in awe the cylinder was built to work with 21st century technology. Someone had a plan.

Billy learned some basic ball programming techniques along with how to communicate with the Troopers through their masks, but he had not bothered them yet. On his center screen he could see four blue dots, each one representing a mask, plus a letter moved with the dots identifying the wearer; E for Ethan, K for Kate and so on. There was a green dot showing Bert.

He could also see them outside on the court from the second floor window above the garage, and they looked tired. Billy scanned the readout on the four screens, one assigned to each Trooper, seeing their heart rate elevated and blood pressure about normal. He decided they would all make it through the first day.

The drills up to now were very basic, starting with Bert placing soda cans at one end of the court and having the four try to knock them over with a ball. Cooper excelled immediately at hitting the ball to a specific spot. And the others, not being the first time they held a racket, were making four out of five shots within a couple of hours.

The Troopers were all hitting the ball faster and with more accuracy than ever before, and it was mainly due to the racket. They all sensed the racket could tell where you wanted the ball to go and it helped get it there. The four had skills, but not at the level they now performed with the new equipment. Their expertise grew quicker than humanly possible.

After two hours of hitting the ball, the next two hours were spent on blocking. Bert used Cooper's Wilson tennis racket to smash balls at the facemask-covered foursome. Several bruises were raised before they could handle Bert's hundred and fifty mile an hour rockets. But again, a feat they should not be able to do, they were doing.

The next two hours they ran from side to side of the court while again knocking down the soda cans with the ball. Likewise the next two hours they ran again, while Bert hit balls at them. Being mobile and being accurate were obviously things they needed to learn.   With eight hours logged from the ten hour practice session, the group began to get in touch with the equipment and what they could do with it. Bert called a break and Billy felt it time to test communications.

Ethan, Kate, Rachel, and Cooper had just sat down in the shade when Billy's voice came through the headphones in the masks. "Trooper team this is cylinder com., do you read?"

They all felt like they had been rode hard and put up wet, but not to the point of hearing voices. Rachel tapped on the side of her mask not knowing she wore headphones. "Is that you Billy?'

Billy could tell they needed a lift and put on his best disc jockey voice. "This is Brother Billy broadcasting from cylinder central, coming to all you cool cats out there training for the heavenly armed forces. I know you've been working hard, so sit back and relax while I wash away those aching muscles with little ditty from the Texas guitar man, Stevie Ray Vaughn. This is 'Cold Shot', enjoy it Troopers."

Billy had the CD loaded in the cylinder's reader and clicked play. The heavy blues tune sprang to life in the kid's headphones and as they moved with the music they smiled, remembering it as the first song they learned as a group.

* * *

Carson Taylor's vision of an easy day turned out to be wrong. He worked hard trying to keep everyone happy, helping with booths and policing the area for stray paper cups. But he took pleasure in the day's chores, using them as a diversion from the duties that would otherwise be on his schedule. He could have been spying on the Christians, trying to find out how to open the cylinder.

Things went well and the Sports Charity Expo was set for a ten A.M. start tomorrow morning. There would be some well-known athletes present, but Carson wondered if any of Spencer's political contacts would come. Carson fantasized about meeting the California Governor and practiced a few lines. "I'll be back," he said looking around to see if anyone heard him. "Asta la vista baby." Carson got giddy at the thought of meeting The Terminator.

Spencer would know if Swartzenager was coming, he thought. Carson pushed the speed dial number on his cell phone.

Spencer answered. "Hello."

"Hey, this is Carson. Just wanted to let you know everything went good today and we're ready."

"Good job. How's Mrs. Prescott holding up?"

"We had a small situation earlier, but I haven't seen..." Out of the corner of Carson's eye he could see the geriatric energizer bunny headed his way.

"Mr. Taylor. Oh, Mr. Taylor." Mrs. Prescott walked up not caring if he was on the phone or not. "I need to talk to your boss. There are some issues I..."

"Mrs. Prescott, I have Spencer on the line now. If you like..."

She jerked the phone from his hand and strolled off into the grass.

Carson heard the backup beeper from a large truck   and turned to see the 10:00x22 rear tires inches from the pristine lawn. All he could think of as he ran was the wrath of Mrs. Prescott, but saw the trailer brake lights come on and the truck stop. He ran to the cab. "Hey buddy, you're almost on the grass back there." Carson yelled through the closed window of the Kenworth.

The window buzzed down and the truck driver stuck his head out. "I know Mack, that's why I stopped. Anymore driving tips before I leave?"

Carson waved him on and turned back toward the country club. He was ready to go after a long look at the straight line of sports pews lining the lawn of the club. "And no trees have lost their lives for this endeavor," he said. "Except the ones the two by fours came from." He laughed as he got his truck keys from his pocket and knew he could make a clean getaway without... Then it hit him. Mrs. Prescott had his phone.

* * *

The Troopers sat in the shade grooving to the music, under the sign they had fashioned with the slogan seeming a little cocky for Bert's taste. Bert needed them confident, and at times even cocky, but he wanted them tempered with some humility. Bert thought of Jesus. Jesus walked this earth confident, yet humble, King and servant. And if any human could mesh these seemingly contradictory yet in reality complementary qualities, they would be unstoppable. But these things would not come by flesh and blood, but by the spirit.

Bert had a way to give their spirits a shake, with a side order of humility. He stood far enough away from the four to speak softly and not be detected. Even though Bert's voice fell almost to a whisper, Ernie in the upstairs room above the garage heard every word.

Ernie stood next to a bobble head Billy swaying to the tempo of the CD playing in the cylinder.

"I need to get in there," Ernie said. Ernie's fingers danced across the letters on the keyboard at a speed so fast Billy could not see what happened. Ernie turned off the music, looked at Billy, and hit enter. On the cylinder's center screen a black dot with a black circle around it appeared in the upper left hand corner. And it moved toward the four blue dots on the right marking the Troopers.

Ernie put the cursor on the traveling dot and clicked. The word 'Demon' popped up. "You may want to warn them," said Ernie.

Billy pushed the talk button on the cylinder. "Look out. Ahhh, alert, alert!" Billy quickly composed himself. "Troopers listen up. Out of the east, directly in front of you, there's a demon about a hundred yards out and he's closing fast. It's about tree top high."

Ernie nodded his head and smiled at Billy. "Good warning."

The Troopers jumped to their feet, watching the trees, but saw only the leaves shaking in the breeze. As they stood with rackets in hand, a black void like a hole to nowhere formed in the branches.

"You may need some ammo," Bert said.

They all realized their rackets were ready but they had nothing to hit.

Bert helped again. "Use the red one."

Four red balls were pulled from the holsters as the ugliest thing they had ever seen exited the void. It looked like a five hundred pound rat with wings. It's tail darted from side to side making a whistling sound as it cut the air, with green glowing eyes and teeth the size of your hand dripping with saliva. The creature bucked and moaned in the air with short bursts of fire coming from its nose.

Bert could not tell, but the Troopers looked frozen and he ventured to find out. "Everyone hit together now," he said.

They drew their rackets. Good, not frozen, Bert thought. "Get ready. Fire!"

The red balls careened off the rackets; all meeting the target in sync with the sound of a distant thunder clap. The demon of ugly disappeared. The Troopers looked hesitant, kind of half smiling and half wondering if it was over; when it became evident it was not. The gnarling fire snorting rodent came back.

Bert directed traffic. "Spread out and retrieve the balls."

Cooper and Kate went right. Ethan and Rachel went left. They all pushed their ball retrieval buttons and the balls flew back, except Kate. She fumbled with the button, dropped her racket, and stepped on it as she ran. Her ankle twisted and her body found the concrete, but she didn't give up.

The creature slowly moved toward them now, hissing and not backing off. From Kate's sprawled position on the court, she retrieved her ball, hitting it side armed with the others. The balls met the demon coming across center court slamming into its head, and the furry flying vermin crashed to the pavement. It lay there motionless for a few seconds, and then vanished.

"You got him," Bert said waiting for their reaction. There were no high fives, no cheering, and no pats on the back, only relief. Bert thought he might be teaching them something after all.

Cooper dropped his racket, bent down and picked up Kate, holding her in his arms. Ethan ran over to check her ankle, and Cooper looked down at Kate. "You all right?" he said.

"I will be," Kate answered.

Rachel wasn't pleased with the idea that Cooper looked way too comfortable holding Kate so close. Rachel walked over, stopped a few feet away, and spoke directly to Cooper. "What are you trying to do, guess her weight?"

Cooper was glad Rachel cared but bungled his words. "I'd guess she weighs a little less than you do. I mean, not that you weigh a lot. I think your perfect Rachel."

Rachel held her hands on hips position for a five count, turned, and walked off.

Kate tapped Cooper on the chest. "You can put me down now. My ankles fine. More than I can say for your girlfriend."

Cooper sat her down and went to fix things with Rachel.

Kate hobbled over to pick up Cooper's racket. "That thing was scary."

"Scary and ugly," Ethan said as he put his arm around Kate to support her. "What was it Bert?"

"Well boys and girls I don't want to disappoint you, but that was a cylinder generated 3-D digital image for the purpose of training."

Cooper and Rachel forgot about their sophomoric tiff, strolling to Bert. "It looked real to me," said Cooper.

"That was wicked Bert," Rachel said.

"All of you gather round." Bert sounded stern "I will surprise you in that manner only once. But there are some 3-D programs we will use for training over the next six months."

The four looked around at one another because that's the first time 'the next six months' phrase had been used.

Bert continued. "The next time you see a fanged demon materializing in thin air; it will be real and not a drill."

"There's going to be real ones coming?" Kate said.

"Truthfully I don't know what's coming. It's my job to get you ready for anything. What I do know is the boundaries of the spirit world are breaking down. We have fallen angels and demons hurting people and influencing life patterns beyond what they should be able to do. You are meant to be a light along the dark borders of the supernatural, and the bad guys are going to want to know, why you. I will leave you with this. 'And the light shineth in the darkness; and the darkness comprehended it not.'"

* * *

Carson braced himself for the Mrs. Prescott encounter as he meandered around the plush lobby of the Clear Lake Country Club. The receptionist sat surrounded by four men in golfing attire, so Carson killed some time looking at the decor. He stopped at a long glass case full of trophies won during club events, which were donated by club members. Photos from the forty-year history of club sponsored functions hung among the golden statues. A photo of a tennis match caught Carson's eye.

Drawn to it at first because of the clarity and movement caught on the celluloid frame, but with a second glance something was familiar. It looked as if the camera sat on the post holding up the net when the action was captured, as the long dividing web loomed large in the center of the picture.

Two players were visible standing three feet apart with only the net between them, and their animated nature suggested this must have been the point of victory and defeat. The player on the left had already begun to celebrate, with his racket over his head and you could tell he was yelling through the smile on his face.

The player on the right was bent over backwards, no doubt headed for a fall, as the ball teased him, suspended four feet over his head and out of reach. The winning player on the left was Terry Green. The losing player on the right was Cooper Holt. The photo dated August one year ago was the last time the two had met on the court. The picture encapsulated the strong competitive nature of the boys, and Carson knew their meeting Saturday would be a battle.

He noticed the reflection in the glass mirrored the just out of high school receptionist alone at her desk, and Carson approached her.

She looked up from her magazine. "May I help you? Oh, Mr. Taylor, how's it going?"

"Good thank you. Mrs. Prescott got away with my cell phone a few minutes ago and I..."

A tall man in an expensive looking gray suit walked up as if Carson wasn't there. "I need to see Mrs. Prescott please," he said.

"Do you have an appointment sir?"

"It's taken me all day to track Mrs. Prescott down, so no. I don't have an appointment."

Carson just stood there waiting to see what's up with this guy.

"Who should I say is here to see her?" The receptionist picked up her pen, ready to write.

The man pulled a business card from his pocket. "Give her this. Tell her Bishop is here. And I will not leave until I talk to her."

The young girl took the card and went off down the hall.

My phone, Carson thought, but it was too late, as the teenager turned the corner out of sight. Carson started to speak to the man, but the stranger stood stoic, looking straight ahead, until the receptionist came back. She handed Carson his phone. "There you go Mr. Taylor. And Mr. Bishop, she will see you now."

"Bishop," the man said. "It's just Bishop."

Carson left just happy to avoid contact with the queen bee, Mrs. Prescott, but was sure he had heard the name Bishop somewhere recently. For the life of him he could not remember where.

Chapter Twenty-One

At five o'clock Friday afternoon, the second day of Trooper training and the most difficult step of the equipment acclimation process was over. The remaining part of the process seemed too easy. Don't use the equipment for twenty-four hours. After that, when the equipment became active, the more weapon like functions could be accessed.

On the court, the Troopers holsters were sagging, the masks were pushed back on top of their heads, and they stood in a semi-circle around Bert, curious about the future. Rachel asked the first question. "What happens after the twenty four hours and we use the stuff again?"

Bert wanted to let the whole thing unfold naturally, but they did well during training, and going against his gut, he thought a few answered questions would not hurt. "When you use the equipment after the waiting period, you can access more advanced functions that will assist you against the enemy."

Rachel wanted more. "What kind of functions?"

Bert felt he should have stuck with his first instinct. Tell them only what they needed to know and only when they needed to know it.

Rachel had only asked two questions and Bert regretted having answered the first. He tried to nip this in the bud. "Look guys, when you use the racket again, the changes will be obvious and then we can discuss them. Tomorrow night at six would be a good time."

The Troopers were not letting it go, and Ethan spoke next. "So, what would happen tomorrow if I used Rachel's racket?"

Bert rubbed his forehead. "You would not be able to access the advanced features on Rachel's racket, only your own racket."

Cooper started to speak when Bert held up his hand deciding a demonstration might satisfy their inquiring minds. Bert stood up three soda cans at the far end of the court. "Even now your equipment has extracted enough personal information to be sensitive to the original user. Rachel, please give Ethan your racket."

Rachel held her racket out. "Don't break it man."

"Now Ethan, using Rachel's racket, knock over the cans with the white balls."

Ethan took aim, let three shots go, and came up with three misses.

"Now try it with your racket Ethan."

Ethan fired three more shots, but this time the cans lay scattered across the court from three direct hits. Ethan looked at his blue racket with the star shape on the strings. "Dude, what's up with that?"

Bert hoped he was near the end of the question and answer portion of the show, but he hung in there. "I'm sure you all noticed your play became better even on the first day of practice. The racket started recording your tendencies immediately. It computed if you were swinging late, or pulling the ball left, and made corrections to get the ball to your intended target. Simply, it just made you more accurate than you really are."

They all had to let that sink in a minute, but Bert wasn't finished. "And don't misunderstand me; you are all very good players, that's why you were chosen. But in a life or death situation, every advantage helps."

For what it was worth, the Troopers suspicions had been confirmed. They were better with the heavenly equipment, than without. But this news soon waned on the heels of a more important decision. What to do with their free Friday night?

"Pool party," Cooper said, and they all ran toward the house.

Bert blew his whistle and they all stopped. "Put your equipment in the cylinder and Ernie will put it in the vault until tomorrow evening."

They all stood waiting, thinking there might be some kind of homework.

"That's it," said Bert. "I'll see you Saturday."

It was like the pause button clicked off and the four continued their sprint for the weekend. As it should be, they were all content to dwell on the Friday night at hand and just having fun.

Ernie and Bert held a contrasting view, knowing the next thirty six hours would be crucial on the quest to turn the students, into warriors.

* * *

The time stood at fifty four hours and counting since Major Henry let the Doc loose, and the subsequent disappearing act of their number one and only angel. There were no communications from the Doc. More important there were no queries from The Center as to Doc's decision.

The Major didn't know what he would say if asked how the Doc responded to the question of having the tracking fluid injected. He could act dumb, exclaiming the Doc inexplicably escaped. But the Major conceded he would take the fall for that too.

Despite Doc's absence, work progressed at ARC's new home with the placement of cages, cleaning out tanks to hold their own special angel juice, and the all-important equipment inventory. The fire had taken its toll, but mostly in the form of the time it would take to rebuild. Nothing irreplaceable had been lost. Nothing that is, if the Doc came back to the team.

The Major understood the futility of searching for his angel friend and went about his work like a good solider hoping Doc would return. Major Henry inspected the doors on the newly relocated cages, when Henderson came up carrying the satellite phone. "Major, it's The Center," he said, holding the phone out.

Major Henry paused before taking the line to the corporate tier of the operation, and wondered if Henderson had been given instructions for an other than satisfactory outcome to the call. The major took the phone. "Major Henry here."

"Hang on sir," the communications liaison said. "I have an outside line with the call sign *Dogpatch*, inbound for you Major. Hold while I encrypt."

He recognized *Dogpatch*. An ARC code used to confirm an undercover status. When the operative became fully imbibed with the target group, and felt somewhat secure, *Dogpatch* signaled I'm in, and okay.

"You there Major?" said the liaison.

"Go Center."

"You're up *Dogpatch*."

Major Henry stood with the phone to his ear a few seconds before perceiving a familiar voice.

"Mission accomplished Major. And you were right, she's a sweetheart."

"Doc? It's good to hear from you, but what are you talking about?"

"Affirmative to that," said the Doc. "And you get all the credit. But it took a couple of days for my charming personality to have an effect on her. I hope you weren't worried."

"I've been a little worried waiting for the other shoe to drop, and if this call was meant to calm me, it's not working. "Doc, are you okay?"

"Of course you can. She's right here beside me."

The Major could tell the Doc held the phone out to someone else, when he heard a woman's voice a couple of feet away from the receiver. "Is this line encrypted?" she asked. "I'm not talking on any unsecured line. No telling who might be listening."

The Doc guaranteed the safety of the connection, and she took the phone. "Major Henry," she said. "First off, let me remind you of your total disregard for our number one protocol. By sending the Doc out here in the real world, you ran the risk of jeopardizing the mission, and exposing me personally. And second, you've made me realize we need to change our number one protocol. Good job Major."

The Major flopped down on the bench inside the cell he inspected, and wondered why Doc was with the head of the board of trustees for ARC: Mrs. Abigail Thornton Prescott.

"Yes ma'am. Thank you Mrs. Prescott."

"You know when my husband Archie died and I took over this operation, I thought it no more than a money pit. But Bishop, as I've come to know him, has opened my eyes to your successes and tells me you're close to a cure."

The Major unsure as to what cure they were supposedly close too, thought it better to go along. "Yes Mrs. Prescott, never been closer."

"Keep up the good work, Major. If you need any more money, let me know."

The Major started to ask for extra funding now, but she kept talking.

"One more thing; I've decided the deal for the Doc needs to be reworked. Injecting an untried tracking fluid into such a valuable commodity would be too risky. I'll talk to the board about that, but for now, Bishop is on the honor system. Are you aware of the honor system, Major?"

He was. You honor the deal or we track you down and kill you. "Yes ma'am."

"It's good to talk to you Major," she said. "Let's don't make it a habit."

Major Henry had to shake his head thinking. It's been good *listening* to you Mrs. Prescott. It always amazed him how the woman could be so sweet and so vicious at the same time. Lucky we don't talk much. Doc got back on the phone. "I'm on my way to Reno. We'll have a sit down when I get back."

"That would be pleasant Doc. Maybe you can unscramble a few things for me."

"Will do Major. *Dogpatch* out," and the Doc disconnected.

Major Henry felt the hard bench beneath him, and canvassed the cells interior with his eyes. *If Doc didn't come back*, he thought, *this could be my home.*

* * *

Professor Kendall, Sara, and Spencer informed the others they were going to San Francisco for an evening of dining and sightseeing on Spencer's nickel. After staying overnight at Spencer's, they were going to check on the professor's dig, where he would show Spencer some earthy sights.

They would not be back before Sunday, so the Troopers had the house to themselves, sort of. The angels would be there but they mostly kept out of sight, and Carson's plans were unknown.

The big house seemed empty before the three left, but as Billy roamed the halls searching for other warm bodies, it began to get spooky. His journey through the upstairs rooms led him to imagine what it must have been like growing up in a mansion. Billy's childhood home consisted of only five rooms. But the home felt large to him back then, and being happy and loved by his adoptive parents is what stood out.

Billy came downstairs, and coming from the doorway just off the great room, he heard the unmistakable sound of a video game. He entered to find Rachel and Kate holding game controllers, and Ethan cheering them on.

"What are you playing?" Billy said.

"Pac-Man," said Ethan. "We got tired of Pong pretty quick."

"Old school stuff," Billy said. "Where's Cooper?"

Ethan pointed out back and Billy went to the window. He saw Cooper on the tennis court with two stools from the cabaña set up as a makeshift net. Cooper hit one ball after the other over the well placed stools, practicing his serve. Rachel joined Billy at the window. "Ten hours on the court today and there he is, still at it," she said.

"The boy is really serious about this match tomorrow," said Billy.

"He's been in some close games with this guy but he always loses. And Terry Green's ego being the size of California doesn't help."

"We're going to go, aren't we?"

"Oh yeah," said Rachel. "You were upstairs when we talked about it. Cooper is using Sara's car and leaving at six thirty in the A.M. We'll go around nine in the Cherokee." Rachel beheld her would be bow still hitting balls at the fence. "I will allow him to serve two more imaginary aces, then I'm going out to get him."

"Yeah, go tell him to come in and play some Pong."

Rachel slapped the back of Billy's head as she left to get Cooper.

* * *

Spencer steered his Escalade with Kendall and Sara as passengers toward Clear Lake and not San Francisco. Kendall wanted to check on his home now that three days had passed since the run in with Major Henry. They pulled into the driveway noticing the front door stood slightly open. They saw no other vehicles or unusual activity outside and felt safe going in.

Sara pushed the front door open and they entered. The three paused, shocked at the Major's handy work. It looked like a mini-tornado had gone room to room spewing the entire contents of the house on to the floor. Kendall walked through the intimate debris finding the same chaos in every room. Upside down furniture, with drawers and closets emptied littering every inch of the house.

They came back to the kitchen finding Spencer returning the kitchen table to the upright position along with three chairs. "I thought you two might need to sit down."

They were startled by a voice from the front door. "You're all going to need to sit down." Carson Taylor stood in the doorway with a two fisted grip on the nine-millimeter handgun.

Spencer walked defiantly toward him. "Is this some kind of joke?"

Carson slammed the front door shut and squeezed the trigger. "Bang!" A bullet flew into the wall by Spencer's head. Carson motioned with the gun. "Sit down Spencer."

Spencer sat with Kendall and Sara at the table, and their previous agitated nature at finding the ransacked house, had now escalated to terror. Carson approached, holding the gun steady, pointed at them. "I hoped it wouldn't come to this," Carson said. "I don't have a choice. Just so you'll know, years ago I made a blood binding deal that's had me serving an unsavory master. By his hand I do this."

Sara could not hold her tongue. "Sounds like a deal with the devil."

"It is as you say Sara. I dealt with one of his top agents, but I suspect he was equally charming and deceitful as the evil one himself. I fear for my life as you should fear for yours, if you don't do what I say."

Spencer sat up on the edge of his chair. "Carson it's me, Spencer. What about all those years growing the business? The good, the bad--- through it all, I thought we were friends."

Carson felt a small pang of remorse and that he had better move on quickly. "Enough. Stop talking. This is what you're going to do. I want cell phones and keys on the table. Then stand up."

Sara spoke in a whisper. "This is the second time in three days I've had a gun pointed at me."

Carson moved the gun to single out Sara. "I said shut-up!"

With their stuff deposited on the table, they stood. Carson waived the gun toward the mudroom. "Everyone down in the basement. When all this is over, somebody will find you. Just be patient."

Carson herded them into the basement, shut the door, and snapped the padlock shut on the outside. The lock, he brought with him. "I'll be back," he said.

Spencer, Kendall, and Sara were not sure if Carson's remark was an attempt at humor. It was not, as Carson came back a few minutes later, unlocked and opened the door. He deposited two cases of bottled water and three bags of gas station groceries on the top steps. He closed and locked the door again, without saying a word.

Kendall went up the stairs to inventory the bags. He found bread, peanut butter, cheese and crackers, beef jerky, cinnamon rolls, and cookies. Kendall pondered the mindset of the man who purchased the diet, and especially the cinnamon rolls and cookies. He thought the last two items strange for someone displaying such a readiness to kill, and decided Carson acted out of sheer desperation.

* * *

Dante's kidnapping plan came off without a hitch. His loyal servant obeyed and responded in a way Dante could be proud. Carson had finally done something right. The taking of hostages put Dante a little closer to the catbird seat, but the plan still hinged on the free will of the humans.

He again cringed, at having to lay the outcome of the cylinder's ownership at the feet of a mortal decision. He ruminated over God's creation of man, and cursed the laws that bound man to the universe.

When Bert spoke of angels breaking the natural order and doing deeds beyond what were designed, Dante's name sat at the top of the list. The murdering of a man, and even a bad man such as Mr. White, broke every law set forth at the beginning. The angel's existence held no circumstances where the outright killing of a human became acceptable.

On the other hand, Carson's actions were of flesh and blood and legal. No matter if they were fostered from a sack of lies. Carson could have said no, but he didn't. Dante needed more Carson-like action, to secure victory.

* * *

Carson rolled into Potter Valley about nine in the evening with gunshot residue on his hands, and glad he hadn't seriously hurt someone back in Clear Lake. His fear accelerated as he headed for the finish line. The deeper he got, the harder it got. He didn't think much about the final outcome anymore, just getting through the next moment was enough.

The next moment meant facing the kids with the kidnapping still fresh on his mind. He found the five Troopers playing Monopoly at the dining room table. He entered with a smile. "I see it's game night," he said.

Kate counted her money. "Yeah it's game night all right, and Billy is the king of Boardwalk. Kate handed Billy two thousand dollars for landing on Boardwalk with a hotel.

"I'll leave you to it, guys," Carson said. "I'm going upstairs to read. Oh Cooper, the match starts at ten tomorrow. Be there early."

Cooper rolled the dice across the board. "I'll be there, and with an attitude. Twelve? Not twelve." Cooper's roll of the dice came up double sixes as Billy rubbed his hands together. "Give it up Cooper."

Cooper's shoe game piece sat squarely on Park Place. The rent would clean Cooper out. Billy held out his hand for payment. "Sorry man, but you lose."

Carson saw an opening to throw a verbal jab. "That reminds me Cooper. I saw a photo of you and Terry Green at the country club."

Cooper looked up from losing at Monopoly, recalling his losing the match. "That picture summed up my day. I lost then too. I have an early wake up, I'm going to bed." Cooper quietly got up and left.

Carson acted apologetic. "I didn't mean..."

"Don't worry about it," said Rachel. "He needs to work it out on his own."

Carson said goodnight and went upstairs. He felt pleased having sparked a questioning of self-confidence among them. He would sleep good knowing Dante would be pleased.

Chapter Twenty-Two

How true it is, Major Henry thought. *The only thing that stays the same is things always change.* Another forced move and another new beginning for ARC. This time in an old evacuated missile silo. The Major stood at the bottom of the eighteen story vertical cavern where the Atlas F ICBM rocket once waited for commands to launch and begin, what would become the end.

The rocket could travel eleven thousand five hundred miles with a potential casualty rate in the millions, depending on the target. So many innocent lives ready to be thrown away for political or religious differences. The MAD acronym was so appropriate. But ARC's success could change the Mutual Assured Destruction scenario forever. One flipped angel or hybrid human under ARC control could take out a handful of strategic prominent personnel, with more far reaching results than killing millions of innocent civilians. At least, that was their plan.

Just like Dante had crossed the line from supernatural to natural, ARC had crossed the same line but from the other direction---natural to supernatural. And the reason for the rift between the realms had its roots in the beginning of creation---self-preservation. The belief that the Earth spun in the final sliver of time had every opposing faction grasping in earnest for a piece of the universal pie.

Major Henry could claim a third of the credit for the inception of ARC. The other two thirds went to the Doc and Mrs. Prescott's husband Archie. With the Major's military training, the Doc's angelic information, and the dabbling of Archie in the black arts, plus his money, cemented the three as a match made in hell. ARC thought their mission noble and simple. Change the way wars were fought. What new agenda the Doc may have conceded to Mrs. Prescott, remained to be seen.

As Major Henry swept the floor of the empty fifty foot wide missile bay, his ranking temporarily fell from founding father of ARC, to silo janitor. The green John Deere cap sat atop the Major's head covered with dust along with the tinted eyepiece he wore. He had not removed it since he put it on in the helicopter three days ago. He even slept in it.

The Major brushed the dust from his eye covering and glimpsed a figure enter from the top of the shaft, landing behind him. The major did not turn; he just rested his chin on the end of the broom handle. "Hello Doc. Or is it Bishop?"

"To you it's Doc. And please don't be..."

The Major spun, swinging the broom through the air and striking the wayward angel on the shoulder. "Don't ever do that again, Doc."

"Okay Major. You feel better now?"

"A little bit. But it might help if I could take another swat at you."

The Doc just starred.

"I didn't think so," the Major said, obviously disappointed. He leaned the broom against the wall. "Boy Doc, it sounded like you were tearing up the pea patch at the country club. Care to explain?"

"Is there somewhere else we can talk," said the Doc, with his voice echoing through the hollow chamber.

The Major started walking. "The people who lived here before..."

"People were living down here?" The Doc said following.

"Oh yeah. It's fixed up pretty nice. Nicer than our old digs. They turned the launch control center into a luxury home---about twenty three hundred square feet of living space. That's where we're headed."

They entered the living quarters passing a spacious kitchen, large recreation room, and down a hall to a master bedroom, where the major had staked a claim.

"We can talk here Doc."

They both sat down and the Doc laid it out. "After the old man died and Mrs. Prescott took over I knew my best chance of being free was a face to face with her. After she calmed down and accepted who I was, she became quite talkative. Her husband Archie died of a rare blood disease and get this; she put him in a cryogenic freeze facility with the hopes of finding a cure."

The Major pushed his cap back, guessing what came next.

"I told her of ARC's extensive experiments with angel's blood, and may have suggested we were working toward a solution for the very same ailment."

The Major just sat there, blank faced.

"Yeah, I lied," the Doc said. The concept is not so far from what we're already doing. And you heard what she said about the money. She's willing to give till it hurts."

"That would be something Doc. We could rework the deceased eighty seven year old Archie Prescott, making him the first bio-engineered assassin ever to be covered by AARP.

"Funny Major. But no, the Prescott thing would be separate from our main cause and I could work on it in my free time. Since now, I'm going to have free time."

"You know I'm with you Doc, just so the main goal stays the main goal. And since we're looking at a month or two before we become fully operational, we have time to integrate the Archie factor."

The angel and the ex-military man shook hands, knowing it would be awhile before a clandestine field trip would have them angel hunting again. But other angel hunters were already deployed. A separate ARC mission began a week ago and Doc was kept in the dark about the unit bivouacked in a foreign country. The Major worried Doc would protest the objective. Doc's involvement would begin, only if and when the angel could be captured.

* * *

Cooper woke before dawn, while everyone else slept, to get ready for his tennis match with Terry Green. He dealt with his demons overnight, and his new intention became just to go out and have fun. If he could simply enjoy the game maybe he could relax enough to win. And if that didn't work he had a backup plan.

On his way out of the house he slipped into Rachel and Kate's room easing up to the side of the bed where Rachel slept. He bent down, kissed her on the forehead saying, "I love you, Rachel."

She opened one eye halfway and closed it. "And it will come back to you, Cooper."

Cooper smiled at her remembering his mother's saying, but realized she might not remember him being there. He crept out of the room, and left for the Clear Lake Country Club.

* * *

A few miles from the country club, Kendall, Sara, and Spencer woke up from a restless sleep after their first night as prisoners---or were they hostages. They could only speculate on Carson's motives. Before deciding to sleep the night before, the three did all they could to escape. The hinges on the door out of the basement were on the outside, so the pins could not be removed. The door and frame were metal, so they were not going to break it down.

The windows were too small for a person to climb through, and after they broke one and took turns hollering *help*, for two hours with no response, that plan was abandoned. All the homes within shouting distance were empty. The owners used them as recreational getaway, and this particular weekend, no one wanted to get away---except Kendall, Sara, and Spencer.

Carson provided them with food, but Kendall considered it good fortune the basement had a bathroom. He didn't know Carson was well aware of the basement's layout, since only four nights before at the north window, Carson laid outside in the dirt as a spy. The captives ate their breakfast, each having a cinnamon roll and bottled water as they discussed their predicament.

"We can take turns watching out the window," Kendall said. "Maybe someone will come by and we can get their attention."

"It's hard to fathom Carson doing this," said Spencer. "I never saw any signs of stress in him. Something made him snap."

Sara swallowed hard to get down her bite of cinnamon roll. "Dante has to be involved. He made it clear he wanted the cylinder and the deal Carson made has to be with him. But I have to wonder why Bert and Ernie don't fly in and rescue us."

"They probably don't know we're here," Kendall said. "We told them we wouldn't be back until Sunday. Them or the kids won't miss us till Sunday night or even Monday."

They exchanged glances and got quiet; trying to process their ordeal would not end soon.

* * *

An hour before the tennis match started, Cooper walked around the country club grounds trying to ease his nerves by talking to some of the vendors before they opened for the day. He saw Carson drive the Hummer onto the adjacent property that was rented for parking and stop. Carson came over carrying some fliers. "It's great weather for tennis."

"It is that, sir."

Carson held up one of the fliers. "Here, take one of these for your scrapbook."

The heading on the flier proclaimed, "Showdown at Clear Lake." It went on to tell of Cooper and Terry's history and their heated competitions in the past. It also gave statistics of who won, and who lost. Cooper stared at the win-loss record and realized he really never calculated it before.

Terry had won fourteen times and Cooper had won three. And Cooper's three wins were the first three times they had played. Once Terry began to win, he was fourteen and 0.

Cooper shoved the flier in his pocket. "Thanks Mr. Taylor. Maybe I'll turn it around today." Cooper left for the locker room for some alone time.

Carson headed for the lobby as Mrs. Prescott came out the front door, and walked briskly in the opposite direction toward the golf course. This time Carson would hail her. "Mrs. Prescott," he yelled. "Just a minute ma'am."

She stopped, looked flustered, and waited for Carson's short legs to traverse the lawn.

"How are you this morning Mrs. Prescott?"

"I heard there was a truck parked next to the eighteenth tee. I'm going to see."

"It's only a sanitation truck ma'am. And they were leaving as I pulled in."

"Are you sure?" She asked as if there was a plot to ruin her fairway. Carson nodded.

"Well, make sure people park where they are supposed to."

"It's being done," said Carson. "One thing Mrs. Prescott, the other day while standing at the reception desk a very insistent man came in looking for you. I believe he said his name was Bishop. The name seems to be important but I cannot remember why. Does he have something to do with the charity?"

Mrs. Prescott acted cool as a menthol breath mint while she diverted Carson's question. "A friend of my husbands, and look at those girls prancing around the golf course in their bathing suits. Don't they know we have rules here?" She departed to chastise the young women for improper attire on the links.

Carson shrugged it off, and took a minute to think hard about where the name Bishop came up. He was blank. With the thought of Spencer and the Kendall's locked in the basement, he continued on with his duties of overseeing the day's events.

* * *

Rachel, Kate, Ethan, and Billy sat in the stands with about a hundred other people, watching the *Tennis Showdown* as Carson called it. The stands were about filled to capacity, and some local news crews shot footage for the evening news. This added an extra scoop of pressure in Cooper's mind, to his already underdog mentality.

With the match into the second set, things were going as they had in the past. Terry Green won the first set, six to three, and was up in the second, five to two. If Terry won the next game, he would win the match. As the players came off the court to take a break and change ends, Terry said to Cooper. "Give it up man."

Cooper debated that very possibility as he waited for the game to resume. With the best case scenario, if he could hold Terry off and win the next game, he would have to win three more games to take this set. And then six games in a row to win the match. That seemed unlikely. But Cooper's decision teetered not on whether to give up, but how to proceed.

He unzipped his equipment bag, threw open the flap, unveiling the red racket he had taken from the cylinder in the middle of the night. The lightning bolt across the strings glistened in the sunlight. He stared at the racket embedded with his DNA, and aware he could win every point from here on out if he used it.

He did not forget Bert's instructions of non-use for twenty four hours, but what was the big deal. He would simply need to start the acclimation process over again, and in three days he could be back with the others. Here stood his major rationalization. But more important than his intended improper use of the racket, was the fact he broke the rules---by stealing and exposing it at this critical juncture.

Bert and Ernie stood by earlier that morning and invisibly watched Cooper remember the vaults combination and remove the racket from the cylinder. This was part of the test, as everything the Troopers did over the last two days was a test. The angels allowed Cooper to take the racket. How the Troopers used their free will ranked in importance with how well they did in training. The angels flew high above the court watching Cooper decide.

"Resume play," the umpire said, and Cooper made his decision at that moment.

He reached into the bag and pulled out the red racket. Cooper's history of losses clouded his judgment, as his resolve grew to go out and crush Terry Green. As the players stood to go back on the court, the crowd clapped and cheered for their favorites. Rachel saw the racket come out of the bag, instantly knowing what Cooper had done, and jumped up and screamed, "No Cooper." The boisterous fans drowned her out.

Terry noticed Cooper's change of rackets, and this time as they went back said, " New toys won't help you."

As he said earlier, Cooper would let the racket do the talking. That's just what he did by serving up four straight aces and Cooper won his third game. But Terry still just needed one game to win the whole thing, and it was Terry's serve. Something Cooper had a problem with throughout the match, until now.

The balls that were flying by Cooper early on in the contest were now being vaulted back at Terry and out of reach. If Cooper could run down a ball, the racket seemed to move on its own hitting the perfect shot. Cooper came back to win the next three games and take the second set. The match was tied at one set apiece.

Terry did not understand Cooper's sudden improvement. *Maybe the new toy did make a difference,* Terry thought, and he went over to talk to the umpire. He lobbied that Cooper's racket might be illegal, and pressed for an inspection.

The umpire motioned. "Mr. Holt. Bring your racket please."

Cooper took his racket over and confidently handed it to the umpire. The umpire studied the strings, the unique shaped body, and the strange hole below the head. He handed the racket back to Cooper and looked at Terry. "However unusual, I can find nothing wrong. Resume play gentlemen."

Cooper needed to win six games to beat Terry. Cooper figured he better let Terry win a few to make it look good. He did just that. With the score Cooper five and Terry four, Cooper had what seemed at the time a brilliant idea. He would maneuver the play to a six-six tie, and force the tiebreaker. It would all come down to one game, which Cooper would stretch as far as possible, and then win. A more exciting finish he could not imagine.

Cooper lived in his own fantasy world of tennis dreams for the past two hours, and was very careful not to make eye contact with his four friends in the stands. In fact he tried to ignore all the crowd noise he could. This felt like the U.S. Open to Cooper as he set his plan in motion. He got the match tied, forced the tiebreaker, and ran that score to a six- six tie also. Victory was there for the taking.

The next player to get two points would win the match. *Two little points*, Cooper thought, *and I can shut this guy up. Two aces and it's mine.* Cooper readied his serve as he rhythmically bounced the ball off the court. The crowd fell silent anticipating the outcome when a woman stepped out of the stands and walked down to the court to stand beside the net. She stood with arms folded staring at Cooper.

Cooper's bubble silently burst eyeing Rachel giving him 'the look' from the sidelines. He stopped bouncing the ball and stood motionless in Rachel's gaze. Terry also saw her and looked at the umpire, pointing at the girl with his racket. The umpire leaned over. "Would you please go back to your seat Miss?"

Rachel stood still a few seconds until the look, emanating from her face, changed to a look of disappointment. She said nothing, but turned and went back to her seat.

Cooper paced around the baseline gathering his thoughts, and it hit him how wrong a decision he made. *Was winning this important? What have I done Lord, please forgive me.* The consequences for taking the racket would play out in time, but what he should do now became clear. He walked up to the baseline, threw the ball up, and smashed it. "Out," said the line judge.

He repeated his motion; hit the ball and, "Out," again from the judge. Terry won the point. Terry needed one point to win. Cooper took a deep breath and tried to rectify his mountain of mistakes. He threw the ball up to serve and hit a hard shot. "Out," said the line judge on the other side. *One more time*, Cooper thought, as he pitched the ball and hit a one hundred fifty mile an hour rocket, purposely long of the mark.

"Out," the line judge said. The game Cooper so desperately wanted to win that he was willing to cheat, he just gave away. The umpire clicked his mike, "Winner, Terry Green."

Terry ran, jumped the net, and stuck out his hand to Cooper. As the two shook hands Terry spoke. "All I want to know is where can I get one of those rackets?"

Cooper pulled back his hand. "Heaven," he said and walked to the sideline.

Terry yelled over the congratulatory fans, "Is that a new sports outlet?"

Cooper put the racket back in his bag and threw it over his shoulder. He looked up into the stands where Rachel, Ethan, Kate, and Billy sat dumbfounded. Cooper did not acknowledge his friends as he headed for the dressing room in the clubhouse. He went to the far back corner of the locker room, dropped his bag, and sat down on the bench alone.

Carson came around the corner. "We have trouble, Cooper."

Cooper just sat there assuming his current trouble could not be matched.

Carson sat down beside him. "Do you remember Dante?"

The name drop got Cooper's attention. "Yeah, bad guy dresses in black."

Carson fished a piece of paper from his pocket. "Dante has kidnapped Professor Kendall, Sara, and Spencer. He told me to give you this."

Cooper took the paper and his interpretation of trouble changed as he read the note. It said: *Cooper, I have your friends. If you want to see them again, you must give Carson the red racket. If he doesn't meet me, with the racket, within fifteen minutes of you reading this, I will kill them.*

Cooper now understood the consequences of his actions. "Is this for real?"

Carson took the note pretending it was the first time he read it, when he actually wrote it. "This Dante guy scared me Cooper. He just popped into my truck out of nowhere. I not only worry about Spencer and the Kendall's, but you and me also. We are dealing with something way over our heads here. We should do as he says."

Cooper thought of his options, but the fifteen minute time period made it impossible to sort things out. Of all the things to run through his head, an expression from his father stuck out. *You dance with the one who brung you*, he used to say. Cooper realized he had not only snubbed that little gem, but he had probably just burnt down the dancehall.

The equipment bag holding the racket ransom lay at his feet. He merely scooted it over in front of Carson with his foot---an obvious sign for Carson to take it. But Carson looked confused. "I can't Cooper," he said.

"Can't what?" said Cooper.

"*Take* the racket, Carson said. "Dante was specific. You are supposed to give me the racket. Physically hand it to me."

Now Cooper looked confused. "What's all that about?"

"I don't know. Some kind of symbolic gesture, I guess. He said it was important."

Cooper could not see what difference it made, so he got the racket out and handed it to Carson. Carson folded the note, put it in his pocket, and slid the racket into a carrying case.

"Okay Carson, what happens now?"

Carson stood up with the racket over his shoulder. "He said he would release them when I brought him this. I better go," and Carson walked out of the locker room.

This was only the beginning of Cooper's troubles. The human mistake, which Dante so patiently waited; Cooper just made it.

Chapter Twenty-Three

Rachel ignored and ran past the men's dressing room sign searching the lines of lockers and finding Cooper on the last row, slumped on the bench. She wanted to slap him, but instead she sat down quietly a few feet away. He didn't move or look up. After seeing him, Rachel's only thought was how to help him. "It'll be okay," she said.

He didn't budge or speak.

Rachel sighed heavily. "We can get through this Cooper. At least you did the right thing by letting Terry win. We both know taking the racket from the cylinder and using it the one day we weren't supposed to is bad, but..."

Cooper straightened up and turned to her, looking mad and frustrated at the same time. "It gets worse."

Rachel scooted closer and clutched his hand. Cooper looked back down at the floor. "The racket is gone Rachel."

Rachel let go of his hand and slapped his shoulder as she stood up. "What happened?"

Cooper told her of the kidnapping, Dante, Carson, and the note.

"Where's the note now?" Rachel asked sitting back down.

Cooper searched, but could not find it. "I don't know. Carson must have taken it. You had to see him on your way in."

"Yeah I did, Rachel said. "He was walking out toward the parking lot. And he did have a racket case. Do you think he's involved?"

"I don't think so," said Cooper. "He seemed scared, Rachel. Dante is the one pulling the strings. We should go to the police."

"I don't know, Cooper. A fallen angel holding three people hostage for a racket---the police would love that. Get it together Cooper. I need to find Bert."

She shot up off the bench, ran down the row of lockers, turned the corner and ran straight into Bert. Bert was posed in human form still wearing the brown sweats. When Rachel hit him her head crashed into the silver whistle around his neck. "Ouch," she said. "That's gonna leave a mark."

Rachel backed away from Bert and held her head starting to speak. Bert beat her to it. "I know Rachel. We are no longer in possession of the racket." He motioned to the back, and they went to Cooper.

"I messed up Bert," said Cooper.

"This is true," Bert said. "But I saw you take the racket from the cylinder."

Rachel and Cooper were puzzled.

"And you didn't stop him," said Rachel.

"I couldn't stop him," Bert said. "The human free will is an amazingly powerful thing. Most angels don't understand it, and are still in awe of it. As a rule we don't have free will. But some of the fallen, darker ones among us are so enamored by this gift they have taken it upon themselves to try it out. And thus we have a growing chasm in the spirit realm, and the reason I'm here---to train you to stop it. One of Major Henry's men was murdered outside the professor's house in Clear Lake. And an angel did it."

"Dante?"

"He's the one we need to deal with. But now were one racket short, and I'm sorry to say Cooper, one Trooper short also."

Cooper's eyes got big. "But Bert..."

"It was your will Cooper. That racket cannot be replaced."

Cooper pleaded. "There's still the holster and mask."

"You wouldn't stand a chance without the racket. Rachel, get the others and meet me at Spencer's."

Cooper looked hurt, now. "What about me Bert?"

"I'm sorry Cooper. But you can go wherever your will takes you."

* * *

Carson drove proudly down Maple Street having secured the racket, and parked in Kendall's driveway for the rendezvous. He just turned the engine off when Dante appeared in the back seat. Carson could see in the mirror Dante's usual smirk change to a grin. Dante made himself comfortable in the Hummer's large leather seat and savored his moment in time.

He had busted up the Troopers, kidnapped three major foes, and his personal property from thousands of years ago lay in the seat in front of him. And all this accomplished while he sat back and watched.

"Carson, you did good."

Carson was grinning now. "Thank you sir and he reached down to pick up the racket.

"Not yet Carson," Dante said. "I want you to keep the racket until it's time. I don't even want to see it. There are still things that need to be done."

Carson pulled his hand back. "What can I do, sir?"

"Put the racket under the floor in the cargo hold. They don't suspect you, so go back to Spencer's. All that's left is to gain control of the cylinder and remaining equipment, and whatever pain we can inflict on the way. In that, I will get personally involved."

"What do I do when I get back to the house?"

"Be upset; talk bad about me, how you feared for your life. I will have one other specific job for you later. But now, I will go down in the basement and mess with these folks heads."

"And you'll contact me sir?"

"Yes. And remember to lock the trunk. Do not lose the racket."

* * *

In the basement Sara found a deck of cards and they played Texas Hold-Em trying to get their minds off captivity. Sara was holding a pair of jacks, and the flop showed a five, a nine, and a jack. She counted her screws and bolts they used for chips and said, "All in."

Spencer and Kendall folded, and she raked in the metal chip substitutes as Dante floated down from the ceiling. Sara and Kendall didn't move. Sara had the truth of the Word of God in her heart, and was given power over the dark ones by what Jesus did on the cross. She determined not to fear. She had told her dad this fact, and at least he acted unafraid. Spencer on the other hand, seeing Dante's wings, assumed he was a good angel there to rescue them and he stood and shouted, "We're saved."

Dante laughed in his face, and took umbrage at Spencer's remark. "Saved? You're not a Christian. Oh, you were not speaking of that kind of saved, were you? As a matter of fact, you don't know what to believe, do you Spencer? Here's a clue. If you do not choose a side, you are then by default, automatically on my side. That's the bad side if you haven't guessed. So sit down, I have no quarrel with you."

Spencer sat, feeling stupid. Dante focused on Kendall and Sara. "However these two are Christians---the older one a babe still needing milk, and the younger one a seasoned veteran craving meat. How ironic."

Sara started to stand and speak, when Dante held up his hand, and she stopped.

"I am not here to hurt you so don't waste your breath. I just wanted to let you in on a couple of things before I am out of your life forever. I've been watching you two for some time."

Dante squatted down with his elbows on his knees to get eye level with them. "It was a Friday morning about eight years ago, and I must admit, I had way too much on my plate. So much in fact, I almost didn't make it. I was in El Paso and my pre-dawn, how shall I say, suggestion session with Major Henry's wife Janice, took way too long. And she proved to be more receptive than I had imagined. All I wanted her to do was use enough explosives to get the cylinder open." Dante paused. "You did know a cylinder surfaced before yours, right."

None of them responded having surmised this from Spencer's information.

Dante continued. "Right. As I was saying, Janice Henry took my suggestions and then some. She ended up blowing up the cylinder and wiping out most of her team. I washed my hands of the whole program at that point, but I was too busy to worry about the loss. There was another cylinder, your cylinder. I needed to start the ball rolling toward procurement."

Dante unexpectedly chuckled. "Start the ball rolling," he said under his breath.

"Sorry," Dante said. "Inside joke."

He composed himself and went on. "It is truly fortunate I can fly so fast. I'm known for that, you know."

They were not impressed.

"Anyway, it was by shear speed that I made it to Chapel Canyon to see the blue Tahoe coming down the road. The weather was nasty that morning---rain, fog, not a good combination for driving. But you know the amazing thing; there was one small rock holding that giant boulder to side of the mountain. I simply removed it, and that boulder took off like a laser guided missile and smashed into the side of that SUV. Too bad, Professor, your wife was driving."

Kendall suddenly realized what the *start the ball rolling* remark meant, and dove from his sitting position, in a rage, toward Dante. By the time Kendall's outstretched body made it across the room, Dante had disappeared. Kendall hit the floor with a thud. Kendall turned over and sat up with tears running down his face. "He killed Beth."

Sara went over and fell next to her father embracing him. "He's a liar dad. Don't listen to him. He works for the father of all lies, and he probably had nothing to do with mom's death."

Dante did his damage and left. He stepped over the line once again. He did not hurt them physically, but the words he shot into their minds and hearts would sting for a long time.

At the house in Potter Valley the somber mood continued for the remaining Troopers as six o'clock rolled around. Time to complete the acclimation of the equipment. No one had seen Cooper since the match, and the kid's hearts were just not in it. Bert sensed their disposition as he entered, and blew his whistle. The piercing sound made them all sit up. "Although this can be a game," Bert said, "it is not a game now. Let's get something straight. People make mistakes. There won't be any blame dished out, to or from anyone. Is that clear?"

"Yes," they all said half-heartedly.

Bert shouted. "Is that clear?"

"Yes Bert," they shouted back in unison.

Bert could not allow the Troopers to mope around while at the same time try to mold them into warriors. Bert looked at his team minus one, *and minus the most talented one in the bunch*, Bert thought. He actually missed Cooper's quips but Cooper was not here, and they needed to move on without him. Ernie came in with the cylinder and opened it.

"Billy, go with Ernie upstairs," said Bert. "You can monitor with the cylinder. The rest of you get your equipment and go to the court. But do not put the stuff on or play with the racket till I get there. Let's go."

Ethan, Kate, and Rachel got their weapons, and Rachel noticed the red holster and mask lying at the bottom of the cylinder. "What about Cooper's stuff?" she said.

"Just put it on the table," Bert said. We'll decide what to do later."

They all did as Bert commanded and Bert stood there alone, knowing the surprises could not be over. His suspicions were correct as he heard a soft voice from inside the room. "Bert. Oh, Bert."

Bert turned to see Dante standing in the corner waving a white handkerchief. Bert knew he would show up. "So, is it truce time again?"

"No. I just didn't want to be attacked before I had a chance to speak."

"So, speak," said Bert.

"I won't be coy, Bert. I have the racket, but I also want the cylinder. You have the cylinder, but you also want the racket. I propose a wager. How good do you think the kids are?"

"After two days?" Bert shook his head. "No doubt they have skills, but you need to work harder at not being coy. What do you want, Dante?"

"A battle. Pitting the three of them against little old me---winner take all---they win, I give back the racket, I win, you give up the cylinder and all equipment."

Bert considered the Troopers might be able to defeat him. But he hadn't shown them the black ball yet. *The ball reacts the same as the others,* he thought, *the only difference is the degree of damage.* Bert had a question. "What constitutes a win?"

Dante pretended to think. "The last one standing."

"Are you saying a fight to the death?"

"Well, if they don't neutralize me, I should send them all to Heaven. How's that for not being coy. So yes, the black ball would be in play. But they're your Troopers; I really don't want them dead. I just want the cylinder. If I can disarm them, that's good enough for me."

"As you know," Bert said, "they're making their own decisions now."

"Yes, I happened to be on the receiving end of one of those."

Bert controlled his urge to attack him. "I'll talk to them and let you know."

"I'll be around," Dante said, and disappeared.

Bert's mind filled with the months of training he planned before facing the Troopers with a battle situation. He considered saying no to Dante's offer and going forward with Billy and the three. But as close as Cooper was to the others, his absence could have an unraveling effect and break the team forever. Bert would let them decide.

"Ernie, send Billy to the court," he said, and went outside.

* * *

Carson spent the remainder of the afternoon at the charity where he was unable to get any info on the name Bishop, from Mrs. Prescott. He still had a feeling of accomplishment as he drove up the tree lined drive to Spencer's. Following the winding pavement he made the curve and saw Dante in the middle of the road. When Carson stopped Dante walked over, opened the door, and got in.

Carson drove on, and raised his eyebrows. "Thanks for not just appearing and freaking me out."

"Turn around Carson, there's a change of plans."

He hit the brakes, did about ten forward and backs to get the oversized Hummer u-turned on the small road, and drove out the way he came. Dante sat perturbed over the starts and stops in Carson driving, but went on with his instructions. "Go back to Kendall's. I will send Alex with your assignment."

Carson moaned. "Do I have to go to Kendall's? I do not want to see Spencer."

Dante realized Carson had done right by him today, so he cut him some slack. "Okay, how about that restaurant where you and Alex met?"

"The Lake Bakery and Café?"

"Yes. Go there, relax and eat dinner. But wait on Alex."

Carson liked the sound of that and started to thank Dante, but he was gone. Carson just smiled and drove.

* * *

Billy came outside with the others, and rightfully so they all looked like they just lost their best friend. Bert felt for them, but Dante's proposal gave a new sense of urgency to re-spark the team spirit before he asked them to go into battle. Bert paced at center court trying to find the right words, and realized the words he chose were not as important as the Trooper's spirits.

He stopped with his hands on his hips, facing them. "There are two things my old friend Ernie says. One, mistakes are for learning not dwelling, and two; if it was easy everybody would do it. The most rewarding and lasting ventures in life take time, and are riddled with setbacks. If we are afraid to fail, we will never succeed. And if we can't persevere through the problems, we will always be short of the solution. Cooper's decision put us all in a position to make some hard choices. First, is whether you want to continue at all?"

Rachel asked, "What about Cooper? Is there any way he can come back?"

Bert decided to play hardball. "As far as *I* am concerned, he should be forgiven, but cannot continue as a member of this team."

Rachel looked at the others and back at Bert. She took her mask and holster, laid them across the strings of her racket, and sat the racket on the court. Down the line Ethan and Kate did the same, and Billy walked behind them stretching his arms around them in a show of unity.

Bert was actually pleased by their response. Even though they were defiant, they acted as a team. The hardball Bert played was hit back at him and now rested on his end of the court. His options were few. If he stopped the Trooper's training and dissolved the whole plan there would be a mad dash from the spirit world to get the cylinder. The humans, the chosen ones, were the fingers in the dike plugging the potential flood of death and destruction.

Again Bert searched for the right words, when he saw something that was self-expressed. He looked at the four making their stand, and pointed his finger to the house. They turned to see Cooper marching past the pool wearing his holster and mask. His red Wilson N Six-One 95 racket propped on his shoulder, like he advanced into battle.

Cooper stepped up beside the others and flipped his mask up so Bert could see his eyes. "You told me to go wherever my will takes me Bert---it takes me here."

Bert's job just got easier. "If you want Cooper back, he's back."

Rachel yelled, "Yes," and hugged Cooper, kissing him on the cheek. The rest of them gave high fives and patted him on the back. The Troopers were whole again elevating their chance for success and lifting their spirits to a new high. *Nothing like a resurrection to give you hope*, Bert thought. But there was one more decision to make.

"There's something else," said Bert.

The celebration quieted down.

"Dante wants to deal for the racket. He wants to fight you, with the winner taking control of the cylinder and all equipment. You must decide."

"What do you think Bert?" Ethan said. "Can we do it?"

"I will quote 1 Corinthians 1:27. But God hath chosen foolish things of the world to confound the wise; and God hath chosen the weak things of the world to confound the things which are mighty; I propose Dante sees you as foolish and weak."

Ethan bent down, picked up his equipment, and stood with a grin on his face. The others followed. Billy waved and went to the house to monitor his friends. Bert had his answer and pulled the black ball from his pocket. He bounced it repeatedly off the court. *Soon*, he thought. After eons of waiting, only hours remained before the fate of the cylinder would be known.

Chapter Twenty-Four

Like the beating of a heart the black ball boomeranged between the court and Bert's hand in a steady rhythm. Bert waited for a question about the before unseen ball, but Ethan had something else on his mind. "It's been bugging me Bert," he said. "Why rackets and balls to fight the bad angels?"

Bert caught the black ball and put it in his pocket. "To explain that, I need to start with the fact angels are immortal. But the way things work with angels; an immortal can kill an immortal. In other words the only way an angel can die, is by the hands of another angel. There are four weapons we are susceptible to, and all four are from the heavenly realm. No earthly thing can harm an angel."

"That's why the shotgun didn't work on Dante," said Kate.

"Correct," Bert said. "The weapons deadly to us are the sword, spear, or the bow and arrow. Now to answer your question Ethan, if we had given you a sword, would you know how to use it? Are you any more proficient with a spear—or would a bow and arrow suited your talents? We had to have something you were already good at. This was a long process and not by accident.

The concept of a game using a ball can be traced back to the early Egyptians, but Christian Monks in the eighth century is where our journey began. They started a game called jeu de paume and they didn't just think it up and do it. It was given to them by a word from God. The game progressed and changed over the years, as planned, to what you now know as tennis. One reason tennis exists at all, is so you four would have experience with this equipment. But tennis needs to take one more transformation to become the game of angels. You will have a part in that also. Does that answer your question, Ethan?"

"And then some."

Bert held up the black ball. "The last thing an angel wants to see flying toward him is this. If this glanced off my shoulder during battle it would cut me. A direct hit on my biceps I could lose an arm. And a major strike to my torso; I could be dead. This can kill an angel. The only down side, it has the same effect on you."

Without warning Bert threw the black ball down at an angle where it bounced up and hit Ethan in the chest. Ethan grimaced as the ball skipped off his body and returned to Bert.

"Oh, one thing I didn't tell you," said Bert. "The ball needs to be traveling at least sixty miles an hour before it becomes active."

Ethan felt around where the ball struck. "Good to know Bert---sixty miles per hour."

"I said before, angels were the only ones who could harm another angel. Starting today, you have the power to reverse the immortal. Tonight you become angel hunters."

"Isn't that what you called the Arc Unit," Kate said.

"Yes, but unlike Major Henry and his men who hunt for profit or political gain, you will hunt the ones who decide they are above the law."

Cooper waved his Wilson racket. "Can I hit the black ball with this?"

"You can. As long as the ball reaches sixty miles an hour, it's lethal."

"Cool. I think," said Cooper.

"But now Cooper you will see some things you can't do. Put on your equipment."

Cooper watched as they strapped on their holsters and slipped on their masks with rackets in hand.

"Hold your rackets out away from your bodies," Bert said. "Keep your arm still and tap the handle three times with your thumb."

On the third tap a metal sounding 'ping' came from the handle as a silver material engulfed their hands like a glove, and shot up their arms to their shoulders. Their hands and arms were completely encased in a protective covering. It looked like knights armor, only lighter and more pliable. The racket also changed. Where the strings once were a colored force field now hummed between the oval frame, and color coded to match the racket.

Ethan hit the sweet spot of the blue light off the palm of his hand. It was solid and made a vibrating sound when it came in contact with the skin. "I'm liking this," he said. He then noticed Cooper inspecting his Wilson racket and wondering what could have been. "Sorry Cooper."

"No Ethan," said Cooper. "I'm the one that needs to apologize. I guess it never seemed real to me, all the angel hunting business. So, I ask you all for your forgiveness, including you Bert."

"We all agree you're forgiven Cooper. And you'll have to do the best with what you have."

Ethan, Kate, and Rachel swung their rackets at the air getting the feel of the new armor.

"It's so light," said Kate. "If I couldn't see it, I wouldn't know it was there."

Rachel rubbed the unusual sleeve shielding her arm. "I think it makes me stronger. Hey Bert, what happens if I..." Rachel grabbed the racket with her left hand, pulling it from the grip of her right. "Hey guys, the armor's still here. Want to arm wrestle Cooper?"

"Not advisable," Bert said. "Rachel would win and Cooper could be injured. The elongated gauntlet increases your arm strength about ten times normal."

Rachel curled her arm as if showing off her muscle. "How do you make it go away, Bert?"

"The same way you engaged it, or until your racket becomes non-functional."

"Non-functional?" Ethan said.

"Broken in the course of battle. The armor gets its power from the racket. Something else I want to show you. There's a hidden compartment above and just behind your wrist. The button to open it is below your wrist in the fold of the joint. Find the button and push it."

They did, and a door the size of a playing card clicked open exposing nine more buttons and a digital readout at the top.

Bert's tone became stern. "I only show you this in case you accidentally opened it. It can take weeks to master the operation of these tools, and you can hurt yourself without instruction."

Ethan looked closely at the buttons and they were inlaid with symbols. A couple he could make out. One had a symbol for fire and one had a pair of wings. He looked up as Bert continued. "Now close the door, and don't open it again until you're trained."

Trained, Bert thought. It crossed his mind he *was* throwing them to the lions by putting them in a battle situation so soon. But he had no choice. The clock was ticking. "Here's the plan Troopers. It's critical you fight Dante tonight. We can't give him time to acclimate the racket. And you're going to have to stop him on your own."

"Stop him? Kate said.

"I mean kill him," said Bert. "Use the black ball and kill him. And no matter what he says, be aware he will be trying to do the same thing to you."

Somewhere deep inside during the thought process of the last few days, the Troopers skimmed over the fact their lives would eventually be in danger. They just didn't think it would be this soon. Rachel raised her mask. "Are you and Ernie going to help us?"

"We can't. Not after it begins. But we will prepare you the best we can with the time we have. We're getting ready to go upstairs for a strategy session and help Billy program the balls so you'll know what to expect. And there are some new things with the masks we will discuss. Go ahead and retract your armor, and let's go upstairs."

They tapped the grips causing the armor to shoot down their arms and disappear. The colored glow on the racket head changed back to woven strings. The mixture of emotions as they went to the house was hard to get a handle on. Cooper tried to sum it up. "Okay guys, this feels like when you've studied too hard for your algebra final with all those formulas bouncing around in your head, and you're not sure you'll recall the correct one when you need it."

"Information overload," said Rachel.

"That's exactly what we have, information overload. So we don't try to sort through it, we just absorb it. Remember we have each other to lean on. And when the time comes, and Dante is trying to do his worst, we just need to focus. Focus on the moment; focus on what's in front of you and we can beat this guy."

Cooper was right. But the hard part would be the focusing.

* * *

At one time or another all the locals ate at The Lake Bakery and Café. You could find the mayor and the judge having breakfast together both wearing t-shirts and jeans. In recent days an angel frequented the restaurant. Although disguised in human form, Alex still made heads turn as she strolled past the front tables. She walked through like she owned the place and flipped her hair as she turned the corner toward the back booths. She walked up on Carson as he took the last bite of apple pie.

"Is this seat taken?"

Carson wiped his mouth and swallowed. "Please, sit down."

Alex sat, and Carson brushed the piecrust crumbs from his pants. His quiet dinner would soon be overshadowed by the payment due on his contract with Dante. Being congenial and making you feel at ease defined part of Alex's makeup, but flirting was her number one weapon with a bullet. Carson wanted to avoid all the usual innuendos, which always left him feeling uneasy, and got right to the point. "What does Dante want?"

Alex ran her fingers through her hair. "What, no small talk? I do so enjoy our verbal games."

"It's been a long week Alex. Get to the punch line."

"So there are orbs under that cotton. Okay mister, this is it. I will take the racket to Dante, and he doesn't want the hostages to leave the basement alive. You take care of that one last chore, and he will tear up your contract."

Carson could not believe he would be free of Dante forever. Go back to his wife and start over. And all he had to do was commit murder.

* * *

At 9:30 in the evening on a Saturday night, only four days after the original discovery, all petitions for ownership of the silver cylinder were about to be settled. It wouldn't happen by earthly methods in a courtroom with lawyers spouting legal precedence and a judge awarding the best argument. It would play out in a grassy clearing a half-mile north of the house in Potter Valley, using heavenly weapons wielded by four kids and an arrogant angel. The last one standing would be the victor.

And it wouldn't go down like Bert drew it up on the blackboard. "Stay together at first," he said. "Start with a volley of four simultaneous shots, then split up in pairs and use the trees as cover. Dante can see through the trees but the masks emit a field that will help keep you hidden. Remember you can communicate with each other and Billy using the masks. Just speak and the microphone will automatically turn on. Try to wear him down with the blue and red balls but save the black ball and make sure of the shot. You only have one black ball. I will be there to start the battle, after that I won't interfere. Bow your heads and let's pray."

The balls were programmed, the prayers were said, and the Troopers walked to the site of the battle a few minutes before time to begin. The three that could, activated their armor, and Cooper advanced with them carrying his Wilson tennis racket. The holsters were girt about their loins and their heads were crowned with the protective masks waiting to be pulled down into place. They stopped at the edge of the clearing bathed in the soft light from the August moon.

"This is it guys," Cooper said.

Rachel stood next to him and leaned in and kissed him on the cheek.

Cooper was surprised. "I love you Rachel."

"Nice try Cooper, but like somebody said, we need to focus."

Kate and Ethan gave the universal finger down the throat signal.

"If God be for us," said Kate. "Who can be against us," they all said.

Ethan looked down the row at Cooper and said, "Vengeance is mine sayeth the Lord."

Cooper looked back and said, "Unless it comes by a Trooper. Let's mask up."

They all pulled their masks down over their faces.

"Whoa," said Rachel.

"What the..." Ethan said.

"This is a strange site for the middle of nowhere," said Kate. Cooper adjusted the goggles on the mask. "Ah Billy. Oh Billy. Hey, come in chief. Are you seeing this?"

"Yeah, hang on Cooper. Let me widen the..." Billy paused. "What is that?"

The view through the goggles and on Billy's screen looked like the lights extravaganza at Disney World. Glowing figures covered the trees surrounding the clearing and they could be seen pushing and shoving for the best vantage point to the upcoming show.

Word had definitely got out. Every demon and angel that could pull out of their current assignments had shown up to see the humans battle the angel. The Chosen Ones coming against Dante with his reputation, plus the first time the equipment was going to be used since the fall of the third from heaven made this an event not to miss.

Rachel asked. "Which one is Dante?"

"You know, I don't think he's here yet. Billy, this is Cooper."

"Go Cooper."

"Can you get Bert or Ernie over here?"

"Already done. Ernie's gone after Bert. They'll be right there."

"Make it fast chief," Cooper said. "We couldn't pick out a comet with brights on in this traffic."

Bert was about a mile away getting some ground rules straight with Dante. "No double morphing," Bert said. "If I see two of you flying around, I'm coming in. What kind of ammo do you have?"

Dante held out his hand containing a blue and red ball.

"That's it?"

"That's all I need Bert. Now when do we do this?"

Ernie flew up. "Hey, Bert. We need to do some crowd control." They both looked at Dante.

Dante tried looking as innocent as his scared face allowed. "I may have told a few friends."

Bert was mad. "A few friends. Give me ten minutes before you come over," and Ernie and Bert took off.

Dante put the balls he had shown Bert back in his pocket and pulled out the one he didn't. He held the black ball up to the moonlight knowing he would use it. The last man standing, he thought, but more likely the last angel.

* * *

The same reflected light highlighting the black ball in Potter Valley gave a soft shine to the 9mm Glock thirty miles away in Carson's hand. Carson stalled outside Kendall's leaning against the Hummer again debating in his mind whether he could or could not carry out Dante's orders. I can't shoot these people. But if I don't, Dante will kill me. No, this is Spencer and two innocent victims of circumstance. Wait, I'm a victim too. I count for something.

It went like this for ten minutes. When Carson thought of his wife, it all became clear. Dante would not only sacrifice me, but also my wife. I cannot let that happen. As he started for the basement he quit thinking of his targets as Spencer, Kendall, or Sara; they would become A, B, and C.

He would do A first, then B and C. Then go home to his wife. Carson unlocked the basement door, went down the stairs and whom did he find. He found Spencer, Kendall, and Sara---A, B, and C vanished somewhere on the way down.

The scene in the basement seemed tense to Carson with Sara and her dad huddled together and Spencer by himself on the other side of the room. Dante said he was going to mess with them and it looks like he did. Carson started waving the gun. "Spencer moves over next to the others. Come on, get beside them."

Carson sat on the steps. His knees got weak at the reality of what he must do. The gun still pointed forward.

Sara's eyes were red from crying at the story of how her mother died. She pleaded. "Let us go Carson. We're all very tired."

Carson did not respond, he just kept pointing the gun.

Spencer leaned up. "Tell him what you told me Sara, about the deal."

Sara took a long breath. "Your deal was with Dante, wasn't it?"

Small beads of sweat appeared on Carson's forehead but he said nothing. Kendall and Spencer urged Sara on with their eyes.

"Okay Carson, listen," Sara said. "There is no binding contract, if you just renounce Dante's boss. You know, Satan."

Carson remembered Dante's warning about the Christians wanting his soul. "That's enough." Carson shook the weapon.

"No, that's just the beginning," Sara said. "All you have to do is say, Jesus come into my heart, I accept you as my savior, and mean it, and every deal, bad deed, or wrong word from your past will be wiped clean. You must think about eternity."

Carson was shaking now with sweat dripping from his chin. Had he done all this for nothing? Was Dante really lying to him? Carson's brain was misfiring, and Sara jerked as the gun went off.

An elderly couple sitting outside across the lake heard the noise.

"Was that a gunshot, Fred?"

"You always hear gunshots Martha. Probably kids with fireworks."

"So, I shouldn't call the police?"

"Drink you tea, Martha."

Martha sipped the Earl Grey. "But what if it was a gunshot. Someone could be hurt."

Chapter Twenty-Five

Bert and Ernie spent about five minutes speeding from tree to tree, and whatever they were saying worked. Angels and demons from the far corners of the earth were heading back from where they came. The sheer number of invisible creatures gathered in one place was an awesome spectacle. But as the spectators dispersed, another spectacle developed at the far end of the clearing.

With arms folded and his body rigged and upright, Dante floated down from the night sky. The entrance was all part of the show. The perfectly combed jet-black hair, smirk in full bloom, and the long black coat fluttering behind him served as a message of superiority. He held his pose as he settled down in the cool grass portraying to anyone who cared he felt invincible.

Dante closed his eyes imagining the cheer that would have encircled his arrival had the meddling angels not run off his fans. He calculated the fight would not last long and didn't understand why Bert let the Christians show up at all. His plan for winning was simple. Fend off their early eagerness, disable them one at a time, then go back and finish them off.

The regal entry of their opponent released a shot of adrenaline through the Troopers. Ethan noticed the red racket and the catalyst for this premature battle was strapped to Dante's back with only the handle visible above the right shoulder. "Zoom," Ethan said, and the new telescoping feature of the goggles activated. He was intrigued by the way Dante carried his racket. "Check out that racket sling," said Ethan. "We need to get one of those.

Billy studied the individual monitors for the Troopers and his voice came over the headphones. "Ethan your pulse is good but the rest of you I'm seeing a slight increase."

Ethan shifted his gaze from the racket to Dante's face. It looked like Dante stood two feet away and Ethan could see his eyes moving from one Trooper to the next.

"Okay Ethan," Billy said, "your heart rate is up with the others now."

"Zoom off," said Ethan.

Cooper chimed in. "Roger the heart rate there Billy, but you might have a little more blood pumping if you were out here."

"No, my hearts beating fast enough thank you," Billy said. "On a more constructive note, there's only one bogie on my screen. All the others have gone. Wait a second---never mind it's only Bert."

Bert flew down landing in the center of the clearing. He looked at Dante still standing statuesque in the same position---then to his warriors who were about to be on their own. "If everyone is ready, let's get to it."

The Troopers each pulled a blue ball from their holsters. Dante was so sure of himself he didn't even pull his racket.

Bert held up his arm. "Ready. Go!" Bert's arm dropped, and he flew out of the line of fire.

The Troopers hit their first volley and Dante waited till the four blue balls got close and he took off onto the sky. What Dante didn't know, was this initial set of balls were programmed to follow his every move. The balls made a ninety-degree turn upward and struck him with the smirk still stuck on his face. His look changed as the blue spheres collided.

Dante's smirk widened to display an open mouth, and his face contorted as electricity surged through his body.

"That's for the professor," Rachel said, as they split up and hid behind the trees.

Dante fell to the ground in a sitting position with his before flawless hairdo now electrified resembling a disturbed porcupine. He jumped to his feet, pulled the racket, and the Troopers were nowhere to be seen.

From Dante's right, Cooper and Rachel appeared hitting another volley. From his left, Ethan and Kate did the same thing. He deflected the two shots from the right and one from the left. But the last red ball went between his legs and exploded when it hit his coat. The bottom third of his calf length coat was on fire. Dante went supersonic straight up. The speed of his flight put out the flames, and he hovered high above the battlefield searching for the Troopers.

Dante was upset with himself for getting caught off guard, but he was upset with the Troopers for messing up his hair and ruining his favorite overcoat. Victory still seemed sure if he just took care of business. The Troopers continued to move using the trees as cover, but they could not see Dante. Kate peaked her head out to get a look. "Where'd he go Billy?"

"I've got him. He's straight up about three miles."

Kate stepped into the clearing looking up. "What's he doing?"

"Just sitting there. Hang on---he's coming down."

Dante saw Kate emerge from the tree line and went after her.

Billy yelled in his headset. "He's coming right for you Kate. Get out of there. Cooper, try to distract him."

Cooper and Rachel both stepped out, each hitting a ball at Dante. Kate was running now, as Dante saw two red balls heading toward him. He pulled up knocking the first ball away and the second he redirected at Kate. Kate was two feet from the tree where Ethan stood and safety, when the ball hit her in the back. She fell at Ethan's feet, and wasn't moving.

"Stay put Ethan," said Billy. "Dante's still about forty feet up on your right."

Ethan just caught himself before he jumped out in the open. He eased up against the tree, starring down at Kate.

"Kate, are you okay? Kate. Kate is down guys. Dante hit her with one of your shots. What kind of ball did you guys hit?"

Cooper looked at Rachel ten feet from him, both in the trees on the other side of the clearing. "Did you hit the red one?"

Rachel shook her head yes.

"Ethan," Cooper said.

"I'm here."

"Those balls were meant to decrease Dante's muscle functions. Maybe keep him from flying."

"This is Billy. Ernie is not sure how that affects Kate. But her vital signs are still good."

"She's not moving Billy," Ethan said. "And hasn't since she hit the ground. Where's Dante now?"

Billy checked his screen. "Still above you. Seems to be..."

Before Billy could say another word, Dante swooped down, picked up Kate, and rocketed skyward. He deposited Kate in the top of a tree at the edge of the clearing and hung her racket on a limb below her. He flew down and defiantly stood in the center of the grassy field. "One down and three to go," he yelled.

Dante looked more beat up than he was with his hair sticking up and the bottom of his coat burnt away. After a long pause, he taunted them. "Oh, Troopers. Come out, come out wherever you are."

"Nobody move," said Billy. He could see Dante ready to fire at the first thing that moved.

* * *

When the sound of the gunshot finished bouncing off the basement walls, Sara opened her eyes. She was still alive. But the microscope a few inches from her head lay scattered in four pieces. The broken microscope wasn't because of Carson's bad aim. He hadn't aimed at all. In fact, he didn't intentionally fire the gun. His hands were shaking so bad he accidentally pulled the trigger.

Carson sat on the basement steps facing the others with his head in his hands and his gun on the floor. The sound of the shot ripped his already frazzled nerves and he dropped it. With his hands pressed tight against his face, Carson postponed any truth as to the bullets final resting place.

Kendall saw a chance to escape, and eased up off the floor. He had to get to the gun before Carson saw him. Kendall was crouched down ready to pick up the weapon when he got close enough. He took one step and Carson raised his head. The sight of Kendall apparently ready to pounce startled Carson. Carson snatched the gun from the floor, freezing Kendall in the process.

Kendall still hunched over and three feet from the barrel of the gun, looked deep into Carson's eyes. He didn't see a killer. But a scared, confused man teetering between redemption and the biggest mistake he could ever make. Kendall felt the fear drain from his body and a surge of boldness come over him. He slowly stood and held out his hand to Carson.

"You don't have to do this," Kendall said. "Sara's right. Dante is a lying thief."

Carson flipped the gun around, now pointing the handle at Kendall. Kendall took the gun. Carson felt the weight of the past week drift away, but it was replaced with the thought he would soon die. To Dante, this would be perceived as cowardice. To Sara, it was the bravest thing she'd seen. She went and sat next to Carson.

"You did the right thing," she said.

"But you don't understand," said Carson. Dante will kill all of us."

Sara took his hand. "Then we'll all go to heaven together."

Carson thought these very brave words. He considered her claim. "I can go to heaven?" he said.

"You can," said Sara.

"Even after signing a contract with Dante?"

"The contract is just one of Dante's tricks---to make you think you don't have a choice. It's not real."

It seemed real enough to Carson twenty years ago as a freshman in college. He had spent the night bar hopping with friends. Considering his inebriated state, he felt lucky to make it home without crashing his car. He lay on his dorm room bed with the room spinning.

This was the first time Dante popped in on Carson, standing at the foot of his bed. Carson was too drunk to move. Dante tapped him on the foot. "This is your lucky day son. I'm here to offer you the world."

"I'll take it," Carson said, and laughed.

The next thing Carson new he was stone cold sober and standing on the roof of a thirty story building in San Francisco with Dante at his side. "You can help shape this town," said Dante. "That twentieth floor office with the big windows can be yours." Dante pointed to the Bryant Building and the floor that was home to Spincorp. Dante proceeded to show him his beach house, boat, cars, and the woman that would fall deeply in love with him.

Carson's most vague memory of the night was the last. He was inside an abandoned brick warehouse and the contract sat on the table in front of him. Over the edge of the table, without moving his eyes from the contract, he could see a girl laying in some kind of liquid on the floor. He didn't remember where she came from, who she was, or what happened to her later. He did remember signing the contract. He signed the contract with a red liquid he knew was the girl's blood.

Back in the dorm room, and feeling drunk again, he thought it was a dream---until he saw his moist, red, fingertips.

"Carson listen," Sara said. "If you really want to be saved and forgiven you have to want it with your heart."

"And it doesn't matter what I've done?"

"Because of what Jesus did, God will forgive you."

"I want to be forgiven," said Carson. "I don't want to go to hell."

Right there in the basement only fifteen minutes after deciding to do murder Carson was led in a prayer of salvation and got born again. It was like all his past was written in pencil and God took a giant eraser and wiped it out with one stroke.

Carson wiped his eyes. "There's still Dante."

"We'll pray about that," said Sara.

Carson looked across the room. "And Spencer."

Spencer looked back at Carson. "I'm glad for your new found faith, but you also will need to find a new job. You're fired."

Losing his job was a ways down on the list of Carson's troubles and he listened intently to Spencer's next words.

"As far as I'm concerned, we don't have to get the police involved." Kendall and Sara both agreed. Because of your loyalty to me," Spencer said. "You're free to go Carson."

"I don't know," Carson said. "I kind of like it down here. Ever think of renting out your basement, Professor?"

Sara, Kendall, and Spencer managed a smile, but Carson was about half-serious. Dante's threats had him worried what awaited him outside.

* * *

Dante's position was the same---ready to fire at the first Trooper who stuck a head out. Dante could see Kate, still propped in the treetop to his left, but the others played hide and seek. Dante had a general idea where the last shots came from, but he wanted specifics. He waited for something to stir.

"Anyone have a plan?" Cooper asked, getting impatient.

"I do," said Billy. "I've located the balls you hit before and they're all behind where Dante is standing. When we're ready, Rachel and Ethan, engage your ball retriever. Dante may turn, thinking an attack is coming from his rear. Cooper, you may get a clear shot."

"Sounds good," Cooper said. "But I'm using the black ball."

"You sure about that?" said Rachel.

"If Dante turns his back," Cooper said, "it would be our best chance."

"I'm hanging on to my black one," Rachel said. "I'll hit the blue one programmed for ice. Maybe I can freeze him."

A soft voice came over the earphones. "What happened?"

Ethan looked up and saw Kate move. "Kate moved her head."

"Yeah, but that's all I can move," said Kate. "Did someone get the license number of that truck that hit me? Hey, where am I?"

Ethan tried not to startle her. "Well, I can see you. I just can't get to you right now. You got hit with a muscle-relaxing ball. You're in a tree, so don't move."

"That'll be easy," she said.

Cooper pulled the black ball from his holster. "Let me know if he turns Billy."

"Will do," Billy said. "Rachel, Ethan, do it."

They pushed the ball retrieval button and both red lights around the hole below the racket head lit up. Two balls lifted off the ground behind Dante. Dante spun, and fired at the first sound.

"He turned Cooper," Billy said.

Cooper jumped out and let the black ball fly. The thing about the black ball, it made a whistling sound as it past sixty miles per hour. Dante heard it and ducked. The black ball flew over Dante's head into the woods.

When Dante hit the ground, he rolled to see where the shot came from. He saw Rachel step out and hit the blue ball. The blue ball sped toward Dante's head, but his racket was ready. He deflected it away behind him. Dante just blocked Rachel's shot not meaning to direct it anywhere specific, but the blue ice ball struck the base of the tree where Kate was perched.

Upon impact, ice started to form around the tree trunk, slowly moving upward. The ice grew to a thickness of one inch as it crept past the first set of branches. The branches quickly froze cracking and popping as they fell to the ground. The ice continued its march up the tree toward Kate.

Dante was up and moving for Rachel.

Billy saw him on the screen. "He's seen you Rachel. Forty feet out and closing."

Rachel pulled her black ball. "Let's get him Cooper."

Rachel and Cooper moved from their cover. When Rachel emerged with her racket high over her head ready to fire, Dante was already there. Dante smiled at her before he employed a feature on the racket the Troopers had not learned. He touched the grip a few times and a silver blade slid out around the outside of the head.

Dante swung hitting Rachel's armor along her biceps. Sparks flew and a metal 'ping' ran out, but Rachel heard something crack and she fell. Dante swung again cutting Rachel's racket head in to two pieces. Dante was too close to Rachel for Cooper to get a shot off. When Ethan started to fire, the sound from the falling limbs of the freezing tree distracted him. The ice was fifteen feet below Kate, and climbing.

Ethan knew what he had to do. "Can you hear me Kate?"

"I hear you Ethan. What's that crashing sound?"

"Never mind. I'm coming after you."

"You what?" Billy said.

"I have to try this Billy. I know Bert said not to, but..."

Ethan pushed the hidden button on the armor on the underside of his wrist, and the concealed door came open. He eyed the button labeled with a pair of wings. "I hope this means I can fly," he said, and pushed the button.

The same silver blades came out of the racket as Dante's. Only this time they went farther out, and looked like small wings. The racket made a whirring sound, Ethan got a tight grip on the handle, and he took off. Ethan was flying. But he had no control. "This might be a mistake," he said, as he went straight up, then across the treetops in the opposite direction as Kate.

Dante saw Ethan erratically fly out of sight. "Trying to get away, huh," said Dante. Dante sped after him.

"What's happening?" Kate said. She could see branches falling from below her now.

Cooper ran to Rachel. "You okay?"

"I think my arm is broken. My armor's gone, my racket's shot, and there's something..." Rachel reached under her with her good hand. She was laying on the black ball.

"Hold on Rachel," Cooper said. He stood up pulling the last two balls from his holster trying to remember which did what. "You still with us Kate?"

"Yeah, just hanging out. What is that stuff coming up the tree?"

"I'm going to try and stop it," said Cooper.

Cooper hit a red ball striking the tree about halfway up. Where the ball hit, the tree immediately caught fire.

"You trying to burn me down?" Kate said.

"Give it a second, Kate."

The fire slowly rose and got bigger. After the flames popped and stretched a few seconds the ice started to melt. It wasn't long before both balls were nullified. The melting ice put out the fire, and the fire stopped the ice. The tree was partially burnt, most of the limbs were missing, and Kate still hung near the top.

"We'll get you Kate," said Cooper. "I don't know how, but we'll get you." Cooper knelt down by Rachel.

Chapter Twenty-Six

Ethan had crashed into a tree a mile away when Dante found him. Dante tapped him with the red racket. "I take it you were absent the day they taught flight training."

Ethan moaned from the pain.

Dante laughed. "You'll get style points and I'll get your racket." Dante grabbed Ethan's racket. "I'll be back brother Ethan. Then the pain will stop."

Cooper comforted Rachel the best he could but he was the last Trooper standing. He used his black ball already and the Wilson racket would not match up with Dante's. Cooper brushed Rachel's hair from her face. "I'll guard you," he said.

Rachel seemed close to losing consciousness from the throbbing in her arm. "Here, take this," she said, and handed him the black ball.

Cooper held the ball looking at it and back to Rachel. "There's still hope, girl"

"Always Cooper. God be with you."

Dante hit the ground behind Cooper. "Well, if it isn't Cooper Holt, tennis player extraordinaire---Oh, you lost that match didn't you?"

Cooper hid the black ball in his pocket and stood. "Where's Ethan?"

"He's out there somewhere crying for his mommy."

"Yeah, I bet."

Billy came over the headset. "Ethan's okay. I don't know how bad he's hurt, but his readings are in the green."

Dante held up his black ball. "You have never seen this do it's work, have you?"

Cooper did not respond.

"You're about to," Dante said. "It is fitting you and I stand here together. You're responsible for me getting my racket back and it is entirely your fault the ones you call friends are waiting to die in the forest."

Cooper inched his hand toward his pocket. Dante stepped to the left, drawing his racket back and taking a bead on Rachel. "If you pull that ball Cooper, your girlfriend is dead. Now, easy, take it out and get rid of it."

Cooper didn't know what to do other than step between Dante and Rachel to protect her. Rachel lay four feet behind him with Dante fifteen feet in front of him. The situation reminded Cooper of two gunslingers facing off in an old western. If Cooper tried to use the black ball, he wasn't sure he could get it to sixty miles an hour in such a short distance. Especially having to pull it, draw back and hit it.

Dante on the other hand stood ready to fire. And with the red racket the ball would become lethal as it traveled the fifteen-foot span. Cooper reached into his pocket and slipped the ball out.

"Be careful what you do next Cooper," Dante said.

Cooper considered his options, which were few, and heard Rachel's faint voice behind him. "Cooper, I think I'm going to pass out. While I still can, I want to say, I love you."

Cooper kept his eyes focused on Dante, but couldn't believe she finally said it. This was the first time Rachel ever said I love you to him. He guessed his persistence paid off. Rachel got out one more sentence. "And Cooper, remember what they say about love." Rachel's body went limp.

Cooper blocked Dante's view of Rachel but Dante heard her. "Now wasn't that special," said Dante. "Kids in love. Makes my skin crawl."

Cooper screamed in frustration as he drew back and hit the black ball off into the forest behind Dante. Dante felt the wind from the ball as it flew past his head. "Fifty two miles an hour," he said.

"What?" said Cooper.

"The velocity of the ball," Dante said. "It was at fifty-two miles an hour when it passed me. You couldn't even get it up to speed." Dante relaxed now that the black ball was gone. He took his racket and spun it off the palm of his hand. "Thank you for my racket Cooper. This was the key to my victory."

Dante savored his upcoming win by rising off the ground a few inches, while he planned his last fatal move. After a bit of suspense, he would pitch the black ball in the air, grasp his racket with two hands, and slam if through Cooper and into Rachel on the ground. Two with one shot, Dante thought, that's one for the record books.

"You know Cooper," said Dante, "you really didn't have a chance against me. And I knew you didn't have the guts to use the ball. But it could have been interesting if you did."

"Guts huh," Cooper said. "You want to talk about guts. I'll show you guts."

Rachel yelled. "Now!"

Cooper dove to the ground.

Dante could now see Rachel sitting up, holding her broken racket high in the air. The red ball retrieval light still worked and was glowing. Dante's expression changed from defiance to disbelief. Then the crunching sound was heard as the black ball came sailing back through Dante's chest and nestled in the frame of Rachel's racket. Dante dropped to his knees, inspecting the fist size whole in his body. The red racket fell by his side.

"Now there's some guts," Cooper said, smiling at Rachel. "Love always comes back to you."

"Just like the black ball," she said. "But I meant what I said. I do love you.

"I'll tell you girl, I almost missed your code about what they say about love. I got excited at the I love you part."

They both looked at Rachel's racket still held high with Dante's insides dripping down the handle. Dante's body had become semi-transparent, and he could not grasp his demise. "This is not supposed to happen. I'm an archangel. You're nothing but kids."

Cooper turned to face him. "We're Troopers chief. Anointed by God and strengthened by his word. I guess you didn't read the book. We win."

Dante's body melted into the earth.

* * *

Carson apologized as best he could to Spencer and the Kendall's, and walked up the basement stairs alone. He assumed Dante would be busy with the Christians. He could get home and see his wife before Dante retaliated. He didn't know Dante would never retaliate again.

Carson walked through the ransacked house and out the front door. He stopped, closing his eyes to savior the night air with his newborn soul. When his eyes opened, Alex hovered to his right. And the strange thing---when the moonlight sparkled off the four-foot sword Alex held ready to strike---it was only then he remembered.

Alex said, "Sorry Carson," and swung.

Carson yelled, "I saw Bishop."

Alex closed her eyes tensing every muscle to stop the swing. She cracked her eyelids, seeing the steel blade touching Carson's throat. She had stopped in time and lowered the sword.

Bishop?" she said.

"It was you. That's where I heard it. The day in the Hummer when you came back from the ARC unit."

"Where is he?"

"I don't know where he is now, but three days ago he walked into the Clear Lake Country Club, and he wasn't leaving until he talked to Mrs. Prescott. They must be acquainted."

Alex floated to the sidewalk. "Information on Bishop has saved your life, Carson."

Carson raised his eyebrows. "Well, that's twice tonight I've been saved. What about Dante?"

"He's dead. The Christians beat him."

"So, I..."

"Go home to your wife Carson. You have another chance."

Another chance was more than he could ask at this point. Carson left Clear Lake, never to return again.

* * *

Major Henry sat sullen in the control room of ARC's new Nevada location thinking about the loss and waiting for the equipment in front of him to be turned on. A smile formed when the monitor came to life. The smile grew as he punched in coordinates and a picture filled the screen. He could see ARC's only other field unit with the code name Black Wing deployed halfway around the world.

Five men dressed in military fatigues passed the time by playing cards at the edge of the rain forest, waiting for the local priest to die. Despite the alternating torrential rain and sweltering heat, they camped for days patiently expecting the padres certain end. They had nothing to do with the clergyman's condition or wished him any harm, only that his soul would hurry up and depart. His death would provide them ideal conditions for completing their objective along with a one-way ticket out of the jungle. The one who would travel to the saint's side at his moment of passing was whom they waited: the gathering one---the special one---the secret escort to the other side. The angel of death was marked for capture.

* * *

By the next morning the large downstairs bedroom at the house in Potter Valley had been turned into a makeshift hospital ward. With Rachel's arm broken, Ethan's concussion, and Kate just getting her muscles back, they were all in bed. Spencer's private physician had just left after treating them. Professor Kendall, Sara, and Spencer talked with the recouping Alpha State Troopers about their thrust into the spiritual realm.

The Troopers reveled in the defeat of Dante, and obviously relieved none of the injuries were fatal. But everything seemed to flow back to the questions why them, and what was next. Were they there to save the world from this supernatural upheaval of angels or just keep things in balance until God sent back his son? Could they prevail if more angels crossed the lines and started taking human lives as they saw fit? Three things they did know. They were stronger now, more of a team than ever, and it had only just begun.

Cooper ran into the room. "I ordered pizza. Here, Professor, Bert told me to give you this." Cooper handed a folded piece of paper to Kendall.

"Hey guys, I saw something strange outside," Cooper said. "It was in the dirt by the swimming pool. It looked like the front bumper from a 57 Chevy."

Cooper was pelted to his knees with pillows.

The professor had a curious look on his face as he read the note.

Professor Kendall---I could not let you be deceived. It was Beth's time to go. No angelic power had a hand in your wife's death. As to why she died, angels do not know these things. Only God. I hope this gives you peace. When you are ready for another adventure, try this: latitude 20.2244, longitude 56.3245. At this spot you will find the torn veil from the holy of holies and wrapped inside---the crown of thorns.
Go with god,
Bert

P.S. Tell the Troopers the training has just started. Ernie and I will return in a few months to help with the following: At latitude 33.0704, longitude 56.3245, is another silver cylinder.

Sara was intrigued by Kendall's face. "What is it dad?"

Kendall stuffed the note in his pocket. "Just another fifty seven Chevy."